Hard, brilliant, and dark as coal, this brand new and necessary volume captures Appalachia today, a place where the old bedrock verities of family, community, belief, work, and the earth itself are all in painful "Upheaval"—to use the title of Chris Holbrook's story herein. From manic to elegiac to rough, raw, beautiful, and heartbreaking, these stories will strike the reader as both absolutely true and as unforgettable, like the high pure ring of an ax on a cold winter morning, vibrating across distance, hanging in the air long afterward. —Lee Smith, author of *Saving Grace* and *Mrs. Darcy Meets the Blue-Eyed Stranger*

Working Lives Series
Appalachian Writing Series

Degrees of Elevation

Short Stories of

Contemporary Appalachia

Edited by
Charles Dodd White & Page Seay

Bottom Dog Press
Huron, Ohio

© 2010 Bottom Dog Press, Inc.
ISBN 978-1-933964-39-3

Bottom Dog Press
PO Box 425
Huron, Ohio 44839
http://smithdocs.net

Credits:
General editor: Larry Smith
Layout and design, Larry Smith
Cover by Susanna Sharp-Schawacke
Acknowledgments
Many of these stories were previously published in
the following publications:

"Bait" by Richard Hague appeared in *Negative Capability*.
"The Beauties of this Earth" by Mark Powell appeared in *Appalachian Heritage* in 2007.
"Casting Out" by Denton Loving appeared in *The Minnetonka Review* in 2010.
"Holler" by Crystal Wilkinson appeared in *Slice Magazine* in 2010.
"Horseweed" by Chris Offutt in the story collection *Kentucky Straight* published by Vintage Books in 1992.
"Into the Gorge" by Ron Rash appeared in *The Southern Review* in 2008.
"Magic" by Jim Nichols appeared in the story collection *Slow Monkeys* published by Carnegie-Mellon University Press in 2002.
"Total Immersion" by Silas House appeared in *Night Train* in 2003.
"Upheaval" by Chris Holbrook appeared in *Night Train* in 2004.
"Worth" by Valerie Nieman appeared in the story collection *Fidelities* published by West Virginia University Press in 2004.
"The Coal Thief" by Alex Taylor © 2010 by Sarabande Books appeared in the story collection *The Name of the Nearest River* and is reprinted with permission.

Table of Contents

Dedication

*This book is dedicated to the 29 miners killed by
the Upper Big Branch Mine explosion on April 5, 2010*

Preface

The stories of Appalachia are the stories of America. This collection is an important step towards understanding Appalachia as it is, and as it has become. It is a step long overdue.

The plight of the people who live in the hills, hollows and river basins of the great eastern mountain chain of North America is both ancient and immediate. Here, you will not find tales replete with folksy charm and backwoods romanticism. There is not room in these writers' hearts for vacant sentiment. These stories ache and roar and testify to what they are—claims on a distinct and strong American identity. In the story titles we find "Upheaval" and "The Beauties of this Earth" as two sides of this place we call Appalachia.

We have endeavored to bring diverse voices to this collection, calling on the rich and complex culture of a region that straddles North, South and Midwest, a place that is other places as well. We do not believe any one view of Appalachia is a Truth entire. But somewhere in the patchwork, we have tried to present the hard beauty of the land and the history of a unique country and its people.

Even as Appalachia affirms itself as it is today, the idea of Applachia is dynamic and a work ever in-progress. For that reason, the reader will find many familiar names alongside those perhaps less well known. This is intentional, placing value here on artistry not notoriety. We believe the natural resource of emerging talent in the region is proof of larger literary goals and predicts future achievement.

It is worthwhile to note that the national and international regard for Appalachian letters has dramatically increased in the past few years, a regard proven most recently by Ron Rash being awarded the prestigious Frank O'Connor International Short Story Award for his collection *Burning Bright*. One of the stories from this prize-winning collection, "Into the Gorge" appears in this anthology. Rash is not alone. Writers such as Chris Offutt, Silas House, John McManus, Crystal Wilkinson, Mark Powell and Chris Holbrook are pushing beyond regional recognition with their formidable bodies of work, rolling back that shadowline where Appalachia ends and America begins.

But for this reputation to continue, we must put forth our best new work from writers not yet established, to discover new ways of looking at ourselves as a people. Innovation and reinvention are at the heart of Appalachian identity. Our goals for this book are to reveal the values and forces of our contemporary culture and to share the exciting change occurring in our writing, and so to celebrate this powerful force in American literature.

Charles Dodd White
Asheville, North Carolina (October 2010)

Horseweed
by Chris Offutt

William plucked beads of hardened plaster from his trowel and wiped them on the bucket's edge. The wall joints had to be smooth as snow. This job might lead to another and the Brants wanted everything perfect. The Brants owned the Sheetrock, the plaster, and the red rug under the drop cloth. Until the job was finished, they owned William eight hours a day. Only the ability belonged to William; he'd had to rent the tools.

Mrs. Miriam Brant walked into the room to check his progress, wearing a loose housecoat with nothing underneath. William looked away from her thighs and dipped the trowel. His wife's legs weren't as good but they were more familiar. Miriam tapped a red fingernail against the wall.

"I want your opinion on a room in back," she said.

He followed her through a long hall to the bedroom. A three-panel mirror filled a corner, and small rugs lay on the carpet. She bent from the waist, pointing to a web of ripples that puckered the wallpaper like a burn scar. The housecoat fell open to her navel.

"Work in here," she said, "is never good enough to suit me."

William looked past her face to the store-bought blanket on the bed, feeling bad for her. She was from Bobcat Hollow but had married a lawyer and moved to town. Her husband refused to let her family visit except during election years. William's fingers brushed the dimpled wall. The room was quiet and big, and he could hear his own breathing. He wondered when her husband got off work.

"Too much water in the glue," he said.

"Always something."

"Man ought not to leave a job that way."

"Maybe you could do better."

William looked at her legs, thinking of his wife alone at home all day. If one of his friends came by, she made the man stay on the porch until William got home. He lifted his head to Miriam, and spoke quietly.

"My daddy knew your daddy."

After a few seconds, Miriam tugged her housecoat together and sat on the bed, shoulders slumped, head down.

"I couldn't wait to get out of that holler," she said. "Now I'm just as stuck here as I was there. You still live on the ridge?"

"Guess I'm stuck there, too."

William stepped past her and returned to the living room. He skimmed plaster over the seam and feathered the edges. The work was nearly complete; tomorrow he would sand. At an outside faucet he cleaned the tools, watching the steady stream of water sparkle in the sun. Miriam waved from the window. William stared at her a long time before getting into his truck. He'd always liked her when they were kids.

William slowly drove the blacktop home, glad to be out of Rocksalt. He passed a new video dish perched among felled trees and wondered what his father would have thought of such a thing. Two years ago he'd told his father about a job with a construction crew in town.

"A man's lucky to have these hills," his father had said.

"I know it," William said. "But they ain't exactly ours no more."

"Town never was either."

William's father spat dark phlegm against the clay dirt yard. Coal dust filled his pores, blending his face into the night. His voice took on the timbre of a father speaking to a son, not to a man he trusted underground, working an illegal mine.

"Don't you do like your grandpaw done."

William stared at his boots. Years back, during the first mine strikes, his grandfather had made whisky to keep his kids in clothes. A government man shotgunned him as he unloaded forty quarts of liquor at Blue Lick River. His body fell into the muddy water and the family buried an empty coffin.

"I'm not Grandpaw," William had said. "And you're not me."

Tools rattled in the truck bed as William drove up the hill and out Crosscut Ridge to his house. Three dogs chased through the dust, jumping at the pickup. William squatted, pushing his fingers in the fur behind each dog's ears. He found several ticks, their bodies stretched tight like kernels of white corn. He twisted one free and squeezed it between thumb and finger. The tick burst in a spray of dark blood.

The heavy scent of venison stew drifted from the house, and William wondered how many meals were left on the doe. His daughters needed more meat. Inside, his wife Connie held the baby on her hip. Sarah sat on the floor, banging a spoon against a pot. Ruth rushed to her father.

"How many'd you get?" she said.

"Eight," William said. "Three off Blackie. Two off Hubcap. So how many ticks off Duke?"

She grunted over stubby fingers. Connie turned and pushed stray hair behind an ear. Afternoon sun washed her skin, softening the shadows below her eyes.

"How's town?" she said.

"About done."

"Take your clothes off before you set down."

"I'll take them off," he said, thinking of Miriam.

Five kinds of paneling formed the bedroom's tight walls. His favorite was a repeated scene of three grouse flying over tall grass. He scanned as if hunting and decided it would take a twenty-gauge with a cylinder bore. From the right position, a man could bring down all three birds. He studied a mirror with taped cracks. White plaster powder coated his face, and he resembled his father except for the color of the dust. William thought of the bathroom Connie wanted. Either that or a trailer, she had said. William was afraid she'd rather move to town.

In the living room, he sat on the end of the couch. Clear plastic covered the other half. As they paid it off, Connie exposed the vinyl in small increments, slicing the plastic with a kitchen knife. William understood that this was a display of her thrift—she deserved indoor plumbing. Town water was nine miles away and moving closer every day. He waved to the crew each morning on his way to Rocksalt, envious of their steady work. To add a bathroom, he needed three times the money from last year's tobacco crop, but the auction brought less every fall.

Connie called him to eat and he walked to the table, watching his daughters rinse their hands in an old lard bucket. Roofing tar plugged a hole in the bottom. The girls laughed around the pail hauled from the well at the end of the ridge. Splashed water clung to their blond hair.

After supper, William slipped into the hunting jacket that smelled of earth and game. He pulled his rifle from the closet and checked the breech. Walnut whorls patterned the stock in light and dark. It had belonged to his father and his grandfather. William often wondered who he'd give it to. He dropped some bullets in a pocket.

"Going out the ridge," he said.

"If I didn't know better," Connie said, "I'd think you had a woman out there."

"What I got is better." He forced a grin. "Back by dark."

"Watch for snakes. They're bad this year."

The dogs followed him as he climbed the hill, gauging fallen trees for winter firewood. Overlapping shadows flowed across the forest floor. When he neared a hickory the hounds began to whine, their dark eyes showing fear. He loaded the rifle and the dogs ran yelping back to the house. He recalled his grandfather's rasping voice, telling William moonshine stories as a boy.

"You take your dogs to a tree where you don't want them to follow you no more," the old man had said. "Let each dog smell of the gun. Then you kill one. The rest ain't much count for hunting after that but they'll not lead the law to a still. I done it many a time."

William stepped around the hickory to stand above his dog's small grave. King had been old and slow, nearly blind, his favorite. He nodded to the humped earth, and walked deeper into the woods. The land crested to a plateau of three hills where two ridges tapered down to the creek. He headed east, away from people, and eased down the hill to a lower ridge. He followed it to a limestone cliff and circled the rocks to a narrow hollow. At its end, he climbed onto a low knob ringed by hills. He listened carefully in each direction. A mourning dove moaned and high leaves brushed on a breeze. He hunched over, eyes intent on the ground. He saw a boot print and tensed his hands on the rifle.

The track was his own from before.

William topped the knob and grinned. Planted on ten-inch centers stood fifty-one hemp plants gently rocking in the breeze. William had never smoked hemp. It simply grew, the same as corn his grandfather had used for mash. Like ginseng and tobacco, hemp had become a valuable weed. Town people would buy a load and he'd sell it cheap. All he wanted were bathroom fixtures, two hundred feet of PVC pipe, and a mirror for Connie.

He walked through his garden, breaking off weak branches and pulling new shoots. He turned the leaves to check for worms. After pruning he leaned against a sycamore and listened to a whippoorwill wail into the surrounding hardwood hills. William knew hemp safer than a moonshine still because the knob belonged to the mine company. A new law allowed the state to steal family land with hemp on it, but the government had always left the coal operators alone. Most of the companies came from out of state, and except for bribes in Frankfort, the money went out of state, too. William's father had said that was why Kentucky had the weakest reclamation laws. Of five miners working illegally during the oil embargo, three went to prison, one got rich, and thirty tons of earth fell on William's father. Everyone on the hill helped dig him out but there wasn't enough left to feed a dog. After the funeral William worked town construction for three months. Instead of drinking with the other men after work, he saved his money and bought his own tools. When the job ended he was laid off while everyone else moved to another site. The foreman said that he didn't mix well. William sold his tools for half of what he'd paid and began searching the hills for wild hemp to transplant on the hidden knob.

Saw briers rattled over the hill. William twitched his head, aiming his ears in that direction. The steady sound was loud enough for large game. He climbed down the back of the knob and circled the downwind side, placing each foot carefully to avoid the noise of leaf or fallen limb. Only a fawn would wander into briers. Its mother would be near. William flicked off the rifle's safety.

At the edge of the woods, he knelt behind an oak and sniffed sassafras blending with pine sap. The whip-poor-will's cry was very loud, a warning. William leaned his head and rifle around the tree. His vision skipped along the ridge to the base of the knob and slowly up the steep bank. Sweat trickled down his sides. A man stood thirty yards away at the lip of the knob. Hemp plants swayed above his head.

William peered through the scope of his grandfather's gun. He lowered the rifle past the man's face to the center of his chest and leaned against the tree to steady his aim, knowing the hills would swallow the sound. He inhaled, and let the air out slow and careful.

The man turned in a small circle, gazing around the hills. William breathed normally again. He would not rush a killing shot. The man limped to a sapling and hauled himself over the knob, panting like a chased fox. With trembling hands he pulled his pants leg to the knee. William moved the scope to the man's bare calf. In the center of a dark swelling were two red puncture marks.

William pivoted around the oak and locked the safety behind the trigger. In three days, he could pretend to find the man and drag him out of the woods. The man would never remember the hemp. He'd lose his leg and not return.

The sun began its final slide behind the far hill when William stood, propped his rifle over his shoulder, and stepped into the deep shade of the woods. Connie expected him home by now. Their daughters would be in bed and he and Connie would lie on the couch and make silent love so as not to wake them. William glanced at the dimming sky and wished he'd killed the man before seeing the snake-bit leg. Now he couldn't shoot him, and worse, he couldn't just walk away.

William moved down the bank and climbed the knob, forcing himself not to look at the hemp. The man was small and wiry and William was surprised that he was so young. His eyes were wide as bottle caps.

"Copperhead got me," said the man.

"Big or little?"

"Big."

"You're lucky. Babies are the worst."

"Lucky," said the man.

William opened his pocketknife and sliced the man's pants along the seam.

"Got a lighter?" William said.

The man slid a sweaty hand into his pocket and handed William a blue book of matches. On its cover the coal company's name was embossed in gold.

"I just work for them," the man said. "I don't own it."

"Shut up."

William lit a match and passed the knife blade through the flame. The shiny metal blackened. He straddled the man's thigh and made a short, deep slit in his calf. He lifted the knife and turned his wrist to cut again. The two lines crossed at one of the holes left by the snake. William pressed his mouth to the wound. Sucked air squeaked, and liquid filled his mouth. He turned his head to spit and repeated the process on the other hole. William cut a patch from the man's shirt tail and covered the wound, tying it with strips of cloth. The man lay on his back, head turned, cheek against the dirt. Vomit pooled beside his face.

William spat until his mouth was dry, then ran his tongue along his gums to check for sores. He knew he'd swallowed some but that didn't matter; stomach acid was stronger than venom. The man rustled dead leaves, struggling to sit.

"What'd they send you for?" William said. "They done mined this land out."

"Just running tests."

"Up here?"

"No. When the snake hit me, I came this way. Figured I'd build a fire and somebody'd see it."

"You'd do that, wouldn't you. You'd burn the woods down."

"Nothing here but some kind of horseweed."

The moon rose above the hemp as if towed by the setting sun. The man's clothes were ripped from briars. A gold band glinted on his left hand and William wondered if he had kids.

"Live in town?" William said.

"All my life," the man said. "We'd like to move out, but I don't know."

"It ain't easy around here."

"Neither is town. Prices are high as a cat's back."

William reached for his rifle and stood, and the man stopped talking, eyes growing wide again. He leaned back, breathing hard. William emptied the rifle of bullets, pulled the man to his feet, and handed him the gun.

"Use this to walk with," William said. "You parked on the fire road?"

The man nodded.

"Try not to bang the scope."

He led the man across the knob and down the back slope into the woods. Tree frogs ceased their noise. Night came over the eastern hills, passed the men, and seeped along the ridge. Starlight spread through open sky. William moved easily down the hill and squatted to drink from the creek. He waited for the man to thrash through heavy growth beside the water.

"Think I ought to wash my leg?" the man said.

"This water might not be the cleanest on account of the mines."

"Then why are you drinking it?"

"All we got," William said. "Ever notice how town water always tastes like pipe?"

"Never did," said the man. "What's your name?"

William stood quickly. "Got a mile to go, uphill."

He began following the creek past tree roots slithering down the bank. A bobwhite call floated through the trees. William remembered that his father and grandfather had walked this creek home from the mines, and he was suddenly glad he'd had no sons. The responsibility of land would end with him. Men's lives ran in bursts of work, drink, and quick death, while women wore down slow and steady, like a riverbank at a sharp curve. He'd urge his daughters to move but they'd probably stay and give him grandsons. One day William would be old and telling a boy about helping a coal man who didn't deserve it. He wondered what the state would find to outlaw in his grandsons' time.

An hour later, William reached the pickup parked on the one-lane fire road. The late-model truck had new tires, high shocks, and the coal company name on each door. William watched the man climb the hill.

"I can make it from here," the man said.

"Nice truck."

"Only reason I took the damn job," the man said. "Free gas and a company truck. It runs better than I do." He patted the hood. "What do I owe you?"

William shook his head and looked away. The man fumbled keys, opened the door, and climbed into the cab. He rolled the window down. William checked the rifle scope and wiped moisture from the barrel.

"That wasn't horseweed up there, was it?" the man said.

"I don't know," William said. "I don't raise horses."

"Far as I know," the man said, "you don't raise a thing."

He started the truck, drifting exhaust along the ridge. Headlights splayed through the trees as he backed along the narrow road. When the engine faded, the sounds of night began again.

William moved through darkness, following the creek. At the fork, he climbed the hill to Crosscut Ridge. He felt momentarily glad that his grandfather and father were dead and unable to know he'd helped the man live. His father would have left the man snake-bit, and his grandfather would have shot him. If William's own grandson understood his decision, he'd give the rifle to the boy.

He chuckled to himself, thirty-two years old and talking to an unborn child. After his grandfather died, he'd once heard his father late at night, telling the old man about the landing on the moon. His father swore that tv people had invented it for money. The proof, he whispered into the darkness, was that nobody ever went back.

Connie was asleep when William came home. He sat on the bed and spoke in her ear, promising a mirror with a built-in light for the bathroom. She wiggled naked across his lap. Moonlight gleamed through the window, outlining his hand along her hip. She unbuttoned his shirt and he remembered Miriam. His eyes tightened to erase her from his mind. His father filled the gap. He stood tall and coal-dirty, holding a dinner bucket. Connie kissed William's neck and brushed her fingers along his back. He thought of Miriam again, and this time let her stay. His father had been smiling. The big seam he'd found would make the family rich.

Into the Gorge
by Ron Rash

His great-aunt had been born on this land, lived on it eight decades and knew it as well as she knew her husband and children. That was what she'd always claimed, and could tell you to the week when the first dogwood blossom would brighten the ridge, the first blackberry darken and swell enough to harvest. Then her mind had wandered into a place she could not follow, taking with it all the people she knew, their names and connections, whether they still lived or whether they'd died. But her body lingered, shed of an inner being, empty as a cicada husk.

Knowledge of the land was the one memory that refused to dissolve. During her last year, Jesse would step off the school bus and see his great-aunt hoeing a field behind her farmhouse, breaking ground for a crop she never sowed, but the rows were always straight, right-depthed. Her nephew, Jesse's father, worked in an adjoining field. The first few times, he had taken the hoe from her hands and led her back to her house, but she'd soon be back in the field. After a while neighbors and kin just let her hoe. They brought meals and checked on her as often as they could. Jesse always walked rapidly past her field. His great-aunt never looked up, her gaze fixed on the hoe blade and the dark soil it churned, but he had always feared she'd raise her eyes and acknowledge him, though what she might want to convey Jesse could not say.

Then one March day she disappeared. The men in the community searched all afternoon and into evening as the temperature dropped, sleet crackled and hissed like static. The men rippled outward as they lit lanterns and moved into the gorge. Jesse watched from his family's pasture as the held flames grew smaller, soon disappearing and reappearing like foxfire, crossing the creek and then on past the ginseng patch Jesse helped his father harvest. Going deeper into land that had been in the family almost two hundred years, toward the original homestead, the place she'd been born.

They found his great-aunt at dawn, her back against a tree as if waiting for the searchers to arrive. But that was not the strangest thing. She'd taken off her shoes, her dress and her underclothes. Years later

Jesse read in a magazine that people dying of hypothermia did such a thing believing heat, not cold, was killing them. Back then, the woods had been communal, *No Trespassing* signs an affront, but after her death neighbors soon found places other than the gorge to hunt and fish, gather blackberries and galax. Her ghost was still down there, many believed, including Jesse's own father, who never returned to harvest the ginseng he'd planted. When the park service made an offer on the homestead, Jesse's father and aunts had sold. That was in 1959, and the government paid sixty dollars an acre. Now, five decades later, Jesse stood on his porch and looked east toward Sampson Ridge, where bulldozers razed woods and pastureland for another gated community. He wondered how much those sixty acres were worth today. Easily a million dollars.

Not that he needed that much money. His house and twenty acres were paid for, as was his truck. The tobacco allotment earned less each year but still enough for a widower with grown children. Enough as long as he didn't have to go to the hospital or his truck throw a rod. He needed some extra money put away for that. Not a million, but some.

So two autumns ago Jesse had gone into the gorge, following the creek to the old homestead, then up the ridge's shadowy north face where his father had seeded and harvested his ginseng patch. The crop was there, evidently untouched for half a century. Some of the plants rose above Jesse's kneecaps, and there was more ginseng than his father could have dreamed of, a hillside spangled with bright yellow leaves, enough roots to bulge Jesse's knapsack. Afterward, he'd carefully replanted the seeds, done it just as his father had done, then walked out of the gorge, past the iron gate that kept vehicles off the logging road. A yellow tin marker nailed to a nearby tree said US Park Service.

Now another autumn had come. A wet autumn, which was good for the plants, as Jesse had verified three days ago when he'd checked them. Once again he gathered the knapsack and trowel from the woodshed. He also took the .32-20 Colt from his bedroom drawer. Late in the year for snakes, but after days of rain the afternoon was warm enough to bring a rattler or copperhead out to sun.

He followed the old logging road, the green backpack slung over his shoulder and the pistol in the outside pouch. Jesse's arthritic knees ached as he made the descent. They would ache more that night, even after rubbing liniment on them. He wondered how many more autumns he'd be able to make this trip. Till I'm seventy, Jesse figured, giving himself two more years. The ground was slippery from all the rain and he walked slowly. A broken ankle or leg would be a serious thing this far from help, but it was more than that. He wanted to enter the gorge respectfully.

When he got in sight of the homestead, the land leveled out, but the ground grew soggier, especially where the creek ran close to the logging road. Jesse saw boot prints from three days earlier. Then he saw another set, coming up the logging road from the other direction. Boot prints as well, but smaller. Jesse looked down the logging road but saw no hiker or fisherman. He kneeled, his joints creaking.

The prints appeared at least a day old, maybe more. They stopped on the road when they met Jesse's, then also veered toward the homestead. Jesse got up and looked around again before walking through the withered broom sedge and joe-pye weed. He passed a cairn of stones that once had been a chimney, a dry well covered with a slab of tin so rusty it served as more warning than safeguard. The boot prints were no longer discernible, but he knew where they'd end. Led the son-of-a-bitch right to it, he told himself, and wondered how he could have been stupid enough to walk the road on a rainy morning. But when he got to the ridge, the plants were still there, the soil around them undisturbed. Probably just a hiker, or a bird watcher, Jesse figured, that or some punk kid looking to poach someone's marijuana, not knowing the ginseng was worth even more. Either way, he'd been damn lucky.

Jesse lifted the trowel from the backpack and got on his knees. He smelled the rich dark earth that always reminded him of coffee. The plants had more color than three days ago, the berries a deeper red, the leaves bright as polished gold. It always amazed him that such radiance could grow in soil the sun rarely touched, like finding rubies and sapphires on the gloomy walls of a cave. He worked with care but also haste. The first time he'd returned here two years earlier he'd felt a sudden coolness, a slight lessening of light as if a cloud had passed over the sun. Imagination, he'd told himself then, but it had made him work faster, with no pauses to rest.

Jesse jabbed the trowel into the loamy soil, probing inward with care so as not to cut the root, slowly bringing it to light. The root was a big one, six inches long, tendrils sprouting from the core like clay renderings of human limbs. Jesse scraped away the dirt and placed the root in the backpack, just as carefully buried the seeds to insure another harvest. As he crawled a few feet left to unearth another plant, he felt the moist dirt seeping its way through the knees of his blue jeans. He liked being this close to the earth, smelling it, feeling it on his hands and under his nails, the same as when he planted tobacco sprigs in the spring. A song he'd heard on the radio drifted into his head, a woman wanting to burn down a whole town. He let the tune play in his head and tried to fill in the refrain as he pressed the trowel into the earth.

"You can lay that trowel down," a voice behind Jesse said. "Then raise your hands."

Jesse turned and saw a man in a gray shirt and green khakis, a gold badge on his chest and US Park Service patch on the shoulder. Short blond hair, dark eyes. A young man, probably not even thirty. A pistol was holstered on his right hip, the safety strap off.

"Don't get up," the younger man said again, louder this time.

Jesse did as he was told. The park ranger came closer, picked up the backpack, and stepped away. Jesse watched as he opened the compartment with the ginseng root, then the smaller pouch. The ranger took out the .32-20 and held it in his palm. The gun had belonged to Jesse's grandfather and father before being passed on to Jesse. The ranger inspected it as he might an arrowhead or spear point he'd found.

"That's just for the snakes," Jesse said.

"Possession of a firearm is illegal in the park," the ranger said. "You've broken two laws, federal laws. You'll be getting some jail time for this."

The younger man looked like he might say more, then seemed to decide against it.

"This ain't right," Jesse said. "My daddy planted the seeds for this patch. That ginseng wouldn't even be here if it wasn't for him. And that gun, if I was poaching I'd have a rifle or shotgun."

What was happening didn't seem quite real. The world, the very ground he stood on, felt like it was evaporating beneath him. Jesse almost expected somebody, though he couldn't say who, to come out of the woods laughing about the joke just played on him. The ranger placed the pistol in the backpack. He unclipped the walky-talky from his belt, pressed a button and spoke.

"He did come back and I've got him."

A staticy voice responded, the words indiscernible to Jesse.

"No, he's too old to be much trouble. We'll be waiting on the logging road."

The ranger pressed a button and placed the walky-talky back on his belt. Jesse read the name on the silver name tag. *Barry Wilson.*

"You any kin to the Wilsons over on Balsam Mountain?"

"No," the younger man said. "I grew up in Charlotte."

The walky-talky crackled and the ranger picked it up, said okay, and clipped it back on his belt.

"Call Sheriff Arrowood," Jesse said. "He'll tell you I've never been in any trouble before. Never, not even a speeding ticket."

"Let's go."

"Can't you just forget this," Jesse said. "It ain't like I was growing marijuana. There's plenty that do in this park. I know that for a fact. That's worse than what I done."

The ranger smiled.

"We'll get them eventually, old fellow, but their bulbs burn brighter than yours. They're not big enough fools to leave us footprints to follow."

The ranger slung the backpack over his shoulder.

"You've got no right to talk to me like that," Jesse said.

There was still plenty of distance between them, but the ranger looked like he contemplated another step back.

"If you're going to give me trouble, I'll just go ahead and cuff you now."

Jesse almost told the younger man to come on and try, but he made himself look at the ground, get himself under control before he spoke.

"No, I ain't going to give you any trouble," he finally said, raising his eyes.

The ranger nodded toward the logging road.

"After you, then."

Jesse moved past the ranger, stepping through the broom sedge and past the ruined chimney, the ranger to his right, two steps behind. Jesse veered slightly to his left, moving so he'd pass close to the old well. He paused and glanced back at the ranger.

"That trowel of mine, I ought to get it."

The ranger paused too and was about to reply when Jesse took a quick step and shoved the ranger with two hands toward the well. The ranger didn't fall until one foot went through the rotten tin, then the other. As he did, the backpack dropped from his hand. He didn't go all the way through, just up to his arms, his fingernails scraping the tin for leverage, looking like a man caught in muddy ice. The ranger's hands found purchase, one on a hank of broom sedge, the other on the metal's firmer edging. He began pulling himself out, wincing as the rusty tin tore cloth and skin. He looked at Jesse, who stood above him.

"You've really screwed up now," the ranger gasped.

Jesse bent down and reached not for the younger man's hand but his shoulder. He pushed hard, the ranger's hands clutching only air as he fell through the rotten metal, a thump and simultaneous snap of bone as he hit the well's dry floor. Seconds passed but no other sound rose from the darkness.

The backpack lay at the edge and Jesse snatched it up. He ran, not toward his farm house but into the woods. He didn't look back again but bear crawled through the ginseng patch and up the ridge, his breaths loud pants. Trees thickened around him, oaks and poplars, some hemlocks. The soil was thin and moist, and he slipped several times. Halfway up the ridge he paused, his heart battering his chest. When it finally calmed, Jesse heard a vehicle coming up the logging road and saw a pale-green forest service jeep. A man and a woman got out.

Jesse went on, passing through another patch of ginseng, probable descendants from his father's original seedlings. The sooner he got to the ridge crest, the sooner he could make his way across it toward the gorge head. His legs were leaden now and he couldn't catch his breath. The extra pounds he'd put on the last few years draped over his belt, gave him more to haul. His mind went dizzy and he slipped and skidded a few yards downhill. For a while he lay still, his body sprawled on the slanted earth, arms and legs flung outward. Jesse felt the leaves cushioning the back of his head, an acorn nudged against a shoulder blade. Above him, oak branches pierced a darkening sky. He remembered the fairy tale about a giant beanstalk and imagined how convenient it would be to simply climb off into the clouds.

Jesse shifted his body so his face turned downhill, one ear to the ground as if listening for the faintest footfall. It seemed so wrong to be sixty-eight years old and running from someone. Old age was supposed to give a person dignity, respect. He remembered the night the searchers brought his great-aunt out of the gorge. The men stripped off their heavy coats to cover her body and had taken turns carrying her. They had been silent and somber as they came into the yard. Even after the women had taken the corpse into the farmhouse to be washed and dressed, the men had stayed on his great-aunt's porch. Some had smoked hand-rolled cigarettes, others had bulged their jaws with tobacco. Jesse had sat on the lowest porch step and listened, knowing the men quickly forgot he was there. They did not talk of how they'd found his great-aunt or the times she'd wandered from her house to the garden. Instead, the men spoke of a woman who could tell you tomorrow's weather by looking at the evening sky, a godly woman who'd taught Sunday school into her seventies. They told stories about her and every story was spoken in a reverent way, as if now that his great-aunt was dead she'd once more been transformed back to her true self.

Jesse rose slowly. He hadn't twisted an ankle or broken an arm and that seemed his first bit of luck since walking into the gorge. When Jesse reached the crest, his legs were so weak he clutched a maple sapling to ease himself to the ground. He looked down through the cascading trees. An orange and white rescue squad van had now arrived. Workers huddled around the well, and Jesse couldn't see much of what they were doing but before long a stretcher was carried to the van. He was too far away to tell the ranger's condition, even if the man was alive.

At the least a broken arm or leg, Jesse knew, and tried to think of an injury that would make things all right, like a concussion to make the ranger forget what had happened, or the ranger hurting bad enough that shock made him forget. Jesse tried not to think about the snapped bone being in the back or neck.

The van's back doors closed from within, and the vehicle turned onto the logging road. The siren was off but the beacon drenched the woods red. The woman ranger scoured the hillside with binoculars, sweeping without pause over where Jesse sat. Another green forest service truck drove up, two more rangers spilling out. Then Sheriff Arrowood's car, silent as the ambulance.

The sun lay behind Clingman's Dome now, and Jesse knew waiting any longer would only make it harder. He moved in a stupor of exhaustion, feet stumbling over roots and rocks, swaying like a drunk. When he got far enough, he'd be able to come down the ridge, ascend the narrow gorge mouth. But Jesse was so tired he didn't know how he could go any farther without resting. His knees grated bone on bone, popping and crackling each time they bent or twisted. He panted and wheezed and imagined his lungs an accordion that never unfolded enough.

Old and a fool. That's what the ranger had called Jesse. An old man no doubt. His body told him so every morning when he awoke. The liniment he applied to his joints and muscles each morning and night made him think of himself as a creaky rust-corroded machine that must be oiled and warmed up before it could sputter to life. Maybe a fool as well, he acknowledged, for who other than a fool could have gotten into such a fix.

Jesse found a felled oak and sat down, a mistake because he couldn't imagine summoning the energy to rise. He looked through the trees. Sheriff Arrowood's car was gone, but the truck and jeep were still there. He didn't see but one person and knew the others searched the woods for him. A crow cawed once farther up the ridge. Then no other sound, not even the wind. Jesse took the backpack and pitched it into the thick woods below, watched it tumble out of sight. A waste, but he couldn't risk their searching his house. He thought about tossing the pistol as well but the gun had belonged to his father, his father's father before that. Besides, if they found it in his house that was no proof it was the pistol the ranger had seen. They had no proof of anything really. Even his being in the gorge was just the ranger's word against his. If he could get back to the house.

Night fell fast now, darkness webbing the gaps between tree trunks and branches. Below, high-beam flashlights flickered on. Jesse remembered two weeks after his great-aunt's burial. Graham Sutherland had come out of the gorge shaking and chalk-faced, not able to tell what had happened until Jesse's father gave him a drought of whiskey. Graham had been fishing near the old homestead and glimpsed something on the far bank, there for just a moment. Though a sunny spring afternoon, the weather in the gorge had suddenly turned cold and damp. Graham had seen her then, moving through the trees toward him, her arms outstretched. *Beseeching me to come to her*, Graham had told them. *Not speaking, but letting that cold and damp touch my very bones so I'd feel what she felt. She didn't say it out loud, maybe couldn't, but she wanted me to stay down there with her. She didn't want to be alone.*

Jesse walked on, not stopping until he found a place where he could make his descent. A flashlight moved below him, its holder merged with the dark. The light bobbed as if on a river's current, a river running uphill all the way to the iron gate that marked the end of forest service land. Then the light swung around, made its swaying way back down the logging road. Someone shouted and the disparate lights gathered like sparks returning to their source. Headlights and engines came to life, and two sets of red taillights dimmed and soon disappeared.

Jesse made his way down the slope, his body slantways, one hand close to the ground in case he slipped. Low branches slapped his face. Once on level land he let minutes pass, listening for footsteps or a cough on the logging road, someone left behind to trick him into coming out. No moon shown but a few stars had settled overhead, enough light for him to make out a human form.

Jesse moved quietly up the logging road. Get back in the house and you'll be all right, he told himself. He came to the iron gate and slipped under. It struck him only then that someone might be waiting at his house. He went to the left and stopped where a barbed wire fence marked the pasture edge. The house lights were still off, like he'd left them. Jesse's hand touched a strand of sagging barbed wire and he felt a vague reassurance in its being there, its familiarity. He was about to move closer when he heard a truck, soon saw its yellow beams crossing Sampson Ridge. As soon as the pickup pulled into the driveway, the porch light came on. Sheriff Arrowood appeared on the porch, one of Jesse's shirts in his hand. Two men got out of the pickup and opened the tailgate. Bloodhounds leaped and tumbled from the truck bed, whining as the men gathered their leashes. He had to get back into the gorge, and quick, but his legs were suddenly stiff and unyielding as iron stobs. It's just the fear, Jesse told himself. He clasped one of the fence's rusty barbs and squeezed until pain reconnected his mind and body.

Jesse followed the land's downward tilt, crossed back under the gate. The logging road leveled out and Jesse saw the outline of the homestead's ruined chimney. As he came closer, the chimney solidified, grew darker than the dark around it, as if an unlit passageway into some greater darkness.

Jesse took the .32-20 from his pocket and let the pistol's weight settle in his hand. If they caught him with it, that was just more trouble. Throw it so far they won't find it, he told himself, because there's prints on it. He turned toward the woods and heaved the pistol, almost falling with the effort. The gun went only a few feet before thunking solidly against a tree, landing close to the logging road if not on it. There was no time to find the pistol, because the hounds were at the gorge head now, flashlights dipping and rising behind them. He could tell by the hounds' cries that they were already on his trail.

Jesse stepped into the creek, hoping that doing so might cause the dogs to lose his scent. If it worked, he could circle back and find the gun. What sparse light the stars had offered was snuffed out as the creek left the road and entered the woods. Jesse bumped against the banks, stumbled into deeper pockets of water that drenched his pants as well as his boots and socks. He fell and something tore in his shoulder.

But it worked. There was soon a confusion of barks and howls, the flashlights no longer following him but instead sweeping the woods from one still point. Jesse stepped out of the creek and sat down. He was shivering, his mind off plumb, every thought tilting toward panic. As he poured water from the boots, Jesse remembered his boot prints led directly from his house to the ginseng patch. They had ways of matching boots and their prints, and not just a certain foot size and make. He'd seen on a TV show how they could even match the worn part of the sole to a print. Jesse stuffed the socks inside the boots and threw them at the dark. Like the pistol they didn't go far before hitting something solid.

It took him a long time to find the old logging road, and even when he was finally on it he was so disoriented that he wasn't sure which direction to go. Jesse walked a while and came to a park campground, which meant he'd guessed wrong. He turned around and walked the other way. It felt like years had passed before he finally made it back to the homestead. A campfire now glowed and sparked between the homestead and the iron gate, the men hunting Jesse huddled around it. The pistol lay somewhere near the men, perhaps found already. Several of the hounds barked, impatient to get back onto the trail, but the searchers had evidently decided to wait till morning to continue. Though Jesse was too far away to hear them, he knew they talked to help pass the time. They probably had food with them, perhaps coffee as well. Jesse realized he was thirsty and thought about going back to the creek for some water, but he was too tired.

Dew wet his bare feet as he passed the far edge of the homestead and then to the woods' edge where the ginseng was. He sat down, and in a few minutes the night's chill enveloped him. A frost warning, the radio had said. He thought of how his great-aunt had taken off her clothes and how, despite the scientific explanation, it seemed to Jesse a final abdication of everything she had once been. He looked toward the eastern sky. It seemed he'd been running a week's worth of nights, but he saw the stars hadn't begun to pale. The first pink smudges on the far ridge line were a while away, perhaps hours. The night would linger long enough for what would or would not come. He waited.

Holler
by Crystal Wilkinson

Turn left where Otha's one-room store used to be and the poplars get thicker, drive past Mt. Zion Baptist Church and across the concrete bridge and on up the holler. You'll be able to see Green River if you stretch your neck, but don't expect something out of a picture book. It's brown, plumb full of mosquitoes, water moccasins galore.

Go to the end of the road and on up the hill a little and this is Mission Creek—this is where we live. You might not expect to find black people in the mountains, not many of us left, but we're here. Keep going until the road levels out a bit and the gravel gets more scarce and turns to dirt, go around the bend and soon you'll see the graying heads of black men nodding as you pass, black children playing Red Rover, black women hanging sheets on the lines.

Tallboy is my brother-in-law. He's six-foot-five, pock-faced and wears a Reds baseball cap pulled down over his eyes. All you can see is a little bit of his broad nose and headphone wires snaking down his bird chest. We all grew up together, and I remember Tallboy before he found Mr. Jessie out in the field, before he went a little off and Miss Mattie had him committed to the state hospital.

Tallboy came back a different version of himself, but Miss Mattie says it's because he stayed away from here too long. The Tallboy I knew was smart and bright-eyed, always had his nose in a book. His hair was the biggest part of him: a wild long Afro that was sometimes braided in sleek cornrows that hung to the middle of his back. This new Tallboy has a close cropped fade and comes up the road to our house to get away from that place out there in the field where it happened.

One night a week ago, Tallboy came in while I was washing up the last of the supper dishes. JB was already gone to work out at Icco making car parts. He's been working third shift for going on a year. Tallboy sat in JB's chair. Like that, with his back turned, he was Mr. Jessie made over. He let out a long breath looking like his daddy for the world.

"Want some cobbler?"

I was already at the stove scooping some out into a bowl before he answered. He sunk his head back into the chair and started telling me about his girl trouble.

He started and kept going like a train through it all.

I knew about Tallboy's group therapy. I knew he'd met his girlfriend, Chelsea, there. Miss Mattie said it wasn't helping him none to sit around with people as bad off in the head as he was.

I handed him the bowl. He took big bites and kept talking. Every once in a while he stroked the bridge of his nose or ran his thumb and forefinger across the brim of his cap.

I'd seen the girlfriend once all hugged up with Tallboy at Dee's. Her mother had driven her up here to see him. We all used to go to Dee's for birthdays, anniversaries, and proms. It was the kind of place that wasn't meant for us, but we went anyway before they tore it down a few months back and built a Dollar Store. They had a jukebox then and we kept it fed quarters even if the songs were five or six years old. We preferred Aretha Franklin and the Floaters, but some nights the lonesome twang of Merle Haggard.

Tallboy had his arm around that girl when me and JB walked in and her hair hung over Tallboy's elbow like kudzu. She wasn't from around here. Nice wire-framed glasses. Average face I guess—you couldn't really tell anything was wrong with her but mostly all I remember is that sheaf of black hair hanging down to the center of her back, shining and waving to the white boys at the front counter.

Tallboy had a proud look on his face and nodded to me. JB slapped his brother on the back like he had just won something, which was unusual because usually he scowled at Tallboy like he was angry or ashamed. Everybody looked. I spoke gently to the girl and kept moving. Her mother was in the parking lot in her Chevy waiting for the date to end.

Miss Gayl waved to us from the back through a wall of steam. She was the one black cook they had and most times we didn't stay if we didn't see her working back there.

We slipped into our booth. But even after we had received our drinks and tapped the hard red plastic glasses together in a toast, I couldn't take my eyes off that girl Chelsea.

"Hair like that make a man go crazy," I said to JB.

He didn't say nothing.

Tallboy lit up a cigarette and pressed it between his lips, took a drag from it then looked into her eyes. He stroked his hand across that hair and chewed her ear a little. They looked normal from that distance.

Normal. He seemed normal that day, happy even, but last week when he came out to the house all that was gone, replaced with a wild-eyed misery. I ended up rubbing his neck while he lay over on my lap crying, hollering out like somebody had just died.

"Chessie's gone," he said.

"You'll be alright," I said but it wasn't something I really believed. He'd be alright? Nobody who'd known him before he found Mr. Jessie believed that.

They say when Tallboy found Mr. Jessie that his face was mostly gone. Mr. Jessie was working on his own land, riding his own tractor. They beat him up, then tied him to the back of the tractor with a log chain and drove around the pasture making huge round patterns like crop circles. Tallboy, fresh home from school, had been the first to find him. JB and Sis weren't home yet. Miss Mattie came home to Tallboy running loops around and around the outside of the house mumbling "Daddy, Daddy, Daddy" and Mr. Jessie out there mangled like something wild had gotten hold of him.

Tallboy curled his feet up on the couch.

After some time, Tallboy's story drifted off to nothing. Chelsea was gone. Her mother had thought it all a bad idea when she had caught them kissing.

I called out his name and tried to rustle him up but his head fell back hard against my legs and I knew he was sleep. Miss Mattie said it was the medicine that knocked him out like that, but I knew the man was tired. I was tired too. His breath on my thigh was heavy and warm. I wanted to stroke his head where that Afro used to be but I didn't. I rubbed his back in small circles like I would a child's.

Sometime during the night I dreamed of Mr. Jessie's body out there in the field being drug behind the tractor but when I looked at him it was my own daddy's face I saw, the way he looked when they pulled him up from the coal mine, like he'd just fallen asleep down there and never woke up. Him and the fourteen others, everybody white but him, lifted up from their graves to be buried again three days later. I woke up thinking about Mama too and how she didn't last long after Daddy passed. It's easy for a woman up here to grieve herself to death.

I roused up a little, but instead of telling Tallboy to move up off of me like I should have, I fell back asleep with his head buried in my stomach, my hand resting on his back, our legs sprawled out along the couch.

Up toward the morning, the front door thumped against the wall and it scared me considering what we'd all been through. Tallboy sat up straight on the couch and braced his hands on my thighs.

JB walked in and dropped the two plastic sacks of groceries and a gallon of milk he was carrying. The milk jug busted and poured onto the floor. I smiled, relieved at the sight of him.

I called out to him, "Baby..."

JB could have been Black Jesus coming to save us all with that halo of light spread out around his head but before I had a chance to tell him that, before I told him the story of Tallboy's woman or of my dream. Before all of this, he hauled off and hit Tallboy square in the face knocking him to the floor.

Tallboy sat in the milk cradling his bruise.

JB hit Tallboy again and I thought I could hear the small bones in his jaw give a little.

When he got back up Tallboy had his hands out in front of him at first trying to stay the blows, then he took a wobbly swing. A look of terror welled up in Tallboy's eyes, and I couldn't help but to think about Mr. Jessie. I scrambled up and in the ruckus was knocked into the end table. The lamp crashed to the floor and Alpha was barking out in the yard.

Tallboy's arms were flailing around but he wasn't hitting nothing. His boyish face was becoming a blood blister and a long strand of red slobber slid from his mouth to the floor.

"Stop, JB. You stop this right now," I said. "He wasn't doing nothing."

But JB rubbed his hands across his face. He was sweating dark shapes through his work shirt. I tried to get to the phone, but JB jerked it out of the wall.

"Just listen," I said and put my hands up to him, but he kept his fists balled up.

Tallboy got to the door and we all went out into the yard where we could see the sun rising up over the mountains.

Alpha ran back and forth in front of the doghouse wagging his tail like he was waiting on breakfast. With all the yelling and moving around the poor thing began to yelp a little. It was already a little cold. The leaves had turned and were beginning to fall.

Tallboy ran to the end of the driveway, then down the path behind our house, past the cistern. He jumped over the barbed wire fence and ran on up the foothill toward the woods. Every once in a while I saw one of his hands go up to his face and I knew he was wiping away tears. JB ran after him and soon they were just outlines of men among the trees off in the distance.

I ran back into the house to grab my car keys, and when I came out Tallboy was bounding back down the hill toward me covered in cockleburs. Once he reached flat land again Tallboy rushed past me and took off down the road his feet slapping the dirt and leaves.

JB followed but was losing ground and I could tell his rage, even though it had nothing to do with this, was getting the best of him. For a moment my heart fluttered a little at the thought of Mr. Jessie having one son so full of anger and the other emptied out of most every thing he used to be. My heart leapt out of my chest for my husband, but JB still had that way about him that called for more fear than empathy.

I jumped in the Pontiac and sped past him.

Tallboy was way out in front and ducked quickly into the passenger's seat.

I could see JB in the rearview mirror his hands on his thighs gathering his breath. He dropped to his knees like a praying man.

I took Tallboy to his mama.

At Miss Mattie's place, Patton, who'd kept an eye out for her since Mr. Jessie died, was next door pulling weeds. He waved to us with a gloved hand.

In Miss Mattie's yard a stack of fresh wood was piled up against the house waiting on winter and a chicken wire cage was home to two pups. The pups barked at us when we arrived and then waved their tails when they picked up Tallboy's scent, but he didn't bend down to pet them.

When Miss Mattie came to the door she was breathing hard and placed her hands on her hips.

"What now?" she said at the sight of us.

"Nothing," I told her. "I brought him back home to you."

Tallboy took his cap off when he entered the house but didn't say a word.

Miss Mattie came out on the porch in her housedress and rubbed the head of the mother beagle when the dog came out from around the house. Miss Mattie pulled a fat tick from the place she had rubbed and burnt it with a cigarette lighter. Then she threw her hand up at Patton and slipped back into the house.

The dog looked back at her with sad eyes, one drooping lower than the other. The trees in the back of the house were full of red leaves, some of which had already fallen.

"What happened?" Miss Mattie looked at Tallboy's face then turned to me.

I could hear the pups whining for their mother because they couldn't reach her through the chicken wire. I tried to explain what had happened, but when she found out it was between the boys Miss Mattie grunted in response and lit a cigarette. The smoke came back in on her and she narrowed her eyes.

"You ate?" she said to Tall.

"Pie," he answered.

She went to the oven and pulled out a tin pan with beef roast, potatoes, green beans and a corn muffin inside and sat it on the table beside where Tall stood.

"Hungry?" she said to me.

I shook my head no.

Tallboy began to eat his supper, though it was early in the morning.

Miss Mattie poured him a glass of cold tea.

"Tea?" she said.

I shook my head no again. Somewhere outside I heard the clanking of metal next door and tried to imagine what chore Patton had moved on to.

"Family ain't the place to fight," Miss Mattie said and turned her back to us and began to piddle with a stack of dishrags.

Tall stopped eating for a second but didn't respond.

I was embarrassed when a harsh sigh slipped from my throat.

She turned to me and rubbed my shoulder. I could smell cigarettes and coffee on her. She hugged me.

"Come sit down," she said.

"Sis at work?" I asked, looking around at the emptiness of the house but Miss Mattie didn't answer me.

I sat beside her on the couch in the living room and could hear Tallboy fumbling around in the sink.

"Leave it," she said. "Come on in here."

Tallboy stood in the doorway waiting for his mama to lay down the law, but she rested her head back on the couch and closed her eyes as if she was waiting for the right words to present themselves. She locked her fingers across her belly and sucked air through her teeth. If you looked at her close you could tell she was pretty once. Even now with all that weight on her she turns heads at church, but her feet are like two balls of brown dough. I've seen pictures of her that I mistook for Sis. But Miss Mattie had a dignified stance about her back then that's been lost to modern women.

Tall walked into the living room and sat in the chair Mr. Jessie used to rest in when he'd come home from work.

A few minutes later I heard JB's truck pull up and heard the door slam. He came through the back door saying, "Y'all needn't worry Mama bout this."

There was a quiver in his voice that made me want to just run to him and put my arms around his neck. Tallboy fidgeted with his cap and rubbed his hands palm to palm.

Miss Mattie pulled herself up from the couch and met JB in the doorway. "We don't need no more," she said. "Can't take no more."

He hung his head down to his chest and then glared at me.

Tallboy got up from the chair and edged himself along the wall toward the front door.

I squeezed the keys into my hand.

JB tried to ease past Miss Mattie, but she stepped firmly in his path again.

"No," she said again. "No more."

Outside, I fumbled the keys around before I found the ignition. Tallboy looked down at the floorboard like he was drowning in his own thoughts. My only thought was to save him from this. By the time we left gravel for pavement, JB was close in his pickup.

We drove on out to the one lane road past Mt. Zion where we saw Frieda Jenkins' boys carrying scrawny poles over their shoulders headed to the creek to fish. Tallboy's eyes followed them up the hill until they disappeared. When we veered past Otha's place on out to the main highway and edged through the white part of the ridge Tallboy flipped the radio on and rested his head on the window.

I just kept driving on through town until we reached the interstate. The day was beautiful and bright patches of midday sun shone off the dark tree line. JB had to cool off sooner or later and head on back home. I imagined that me and Tallboy would spend a day in the city, maybe get some ice cream. We might go up to the mall and I'd buy him a new ball cap, make him feel better.

In two hour's time, glass and steel buildings were sprouting up toward the sky, and traffic was so thick that we could see the faces of people in cars on both sides of us.

When we reached a main artery in the city and buildings rose up from the ground where trees should have been, Tallboy glanced up at the mirror and saw that JB was right on the bumper. He hit his fists against the dashboard and his head jerked a little. "Quit!" he said with that humming whine in his voice like JB had him in a headlock, knuckle-burning his scalp through that thick Afro he used to have. I thought he was talking to me at first, but his eyes were focused on JB who couldn't hear him because he was behind us in his pickup truck. "Quit it! Quit it! Quit it!" he said.

When the light changed, JB gunned the truck into the back of the car. The tires squealed and my forehead smacked the glass.

JB punched the gas again and I heard the shriek of metal, smelled rubber burning. There was a little bit of blood on the windshield. When I turned my head I caught the blur of Tallboy's jacket. He was gone.

He had bolted from the car and was running down Main Street and all I remember thinking was Damn, that boy can run, but Tallboy could always run faster than JB when we were kids.

I still see them shirtless running across Mr. Jessie's field elbow to elbow, the sweat flying off their shoulders like rain, Tallboy's fro waving like a flag, JB's face like stone, his jaw tight, and me and Sis standing in ankle-high grass getting bit by chiggers cheering them on. Mr. Jessie standing at the end of the fencerow with his chin tucked over a rake keeping us all safe.

But this time Mr. Jessie wasn't here and JB wasn't running trying to catch Tallboy; he was standing on the driver's side of my car beating on the window. He looked around in the car, but there was nothing there now but me balled up in the seat holding my head.

His lips trembled, they were a little chapped, and he licked them but he didn't say nothing. He could have called me out of my name, said things no woman ought to hear and I'd understood it but he didn't. He jerked on the door handle, but it was locked and then suddenly the law was everywhere.

The law don't carry on like that down here no matter what. One sheriff, a handful of deputies and that's all you get. Might not even get that much if you live out where we live. When somebody did that to Mr. Jessie the law come around and grunted at each other and shook their heads, but still to this day don't nobody know who done it.

JB's fists turned open on the window and then he pointed down the street toward where Tallboy vanished. He called out his brother's name and mine then thudded the window one last time with his open hand before they pulled him away.

After the wreck I woke up in the hospital to that sickly smell of antiseptic with a bandage wrapped around my head. Sis starts telling me the story like it had happened to somebody else and then leans over me and says, "The law wants to talk to you." Her face looks like a globe leaning over me like that and she talks loud like the knot on my head has made me deaf.

Miss Mattie, Sis and the girls circle around my bed and Miss Mattie makes them hold hands like I'm on my death bed and they all begin to pray. Miss Mattie calls out Amen three or four times and the girls say Amen back and then they all get quiet. Their eyes are on me and I grimace a little then turn over on my side. Miss Mattie places her hand on my head and something trembles inside me. Black women are like that down here, ready to lay hands if ordinary prayer ain't enough.

"You rest," she says and moves away from my bedside.

The nurse comes in and says, "Only two visitors at a time please."

Pudd, Sis's youngest, is playing with the toiletries on the night stand. Miss Mattie holds her Bible to her chest like armor and I wish I could feel more of the sunlight from the window but Keisha, the eldest, is leaning across the radiator along the window sill in red culottes and boots looking down at the city. It's then I notice that she's filled out just over the summer.

"I'm alive down here," she says and keeps on looking out into the sunlight at what she thinks is her future.

Miss Mattie says, "Now y'all know what the nurse said," every few minutes and paces back and forth with her ankles spilling out around her shoes, but nobody leaves until the law shows up and even then not right away because that's when Miss Mattie has a spell and has to be helped into a chair.

The law man is a black man and asks me how I'm doing. I can't help but stare at him for awhile. He holds his head to the side when he talks and reminds me of Cousin Ronnie.

"Better, I guess," I say after some time. I smile.

I try to press my hair into the blue silk scarf that Sis brought with her. I clear my throat and drink some of the ice water the law man hands me.

"So we've interviewed your husband, but do you think you're up to telling me exactly what happened? At least what you remember?"

He poises his ink pen over the notebook and looks at me above it and waits.

"Why'd your husband do this?" he says raising one of his eyebrows like a scythe.

And of course all the women of the Brown clan are in the room waiting for me speak, to tell it all. So I sip the water like I've never had a drop in my life and I wish I had on just a little bit of lipstick so I could look a bit more presentable. I pull the flimsy white blanket up to my neck with my hands underneath resting on my belly and I'm still trembling.

The law man notices my nerves, so he asks the family to step outside for a minute, but I can still see their feet in the hallway through the slats in the bottom of the door.

This is a story I don't know how to begin so I start with, "I don't think he did this on purpose." Then I go back as far as I can. It's the kind of thing that a body can't understand in snippets. So I say, "We all grew up together back down home, I've known the Browns my whole life. Our families knew one another..." and start it over there. Then I realize that it will take at least one lifetime to get him to where we live. And another to explain all we've been through.

Almost immediately I see the law man's face and shoulders get set a certain way as he listens to the way I talk with all of the Mission Creek in me spilling out into the room.

And it's then, when he acts like each word I speak is throwing shit on him, that I know it doesn't matter what else I say so I stop talking all together. I look in the other direction toward the door and see Sis's shoes through the slats. Her feet are beginning to puff up just like Miss Mattie's.

The law man stands up beside me with his legs all straddled out with his face already fixed and I know his tongue won't form the words when he tries to tell it later. He'll be thinking we are all just a bunch of country niggers. I reach for more water and suck the cup dry then eat the ice.

Before he leaves he says with his voice as smooth as butter, "Mrs. Brown, would you like to talk to somebody about all this, a social worker maybe?" And I say, "No."

I see the sun setting behind him through the window against all those tall buildings and close my eyes.

Some of the hollers back home are full of women with bowed heads and black rings around their eyes, but I am not one of them. Sometimes JB comes home sulked up like hitting me might soften something hard inside him, but he has never laid a finger on me.

One night when one of the boys down at the factory called him out of his name, he hit his knuckles on the wall and marched out into the dark. I lay on the couch and listened to him out on the porch breathing and pacing until I fell asleep. I woke up in the middle of the night and went to him. He was still out there in his work clothes staring out into the knobs.

"Daddy sure loved it up here," he said. "Sometimes I wonder if we ought to just go on and leave."

I looped my arm through his. I heard a dove cooing from the rafters of the house and me and JB and the bird were still and quiet like that for a long time.

Sis spends that night in the hospital with me and for a minute I can imagine us back home on the den peeling potatoes or cleaning greens. But this feels like a sort of vacation with no husbands or piles of something that needs doing.

She puts her bare feet up under her in the chair and drapes a blanket over her knees. She shifts her hips in the chair and I can see her feet threatening to show themselves.

I think of her kids back home with Miss Mattie and her husband Gene up the road sitting down to supper by himself. I ask her if she misses them and she says, "Shoot no," and laughs, but I can tell she does and I can hear the worry.

She combs and plaits her hair for the night.

Us together like this makes me think of when we were girls and couldn't wait to get out of the country and join the movement. "I'm going all the way to Baltimore," I remember telling her because I liked the way the words lifted off my tongue when I got to the *more*, up and out into the dark and mixed with the song of the bobwhites across the river.

I start smiling at the memory and Sis says, "What?"

"Nothing."

She looks out the window at the city skyline and starts talking about what all she needs to do at home—washing clothes, canning the last of the beans, painting the den—then she stops and says "You gonna leave?"

I lean into the sterile smell of the hospital bed for a few minutes just wishing I was standing on my back porch breathing fresh air, but I don't answer her.

The phone rings and I can hear Miss Mattie's breathing before she speaks.

"I ain't heard nothing from JB, Miss Mattie," I say.

Sis sits up straight in her chair and rubs her neck a little and puts the comb away in her pocketbook. Miss Mattie pauses on the other end. Then she asks about Tallboy.

"Nothing from him neither."

I can see her in Mr. Jessie's chair spread out over its sides and Sis's girls beside her on the living room floor like they are there just to worship that entire mountain of her. And I'm sorry I'm missing that sight though I've seen it a hundred times since I became a part of this family.

I can hear Pudd in the background saying something, but I can't make out what.

Sis reaches over and cuts the TV on Channel 14 News, which is the same thing we watch back home.

"I'm sick to death," Miss Mattie says, "all our men..." And then I hear nothing else but her heavy breathing.

The reporter on TV is a white woman with bobbing red hair and too much eye shadow.

She pronounces JB's name Jessie Brown Junior like he's some vagrant up the holler and I can see everybody back home-black and white-gathered around their television sets over suppers of pork chops and fried chicken thinking Jessie Brown's boys finally lost their natural minds.

I look up and see a picture of JB's truck sitting up against my car on Main Street. They cut back to the studio, show pictures of JB's mug shot, Tallboy's driver's license and the front of the hospital. Then the law man comes on looking just like Cousin Ronnie standing out in the sun and says Tallboy (only he calls him by his true name Terrance Brown) is wanted for questioning but mostly he talks about how none of us are from the city.

And I want to say to Sis, "Don't he look just like Cousin Ronnie?" but I don't.

I hold the phone and can hear the TV on the other end too with Miss Mattie and the kids. I hear Miss Mattie gasp and Pudd is saying, "Don't worry Grandmamma."

After I get off the phone, me and Sis don't say nothing for awhile and I rise up and look out the window out over the city. All of those lights down there remind me of Christmas back down home and I start to cry. Sis notices but don't say nothing. She just looks out the window and says, "I wouldn't live down here for nothing in the world."

The next evening back at home I stand on the porch looking out into the woods and hear something skittering around in the dark. Alpha comes out of his doghouse and barks, and I throw him a few table scraps. I holler out to him and hear my own voice echo off the knob.

The air is cool but I stand there until I can't stand it no more. The first frost is close, but I think of spring and tomatoes growing in the backyard. I think of JB and his hands on the roll of fat that circles my middle. I place my hand on my stomach and peer out above the tree line hoping the stars will bring us back everything we've lost.

Just as soon as I go back in I call to check on Miss Mattie and settle myself at the kitchen table to pay a few bills. I hear a knock on the door. Tallboy stands in the yellow light of the porch bulb looking haggard, his eye a bruised plum, his face and arms full of small wounds like he's come from way across the water, from war.

I invite him in but we don't sit on the couch. We don't talk. I put on a pot of coffee and pour us both a black cup and scoop out two bowls of the chocolate pie I made.

He sits at one end of the kitchen table, me at the other. He stares at me for a long time then eats his pie. When he's finished he reaches across the table for my hand, but I pull further away. We are inside the house, but I can still feel the bite of frost in the air and I can see twelve thousand stars in the sky. I rest my head in my hands and run my hand through my hair. Alpha barks at something outside and I think I can hear a lone whippoorwill calling somewhere out in the dark, high up on the mountain, in the tops of the barren trees.

Magic
by Jim Nichols

The last time I was in jail, the Sheriff told me to jump off the Bucksport Bridge. He thought it would save us both a lot of future trouble. And I tell you, it was starting to sound like a good idea. I even walked out the trestle a few times and looked down into the gorge. I dropped rocks over the side. It took about four seconds for the rocks to fall, and I remembered from physics class that it would be the same for me, despite the difference in mass.

Four seconds.

In school I'd been happy enough. Under my yearbook photo: *Always Quick With A Smile Or A Trick.* That's because I was the school magician. And I was still capable of putting on a show. I could make coins, handkerchiefs, cigarettes disappear.

I just couldn't get rid of my gloom.

I lived in a trailer park, and when I could rouse myself, drove an airport taxi for cash. For days at a stretch, though, I wouldn't leave the trailer, and when I finally did it was only to walk to the bridge.

It was breezy over the river.

The bridge shimmied beneath my feet. When I dropped the rocks they fell straight down until the river breeze caught them and then swung outward and plunged at an angle into the water. I would watch those rocks and sometimes I would be only a thought or two from swinging a leg up over that flaky green railing.

I had a friend named Bobby Kincaid. One night after I'd missed work again he showed up at the trailer with a bottle of Coffee Brandy and a gallon of milk. "Enough of this," he said, barging past me inside. "You're making me look bad."

"Come on in," I said. "Make yourself at home."

He stomped down to my little tin kitchen, dumped half of the milk into my sink, emptied the bottle of coffee brandy into what was left, put the cap on the milk container and gave it a shake as he came back. "I went out on a limb to get you that job."

"I know you did."

He sat down beside me and passed me the jug. A Sombrero, the blueberry rakers called it. I took a gulp and handed it back. We worked at it silently, and before long the booze was half gone, and so were we.

"So what's the big deal?" Bobby said then.

"I wish I knew."

"All you gotta do is drive the damn car."

"It's not just work. I can't do anything."

"Was it the jail?"

"Didn't help."

"What else?"

"Jeez," I said. "Pick a card." I waved a hand. A few feet to my left was the little kitchen nook, and to my right the bathroom. Clothes and magazines were stacked on every flat surface because I didn't have any closets. I couldn't fold the sofa out without moving a junky lampstand that stood against the opposite wall.

"You ain't the only one lives in a trailer."

"That doesn't help."

Somebody hollered from outside. It was the green trailer that sat kitty-corner to mine. They'd been partying for a couple of days, off and on.

Bobby laughed. "Somebody don't mind living here."

"Blueberry rakers can live anywhere."

The trailer park had lots of them, and they had a million kids that ran around loose, like dogs or cats. I liked the kids, though. Sometimes I performed for them. They sat in the dust around my front door and I stood on the stoop. I felt bad for the way they lived. I could remember hiding in the boot closet, making myself invisible, while my old man prowled the house looking for me, and I figured these kids had the same kind of stuff going on.

Bobby said, "I get the old blues myself, sometimes."

"Bad?"

"Pretty bad."

"Bad enough so you start to think it isn't worth it?"

"I don't know about that," he said.

"How do you pull out of it?"

"It just happens."

"Like magic?"

"Like one of your tricks."

I swallowed some brandy and passed it to him. My ears were starting to ring a little. "The Sheriff thought I should jump off the bridge."

"Kind of radical."

"Works every time, though."

He shook his head, took a big drink. There was a little left, and he gave it to me. "Don't jump off the bridge," he said. Then he stood up. "I'm gonna call you in the morning."

I sighed.

"You'll be fine," he said. "Coffee brandy." He gave me a thumb's-up. There was a tap at my door just then, and his eyes widened. He turned his thumb over and followed it to the door. Typical Kincaid. It made me laugh in spite of myself.

Three little kids were crowded onto my stoop. Here it was after midnight. I knew two of them: skinny Carlo and his sister, Eva, who never talked. They lived in the green trailer. A third kid, built like Carlo but with a tough little fighter's face, stood with them. I didn't know where he lived.

"Well?" Bobby said.

I leaned out from the couch, looking back at the kids. They weren't saying anything. I got very tired all of a sudden, waiting for them to speak. I was too buzzed for magic anyway. I said, "Sorry, not now," and fell back onto the sofa.

Bobby said, "Try him tomorrow. He's not feeling too good." They scampered off. He clicked the door shut and looked at me. "You're pathetic."

I reached for the last of the Sombrero.

"I'm calling you in the morning," he said. "Forget about jail. We've all been to jail. That ain't no excuse for nothing." He pointed a finger at me, and then he turned it over and followed it to the door.

I'd gone to jail for fighting one of the blueberry rakers at Country Rose's Bar and Grill. Rose had Karaoke every Friday night, and I'd taken to drinking there so I could listen. I liked it best when it was slow because the waitresses would go up onto the little stage, and I liked the angelic expressions they would get singing.

That Friday they had this busboy up on the stage, trying to get him to perform "Wasted Days and Wasted Nights." He was a shy, chubby kid who couldn't keep his shirt tucked in, and they were teasing him by making him sing, but in a nice way. His face was bright red, but he was happy about it and doing all right. Then this big, old raker with a voice like a bullfrog yelled, "I'm wasting tonight, listening to you!" from a table right behind me, and the busboy stopped singing.

"Ha!" the raker yelled out. "Get the waitress up there!"

He had a dirty denim vest on over his flannel shirt and a checked bandanna around his neck. There were a couple of other guys sitting at the table, enjoying the ruckus.

The waitress told the busboy to ignore him, and he tried, but as soon as he opened his mouth again the blueberry raker yelled, "Get that fat kid off the stage!"

The kid shook his head then, and stepped down.

The blueberry raker clapped his hands loudly. His buddies crowed, and he looked around the room for more admirers. When our eyes met, he winked.

I threw what was left of my beer right into his smirk.

He sputtered and ran at me, and when I punched him in the face he sat right down on the floor. But he bounced up swinging and off we went. We took out tables and chairs, glass busting all over the place, and kept at it until the cruiser arrived with its siren whooping.

Bobby kept his promise and let the phone ring and ring. I wrapped a pillow around my head. My brain was pounding and I couldn't remember going to bed. I felt like hell because I knew I wouldn't get back to sleep, and I'd have to lie there miserable, thinking about those kids, wondering what in the world was wrong with me.

The ringing stopped, finally.

I lay there in the dark and pictured the bridge, high over the narrow, rocky river. I took the pillow off my head and sat up. My windows were open, and as early and dark as it was, the smell of coffee was in the air, and a country western tune twanged faintly from the other side of the trailer park. It was blueberry rakers, ready to head for the barrens. A couple of driveways over a car started roughly. Someone kicked the idle down, put it in gear and drove it to the intersection. He headed off on Dearborne Road. A little later another car whooshed by.

It's a lonely sound: traffic before dawn.

I couldn't lie there listening to it. I went into my little tin box of a bathroom and did my business in the dark, then ran water in the sink and took six aspirin. Then I went into my little tin corner of a kitchen and had a cup of coffee by the light from the stove hood. I looked out the window at the kids' dark trailer and wondered what time the party had ended, and whether they'd managed to get any sleep.

I took another cup of coffee outside and sat on my front step. The stars were still out. Way down at the entrance to the trailer park a traffic light flashed. It was the only illumination in the park since somebody had knocked out the last streetlight while I was in jail. I looked around, saw, off in the distance, the early Boston flight angling into the sky. I pictured Bobby swerving along the dark roads toward the airport, cussing me out for not answering the phone.

I sat back, lit a cigarette and drank my coffee. I looked around the trailer park and tried one more time to figure just how I'd come to this time and place. The Sheriff's fat face came into my mind, and I remembered how disgusted he'd been, and how the kids had peered into the cage at me. I decided to finish my coffee and head on out to the bridge. I'd watch the sun come up, drop a few rocks and see what happened.

It had been a bummer to wake up sore and miserable again in jail. The bright lights had hurt my eyes. And it didn't help when the Sheriff came waddling down the corridor and said, "By God, you must love it here, Joe."

"Home sweet home," I said.

"How many times this year?"

"I don't keep track."

"Maybe you should." He took a damp washcloth out of a plastic bag and tossed it into the cell. "Clean yourself up," he said. "You've got company."

"Who?"

"Schoolboys," he said, and this smile crawled over his face. "Our annual tour. Usually it's kind of boring. It's much more interesting when we have a real, live asshole to put on display for them."

I sat up on the cot. "I don't want any kids looking at me."

"Too bad." He nodded at the washcloth. "You can use that, or sit there with blood on your face. I don't give a damn. It's up to you." He waited while I wiped my face and knuckles, then stuck the plastic bag between the bars and said, "Drop it in here. We wouldn't want you tearing it into strips and hanging yourself off the light fixture. Isn't that what you drunks like to do?"

He was some Sheriff.

I went over and dropped the washcloth into the bag. He twisted it shut and said, "Hey, I got a better idea, Joe. Don't hang yourself, jump off the bridge. Somebody does it every year; this might as well be your turn. It'll save me a hell of a lot of trouble. By the time they find you you'll be ten miles downriver and somebody else's problem."

"Anything for you," I said.

He shuffled off, laughing to himself. Five minutes later he brought the schoolboys back. That was an experience, sitting there as a living example of asshole-ness. The Sheriff told them that I liked to get drunk and fight, and that if they wanted to be like me they could look forward to enjoying the County's hospitality, too. He told them what it was like, the food, how much exercise you got, that sort of thing, and let them look into the cell.

They were typical eighth-grade boys.

Some were almost grown with long hair and fuzzy mustaches, others still little kids. When it was time to go, one of the bigger ones got brave and said, "Too bad you're not Houdini, huh?" and the rest of them glanced one last time into the cell and laughed nervously. I didn't say anything back. They were just being kids.

Slowly a red flush seeped along the horizon. A few more people knocked around in their trailers at the other end of the park. Another car started. It was still quiet at my end, though, quiet enough that when the door of green trailer banged open, I jumped a foot.

They came outside, the three of them, and stood rubbing their eyes. My first impulse was to tell them to go back to bed. I still didn't want to talk to anyone. But I'd already hurt their feelings once, so I stayed put. They didn't move, and after a minute I pointed at Carlo and said, "What's that on your PJ's?"

Carlo looked down at himself. "Ducks," he said.

"Come show me?"

They walked across and stood in front of me, looking down at the ground, hands at their sides. There were rows of ducks swimming, ducks splashing, ducks waddling, on their pajamas. "Nice," I said. "Listen, I'm sorry I was rude to you guys."

Carlo's bright eyes flickered up. "Okay."

"Eva?"

She gave me the briefest of looks.

"You know she don't talk," Carlo said.

"That's okay," I said. "She doesn't have to talk. Any girl with ducks on her PJ's doesn't have to do anything she doesn't want to."

Eva turned away.

I looked at the third kid.

"Joaquin," Carlo said, and made a face. "You like that name?"

"Sure," I said. "That's a fine name."

Joaquin peered at me. He was wearing different PJ's

"He lives over there." Carlo pointed toward the far end of the trailer park, where the bushes came up close and where a row of privies had been built across a trench. It was funny: even a trailer park had its slums, in relative terms.

"Uh-huh," I said. "So, you come over for a trick?"

"Invisible ball!" Carlo said.

Eva turned back, her eyes as dark and shiny as polished chestnuts. "I don't have a paper bag."

Carlo ripped one out of the hip pocket of his PJ's

I looked at it skeptically. "I don't know if my magic works on old, wrinkled-up lunch-bags."

"Aw, man..." Carlo said.

"Wait a minute," I said. "Don't give up the ship."

Carlo and Eva looked at each other. I stuck a hand in the bag, whacked it around. "It might work."

Carlo nudged Joaquin, who slapped at his arm.

I cracked my knuckles, made as if to pluck something out of thin air and quickly stuck it into my mouth. Then I moved my tongue around, figure-eighting it from cheek to cheek.

"That just his tongue!" Joaquin said.

"You wait!" Carlo concentrated on me.

I pulled the invisible ball out of my mouth, walked out into the lane and looked around. Then I flung it high into the ink-wash sky, and held the paper bag out. The ball fell into the bag with a satisfying *snap*.

"See!" Carlo said.

"Again!" Joaquin said.

I tossed it up again, this time crookedly so that I had to trot along the lane to catch it. *Snap!*

Carlo did a little scuff-step, clapped his hands.

I threw the ball higher and higher, circling under it like a catcher after a popup, the last dim stars spinning above me. Finally, going after a very high toss, I lost my balance and lurched sideways, staggering between two of the trailers, tripping and taking a heavily-laden clothesline down with me.

I sprawled on the warm grass, tangled in damp shirts, jeans and Holiday Inn towels. There was a wet towel over my face, and when I laughed, I could feel my own warm breath. I didn't move until the kids scampered up, and then I snaked an arm free, held the bag out and let the ball, airborne for a long time now, *snap* home.

"Caught it!" Carlo said.

Somebody—Joaquin—snatched the paper bag away. I heard him crinkling it, looking for the ball. Meanwhile I lay under the damp clothes. The grass was soft under me and the weight of the clothes sort of comforting. It reminded me of the boots in the boot closet, when I was a kid, hiding from the old man's temper. Then I felt something gentle, a corner of the towel lifting, and Eva's solemn face hung before me. She leaned closer. Her eyes were shiny. I felt her breath, and then she folded the towel all the way back, and I saw the sky filling with oranges and reds.

The boys came up to help and quickly I was free of the damp clothes. I swatted grass off my pants, looked around to see if anybody was watching. The trailers nearby were still dark, though. No blueberry rakers there, or they'd already gone. I found the end of the clothesline and held it up. The clothes were heavy. I walked it back to the trailer and stretched the loop over its rusted hook.

We all strolled back to my stoop.

I took the bag from Joaquin, dug the invisible ball out and screwed it back into the air. "That's that," I said, and dusted my hands together.

Joaquin frowned at me. "How you do that?"

"Can't tell you," I said. "Get in big trouble with the Magician's Union."

"Another trick!" Carlo said.

So I went into my two-bit routine. I made coins disappear and pulled them out of the kids' ears; I broke my forefinger in two and put it back together. I went inside for three Dixie Cups and three balls of cotton and moved the balls through the cups without touching them.

The kids, even Joaquin, laughed.

Eva didn't speak, but looked as if she might. I tried to think of a trick so good she would have to say something, but before I could, a car peeled off from Dearborne and whistled around the corner toward us. It was a taxicab, trailing a cloud of dust, and Bobby Kincaid was driving, face crowded up close to the windshield, elbows stuck out to the side. The kids shrieked and flew back across the street. I laughed at them running in their PJ's. They scurried up the steps and into their trailer. The taxi skidded to a stop, and Bobby shoved the door open.

"It lives," he said.

"It wanted to sleep," I said. "But somebody wouldn't let it."

"Get in," he said.

I slumped into the front seat and shut the door. He pulled a U-turn and headed toward the intersection. We slid around the corner onto Dearborne, and about a mile along stopped for coffee and jelly donuts. Then we left town, riding out past the barrens, where hunched people in silhouette rhythmically swept the hilltops with their blueberry rakes.

The sun was up when we started across the Bucksport bridge. I looked out the window at the water far below. The tide had come up the river, covering the rocks. As we passed, gulls jumped off the railings and wheeled underneath the bridge, catching the breeze, looking clean and white as angels in the new morning sunlight.

We ramped off the bridge and followed the road around a curve into the woods. In twenty minutes we were cruising down avenues lined with oaks, through squares with brick office buildings. At the taxi shack I signed out my car and followed Bobby to the airport. We parked at the cabstand by the Delta Airlines gate. He slammed his door and walked back, and we leaned on my cab to wait for the first flight.

"Nice morning," Bobby said.

"Not bad," I said.

The airport came slowly to life. A half-dozen flight attendants got out of a Ramada Inn van and pulled their little wheeled bags into the building. The maintenance crew was sweeping, cleaning. Hertz girls arrived for work, crossing the parking lot toward the terminal, wearing their bumblebee dresses. One of them even gave us a smile before she went inside.

"What do you think of that?" Bobby said.

"Sweet."

He raised his coffee cup and I reached over and tapped mine against it. It *was* a nice morning. I didn't feel all that bad for a sorry son of a bitch with a hangover who'd been a jail exhibit for schoolboys.

I leaned back against the taxi and shut my eyes. It was the trailer-park kids, I knew. Their sleepy eyes, the ducks on their PJ's, the way they could still believe in magic. It was Eva, especially. Next time I would get her to talk. Meanwhile I would remember the way she had looked at me, her sweet breath on my cheek. And how she had swept the towel off my face, dramatically, like a real magician, and then had stepped aside to let the morning fill with light.

Country Boys
by Rusty Barnes

Reena puts the rifle down and leaps out the back of the truck in one smooth motion like drawing the curtains closed. I click off the spotlight and follow her into the sudden dark. There's a high lonesome moon and I wish I'd brought earplugs, because my ears are still ringing. By the time I've gotten out of the truck she's hopped the drainage ditch and is hoisting one leg over the barbed wire. She's a short little thing, so I catch up with her as she hangs the crotch of her shorts on a barb, swearing.

"Jimmy," she says panting, "you better lift my leg out of there." I shoot a glance back toward the truck. She's left the door open so we can find it easier, but it's like a bug and a bug zapper to a game warden. We should hear him coming long before he'd get here though. We're back on a logging road off a dirt road off a gravel road and surrounded by trees. I reach under her ass and hoist her over. The doe is lying about seventy-five yards from the road, I figure. It should be easy, but the truth is I have no idea how to do this, so I'm following Reena's lead. She knows this from her brothers who've been jacking deer since Hector was a pup. I might marry into this, so I will hold the light and help drag the deer like a kid learning how it all ought to go.

I can see the doe in a huddled lump now. Luckily it's small, so with Reena's help I hoist it up into my arms and hustle it out to the fence walking heavy and toss it over where it lands in a heap of thud. I have dirty hands now, so when I lift her over the fence I leave a bloody handprint right across the pocket of her shorts. "Sorry baby," I say, and slap her on the ass again, just because I can.

"Just get the deer into the back of the truck." I wonder if this is another test, as I manhandle the deer into the bed and put up the tailgate. I've been through a bunch of them since dating Reena Stone, some I didn't know were tests. Don't throw out the coffee can spittoon. When you're finished eating, put the plate on the floor for the dog to clean up. Don't call anyone in the family or extended family an outlaw. Don't brag about your town upbringing. The town has four hundred people, and my dad is the township supervisor, so I'm city as far as the Stones are concerned. My odds weren't good, but I have survived a year so far. Reena likes me around for a couple reasons, one of which is that I'm willing to go along for just about anything.

Life was not exciting until I met Reena Stone. She stood by the smoking barrel at the Vo-Tech High School next to the delivery door, where I was delivering computers from the Best Buy where I work. She and some of her girlfriends, the Shaw girl and Laskey Miller's daughter, were on a break from their senior-year cosmetology classes, so they had on crappy t-shirts that they didn't mind getting all stained from the various dyes. All of them were in various processes of dye jobs, and Reena had her hair tricked up in tinfoil. You could see what she was holding body-wise, though, and it made me look, I have to say.

"You see something you like?" she said.

"Maybe." I didn't want to play it badly.

"Maybe you'd like some of this," she said, and lifted her t-shirt up to show her bra, while her girlfriends screamed and flapped their hands like chicken wings. Then they ran back inside. I waited by the back door until she got out of school and offered her a ride home. That began the whole thing. Four nights later I took her to the movies and on the way home she slipped out of her jeans and showed me what a wild girl she was, by which I mean she showed it to me all right, but I couldn't quite get it yet. For a girl like that she held out a lot longer than I thought she would, almost a month. She couldn't abide a liar, she said. She wanted to see if I would lie just to get at her stuff. I should have seen that for the first test.

From then on, though, we were tight like a nut and bolt, and I slowly learned what it was like to be an outlaw, though I could never say the word out loud for fear of pissing off someone in her family. They weren't outlaws. They were country boys, as her dad Carlton never failed to tell me. He made it clear he didn't want me around as he said it, spitting at my feet. Country like you ain't, he would say. I wondered what was his deal. You could figure out everyone in Reena's family. They weren't simple, per se, just easy to figure out. Carlton though, had something simmering back in his brain that you couldn't touch. Reena didn't talk much about him except to say what he would and wouldn't allow her to do. He'd stare me down like death, though, which was why I went along with all of Reena's shit. I needed to crack him if I wanted anything further from Reena. If that day were to come, anyway.

I jump into the driver's seat and ease the truck into gear. I'm still slow on the manual transmission, too. Don't get me started on how that looks to the Stone clan.

"Well, that was a pretty fine piece of work for your first time." She draws a joint out of the glove compartment and fires it. I take it from her bloody fingers and hit once and hand it back. She hasn't put the rifle, a .25-06 Remington, back into the rack yet, and her hand is wrapped casually around the barrel to keep it from rattling around. It's sexy to see a woman with a gun.

"Where are we going with this thing?" I say. It'll be to one of her other relatives. Her dad doesn't trust me yet

"Up to Uncle Verlin's." We were nearly off the gravel road now. To hit Verlin's I have to hit Coryland Road to Ameigh Valley Road, but I have to hit 328 first, which is a state road and more heavily traveled and I'm suddenly uncomfortable.

"Can't we just take it to your brother's?" Her brother Richard's is closer, too, and they have satellite TV. I can see the scene now. My dad's driving the back roads checking potholes or some stupid shit, thinking about changing the snowplow route, and here I am in a farm truck with no tags and no insurance and a jacked deer in the bed

"No. Richard isn't home anyway. He took Marnie and the kids to Darien Lake this weekend."

"Shit." I don't mind being an outlaw. I'm hoping for the best here. I want to get their approval, all of them.

"Are you turning on me? I had big plans for you, you prick." I can't tell if she's serious, as her face is in shadows.

"I'm not turning on anybody. I'm just worried, is all." Reena looks at me like I've gone crazy. She's never been caught at anything. She doesn't plan on starting now, and I can feel my grip on her beginning to slip a little. How far can she push me is the thing, before I revert to type and refuse to do something she thinks I need to do to get an in with her family. It's a good question, and one I can't answer well. It's a good thing I haven't hit the thing I won't do yet. We turn onto route 328; if someone's going to catch us, they're going to do it now.

After we'd been seeing each other for about three weeks, she asked me to buy beer for her. It was early at night and we were just over the border in New York. She handed me a ten dollar bill and like we were married, said "Run on in there and get me a six-pack, would you?"

"Why you need a six-pack? We haven't hardly got where we're going yet."

"I don't need. I want." Reena had dressed herself carefully tonight, I could see. She wore those poured-into jeans and a white t-shirt with the arms ripped short and a cut down the front all the way into her cleavage. This was early on, remember. I had a notion how the night would end if I bought her the beer, and my saliva went electric. I bought it for her all right, but she never drank a drop. I drank two and before the end of the night, I'd spattered her chin with my semen and she'd used the shirt to wipe her face, never taking her eyes from mine. "You may work out yet," she said.

Verlin's comes up fast, quicker than I expect since I'm looking behind me at every turn and every set of lights that come up. Reena has her leg bent and propped up on the dashboard. I watch the meat of her calf flex in the soft light. There's a light on in Verlin's front porch, and I can see the blue light of the TV in the family room, but there's no action otherwise. I drive the truck down the front yard and nearly up to their kitchen door, and the back porch light comes on. Verlin's wife Marty stands by the back door with her hand on the switch, shielding her eyes from the brightness with her hand as she figures who we are and lifts a hand in greeting.

"We got something for you," Reena says as she jumps out, and I drag the doe by its hind feet out of the truck and into the porch light. To her credit, Marty doesn't flinch.

"Bring it through here and into the back." She holds the door open for me. "You shoot this thing?" I know the wrong answer.

"Nope. Reena did." I flop the deer down on Marty's metal kitchen table.

"Huh." Behind her Reena pulls out a knife. "Best be careful of what she asks you to do, boy," Marty says. "She's either a liar or that girl has some life in her nobody else sees. I don't understand her yet." I watch as Reena winks quickly in my direction, then begins to gut and skin the doe. Verlin comes out then and offers me a beer which I take.

"I like some backstrap," Verlin says. Verlin's smoking and drinking both, his hands shaking. I don't know if he's tweaked or not. Supposedly he cooks meth, though I've never seen evidence of it, other than the shaking. "You all better hurry up, though. Carlton's due up here tonight, and he's not going to take too well to you throwing his girl into jacklighting deer. That's not for women to do."

"Shit," Reena says. "Uncle V—can we put the truck in the lower barn?" She looks almost excited.

"Suit yourself. It'd be better if you were gone. I can lie for you, but he might not believe me." Verlin leans back and studies me. I'm not sure what I'm supposed to do. I want to be gone, but it's Reena's call as to what she thinks we can get away with about her father. Marty says we should just go now, and my pulse is raising a little.

"Go park the truck in the barn, Jimmy. I'll be out to meet you in a second," Reena says. I figure it's just more crazy shit in this crazy thing I've gotten myself into, but I have to be honest about this—I like it. It's always something. It's never boring, and it's nothing I've been uncomfortable with, just things that every country boy does at one point or another. I back the truck across the lawn and jump out to open the door to the lower barn. I park it inside, and shut the door. Reena comes inside and slips me tongue like I've never seen her, twisting and darting like a lizard inside my mouth, tears on her face. "Oh baby," she says, rocking back from me for a moment. "I love you so much." I take it and give it back to her as good as she's giving. I can hear the sound of an engine in the front yard now, and she stops kissing me suddenly, pushes me back and opens the truck door. She pulls the rifle out and hands it to me. I can't figure what she wants me to do. "Jimmy. I've never told anyone."

"What the fuck?" I hold the rifle, but I don't know what she wants. Maybe it's to shoot out the pole light. I did that once at a Future Farmers of America dinner. Maybe it's the same sort of thing again.

"My dad used to make me blow him." I can see the tears shining on her cheeks.

"What?" I'm numb.

"Kill him." Her eyes are shining now too.

"You're fucking kidding me." I can't kill Carlton. Or anybody.

"Kill the bastard."

"Jesus Christ." I'm thinking of places I've been with Reena: the top of the fire tower; sex in the Catamount motel outside of Binghamton; flying box kites at the Fairgrounds, and riding the coaster; jacking deer on back roads at night. I can see her lifting her shirt at me that first time. I can see her and Carlton. I raise the rifle and point it out the barn door, in the cracks between the two sliding doors. Carlton and Verlin are standing by the back door talking. I can see Carlton's head in the sights.

"Do it. Do it. Fucking *do* it," she says. "For me. He made me suck his *cock*, Jimmy." I lower the rifle and watch Carlton and Verlin.

Verlin's looking at the barn, toward us. I wonder if he can see. I look back at Reena dancing from foot to foot on the barn floor, kicking up tiny puffs of chaff with every stomp.

Snapshot '87
by Sheldon Lee Compton

George huddled next to a split-end oil barrel loaded with chunks of coal picked from the belt line, the insides of the barrel on fire. He fought the urge to take two more pain pills. Instead he focused on his work. Charged three coal scoops, held the pills for two minutes, took a connector to the crew foreman, Torch. When the guts of the barrel went cold, George added coal. If anyone came looking to steal cable or batteries, he didn't notice.

He felt nova-like, bursting in all directions. He could split apart and send flying a blast of blue uniform, arms, legs, a chipped tooth from a high school fight, a birth-marked left shoulder, a busted backbone sent careening into the night. He felt kinetic, the way Julie could once make him feel during an argument, the same way she could make him feel during sex, trembling with a basic emotion older than either of them and longer lasting.

The night sky mixed with the tops of the trees leading up and away from the mine, and George didn't look at a clock until four hours of the shift had gone past in a wave of coal dust and dizziness. While trying to keep his balance on the walkway crossing over the belt line, he felt the pill bottle pushing into his leg, reminding him that within that bottle was relief of some kind, and then, beyond that, oblivion. But it wasn't oblivion George thought about when he shook two more pills from the bottle and stood thinking for more than five minutes about chasing them with two waters from the supply shack.

His little boy slipping behind the kitchen counter. Russell with his little hands fumbling with a drawing before it was time for George to leave for work. Coloring lightly in circles, adding two large ears and then two smaller circles inside for the eyes. A looping frown for a mouth. Russell holding the drawing up to him, the crayon face there dripping large, oval tears and crossing the looping frown.

His own father, standing in the doorway outside the bedroom he and Russell had shared for the past three months since everything that happened had happened. Then on the front porch where the two of them stood, shadowselves against the kitchen window, close to one another while listening to the sounds of winter floating there, a backdrop for their silence, the rattle of the warming truck off in the distance.

Julie smiling at him at him across the kitchen table, pouring them glasses of whiskey. Later the whiskey bottle between them on the bed, singing songs to one another. Julie hiding the pills after the second surgery, crying as he yelled, accused her while she begged him for quiet, begged him not to wake Russell, sang songs to herself while he slept in the living room floor.

Hours early—but George pulled another pain pill from his pocket, felt it familiar there like a cigarette or the handle of an old coffee mug. It would be a bitter thing to chew, but it would be all he could have until tomorrow. Three a day, no more. It had to be chewed. It wouldn't take long for the medicine to mix with the rest, get into his blood and start working on his back, being chewed like that. So he chewed, choking down clumps of wet powder.

A muffled voice—*Hey, hey, you*—upset but soft in sound, drifted like a flat whisper from the black mouth of the mine. But the voice was no more significant than any of the other sounds that slowly peeled layers from his skin. The hum of the charging machinery, the rattle of the bottle inside his fist, rats the size of beagle pups pushing empty potato chip bags across cracked and roughly poured concrete flooring. George was lost somewhere in the night sky and the tree-line. He perched himself on a hillside in the back of the main garage where night watchmen and outside workers pissed during the shift. He felt the pill bottle bite into his leg again, and then a single shining light emerged from the mine, the single headlight bouncing across jagged ground, pock-marked with tire tracks frozen in place like thick scars. At the wheel was a man covered in hanging chunks of thickened coal dust and sludge. When he passed under the conveyor belt line, he didn't have to duck or move his head an inch. He kept his eyes straight ahead to the garage, stopping abruptly and hopping off, an action as common and natural to him as stretching. Bowlegged, the miner pushed through the garage and made a quick path for George on the hillside beyond the swinging back doors.

"Hey! Jesus Christ!" Flinging of arms, slabs sludge falling from his shirt sleeves, drops of murky water. "First night, right? You want seven dead miners on your hands your first night out? Did you hear the phone? We've been trying to get you for ten minutes."

"I started the fan when you all called out," George said. His back muscles twisted together as he stood up, tense.

The miner stopped and squinted at George, then stomped across to the fan, dropping a switch. The fan came to life like a helicopter taking off sideways into the night. The cold void of winter silence was sucked into the fan and spat back out, changed, twisting everything different in the atmosphere. The miner took off his hat. The battery light flinted and flopped across darkness, a spear of bright dust splitting through the tree-line, the night sky. George climbed down from the hillside and pulled his coat closer around him.

"Is that Torch's coat from storage?" The miner asked. "Don't you have your own coat? Jesus."

The miner tossed three large chips of coal into the barrel. Flames popped up and then settled again. He took a long look back to the face of the mine and then took a cigarette from a pack left for later on top of a busted battery. George noticed right then that about the only part of the miner that wasn't coated in black, sparkling dust was his hair. It was gray like white fire off the top of his head, springy and odd from being pushed down by his hat. His eyes were blue buttons trapped in ebony and they had a look about them that made George uncomfortable.

"Well, might as well take a little break while I'm out here. I'm Kelly." He stuck out his hand and George shook it, making sure not to wipe his hands on his pants afterwards. "What's that?" He pointed to the pill bottle still in George's hand.

"Medicine."

"Let's see it."

George hesitated. It was an awkward hesitation no matter how hard he tried. Kelly stuck his hand out again, shaking it and wiggling his fingers. "Jesus. Give them things up." He turned the bottle into the light. "For pain?"

"Yeah. My back."

"Your back." He smiled widely, white fire, button blue and now the smile, sweat-stain yellow. "Your back, huh? Well, okay." Kelly gripped the bottle in both hands so that the white label was left smeared a deep gray and bent over to look closely, buried up in thought. "I say okay. Let's have us some, new guy."

"Well, they're for my back," he said, but didn't ask for the bottle back.

No chewing.

No need.

There were twenty pills and then there were fifteen, and then ten. George swallowed his with bottles of water from storage. Kelly crushed and snorted two and then chewed the rest but one. George snorted the last, gagging from it while Kelly laughed and drained a another bottle of water.

"Goddam, what a beginner," Kelly said and laughed some more.

"Yeah," George said. His voice fluttered, broken wings inside his head.

The night sky opened up and the hours clinked past after Kelly crawled onto his scoop and went back under the mountain. George didn't feed the fire any after that. For two hours it was only the dead cold and the blurred vision and him stumbling up to the belt line and then back again, afraid to grab more chunks of coal, afraid he'd get swept up in the belt and pulled apart and tossed aside, and he didn't want to die tired. He didn't want to die messed up. A couple of times he tried to burn a box or two in the split barrel to keep warm, but it was no use. And then it didn't matter. Oblivion kept him warm. His laughter was out of place and the rats stayed away.

Across the porch, too loudly, through the front door, too quickly, George slowed himself to an easy glide inside the kitchen. He had pretended to be asleep during the ride home with the foreman and now, with hands thick numb slabs of meat and bone, he pulled at his boots until they fell to the floor. He made it through to the living room trying not to touch the walls with his dirty hands for balance and at once noticed Russell's drawing from hours before on the coffee table, held to the edge with a school book, leaving the yellow page to flutter in the slight breeze of a nearby heater vent. He didn't touch the drawing, not right away. He did not take one step toward it, but it made the frozen muscles of his wild-wired body tingle and brought feeling into his forgotten stomach. He saw every pill, one after another, running around inside him there, torturing him, grinding a fast path to his heart.

At the edge of Russell's bed, a twin-sized thing tossed crooked in the corner of the bedroom, George watched the small smooth face lying still against the pillow, smiled when the soft lips puckered in sleep, smacked together, and then went slack again. He rubbed his fingers through the fine blond hair, leaned in close and kissed the forehead. Shampoo and soap.

Outside, the world was waking up. Truck engines turned over stubborn and cold and started. Men, pulled from their beds for work, coughed into the stinging winter air, gripping cups of coffee like lifelines, moving through the thick and dark morning like tired fireflies, their light almost spent and gone.

George tucked his lunch bucket beside his feet in the floor. It rattled against his leg, empty cans of Vienna sausage knocking around inside. He put his fingers to his lips and hissed at the bucket. Dust was smeared across his face, blotching his hands and covering his fingers. A wedding ring that sometimes still held its shine shot occasional glints of pure yellow across the room. He still wore the ring but kept his left hand stuffed into his pocket most of the time, ashamed of the fact that he still loved a women who had hurt him so badly, had walked away from him and from Russell when they most needed someone to stay. Holding his hand close to his face, he stared at the ring, noted the deep scratches across its surface, scratches as long and deep as his own. His hands and clothes smelled of rust and grease, smoke and the faintest scent of gasoline. From his coat pocket, he pulled out a piece of yellow chalk used for marking tears in the belt line.

"Hey little man, wake up," he said.

Russell moved sideways in the bed, yawned once.

"Daddy?" His voice was broken and stuck against the softness of the pillow, sliding off the thick quilt pulled to his chin.

The room was stitched together in patches of black and artificial light. Headlights from a diesel garage across the street were scanning Calvary as drivers pulled in and out, backing up for repairs, pulling out for familiar destinations. George sat quietly beside Russell, his features dripping tiredly from the gaunt bones of his face. Russell smiled and reached out to touch George's hand. George pulled his hand close and held it there, circling the knuckles with his rough thumb. Soon Russell's eyes were closed again, flickering under the eyelids, searching for a lost dream or just darkness.

"Hey little man, let's go outside," George whispered. "I brought something back from work and now we can play. Now we have time."

Russell stood weaving in the middle of the room, and George took him by the arm. He could feel warmth from the bed covering Russell's skin like the first hour of an easy sunburn. Russell wrapped his hands around his elbows and blinked several times, his chin lowered, lips pushed out. He then sat back down on the bed and fell onto his side, his eyes closing before his head was back into the pillow.

George allowed a long breath to ease from his lungs, patience slipping from inside him in a slow gush. His insides were turning on him now. Moving and shifting energy, an old energy, that nova blast that could create explosion from nearly nothing at all. That wild-wiring that had grabbed him away from the world once before. Only now there was nothing to hold it down. It spun and ran and shifted and did as it pleased. Anger management classes after the divorce had taught him only one thing—everybody was angry at something, just some more than others. But it was always something, and usually that something was small at first before it caught fire enough to burn entire towns, entire families, into heaps of ash. By then, it was always too late. Always too late.

"You sure was awful sad to see me going last night to be laying back down there now acting like you don't even care what I brought home," George said and coughed deeply, felt the film from the crushed pills crawl up into his throat, burn his nose. His voice was tangle vine and thorn, slashing out.

Russell quickly sat up in bed and when George looked at his son's eyes, it was the slow rippling surface of tears he saw floating across that sleepy blue. George held the drawing out in front of him like a bad report card. When he saw Russell looking at it, he dropped it onto the bed.

"Forget it. I'm going to bed. I'm tired anyway," George said flatly. He started out of the room, wobbled in the doorway of the bedroom, caught his balance and rubbed the back of his neck. He was only trying to make things better from earlier when he rushed out to get to work, but it was only getting worse. He heard Russell plucking wildly at the floor behind him, finding his pants, tossing them out in front of him and pulling them up over his hips.

"What did you bring, Daddy?" Russell asked. "Let me see. We can play now. Okay?"

George turned in the doorway. He stood still, his hands down to his sides, and his expression changed from angry to hurt, a brief and passing moment of lucidity, a reprieve from last night's high with Kenny. He saw his son, the sadness, the love, and then, building from another fit of anger fueled from fighting pain, it was gone again, replaced with dizziness and thickness of tongue and the old anger. The room offered only silence. It was only the two of them.

Bending to Russell, George wrapped him in his arms, smelling himself as he did so, the heavy scent of grease and rust and old sweat. And then George dug far into his coat and brought out the jagged chunk of yellow chalk.

"Remember what we used to do with sidewalk chalk, little man? This is the same thing. I brought it from work and it's pretty much the same kind, I think. Let's go."

George's face fell into a sloppy grin, transforming in no time at all from that hard granite, that volcanic rock and lava that could bubble just beneath the surface, and he took Russell's thin, bare arm and helped them both get quietly out the front door into the dancing cold.

A thin frost coated the front porch and the tops of parked cars glistened and sparkled under the pole lights. George walked in circles in the street, searching for a section of pavement without oil spots that would be good for drawing. He searched the ground for the right spot and missed Russell's shaking body and his tiny bare feet pushing into the chilled pavement and the cold splotches along his bony chest, the arms bright red and bluish in places. He circled and circled and spun in the street, stopping momentarily here and there and then moving on again, hand pressed firmly to his chin.

"I should go in and get something to put on," Russell said, but the voice was lost, passing across George and moving away and up into the predawn cloud cover.

George dropped to his knees, clutching the piece of chalk between two gloved fingers. Writing frantically, dirty black hair springing out above the thick wrinkles of his forehead, he worked the chalk against the pavement in complete concentration, pressing down so hard flecks of broken yellow chalk fell to either side onto the street. He wrote in bold letters—BY RUSSELL AND DADDY—then stood up and sucked in a long breath, turned his head sideways to review what he had written and handed the chalk to Russell, watched as his son fumbled with it between his fingers, dropped it and then bent slowly to pick it from the ground.

"Go ahead," George said.

George squatted and wrapped his arms around himself, bouncing gently, feeling the lack of pain in his back. The winter air rushed through him and he studied his son drawing circles and loops on the pavement. A chalk drawing on pavement. Scrawled symbols dashed off on the cave wall. Some promise at last made good between he and his son, and somewhere the blood of both tangled in that moment.

Proof
by John McManus

Everyone in Curd knew me and Burl's shotgun cabin on the
Curd River had just one bedroom, but since Burl always dropped the
charges Sheriff Hahn brought against townsfolk who drove home drunk
from the Horseshoe, they put up with us. Curd was an old mill town in
the foothills of North Alabama, and nearly all its drivers had been
arrested over the years—all but Dinah, who was Burl's wife and the
sheriff's girlfriend. She showed up to the river on Christmas to say,
"I've had it with how this town admires you. I wish somebody would
kill you." Two weeks later, when I found Burl sprawled on the couch
dead from a gunshot to the head, I told of her threat to Sheriff Hahn. I
repeated it six times. I was focusing on my calm. "Perfectly in control,"
I kept announcing as Hahn's men measured the room.

He said he'd talk to her, but the next day was Sunday and then
Monday the state caught the castration killers who'd fled from Curd
Bluff. Back in November there'd been a 911 call from up there and the
firemen had arrived to find a man bleeding to death from a botched
castration. Now they'd caught the owner of the house, and he'd admitted
to cutting the balls off a dozen men, never forcibly, which I learned
from the national news as I watched it alone.

The first call came from my editor at the paper. "I know you're
grieving over your friend," Henry said, "but I've gotta put you on this
story."

"My friend? Fuck you," I said before hanging up. The second
call came from Hahn: "Hunter? When's the last time you went up Curd
Bluff?"

"You think I know those freaks cause I'm gay?"

"Word is you cheat on Burl left and right."

"I'm going to call the ACLU."

"You wasn't even sad the day he died."

"His crazy bitch wife's still running free."

"If I arrest her, she'll just post bail and hire that black lady."

What I did, I hung up on him and called Henry back. "Henry, I'll do it," I lied, so that I'd be in good standing for him to publish a piece in which I quoted Sheriff Hahn saying, "If I arrest [Dinah], she'll just post bail and hire that black lady."

As I'd hoped, it caused a stir on the black side of town. They'd all thought Hahn was their ally against Burl. It stemmed from when Cara Biddle's son got killed last year as he was walking along the highway. Burl's office charged that guy with manslaughter, yet Burl somehow became a villain to black folks, so much that the manager of the grocery came up and asked us to go elsewhere to buy groceries.

After my story Hahn could only arrest Dinah and drag her downtown. Within hours she posted an absurdly low bail, pled not guilty, and went free. I told Henry I'd work from home on the castration killers, and then I holed up in the cabin to finish my book about meth addiction, which I'd been keeping from Henry. For one year I'd interviewed gay methheads in the foothills, and I was assembling their stories in a book. It took my mind off things. I stopped answering the phone, which rang too often. One day I was revising a bit about addict cops, watching the sun set over Curd Bluff, when a knock came. It was a middle-aged black lawyer I recognized from Burl's divorce.

"Hunter Tillman?" she said. "I'm Tamiquah Williams and I represent Dinah Carter. May I enter?"

"Let's just talk on the porch," I told her, standing in the doorway.

"A trial date's been set for May," she said, unfazed. "I'll be asking embarrassing questions, so I hope you're prepared."

"I'm moving to Atlanta in April."

"The state will pay to transport you along with your interview subjects who plan to testify. Have you been following that case?"

"How would you know who I've interviewed?"

"We subpoenaed your manuscript from Grove, and Duane Draper and Billy Ripley have both agreed to appear as defense witnesses."

"Tamiquah, those are pseudonyms."

"I showed the text to the castration killers. They believe they're Duane and Billy."

For several seconds I stared past her at the scar where the road switchbacks up Curd Bluff. I must have looked like there was a turd on my tongue. "Why would you warn me?"

"It seemed like it might stifle your memory to consider telling your plans to let Duane—"

"You're right, I don't recall Dinah's threat anymore."

"In Birmingham they sell some stuff called gingko to help your memory, but I doubt Curd's got any."

When she was gone, I unplugged the phone and bolted the door. It was obvious now my editor had been calling along with Rudolph, aka Duane. Did he know where I lived? No, I reminded myself, he was in jail. I stared at my notes on him and his partner Billy, who was named Paul Overton. My names were better than theirs at conveying their essence. I wanted them to sound as restless and depraved as they'd struck me the night I met them. They'd been looking for "dudes who party," which is code for either coke or meth. "What sort of party?" I wrote, and they replied "tina," and then Burl passed out drunk on the couch.

He knew I went out for fun, and he knew I was conducting interviews, but he didn't realize I'd been getting my interviews and fun from the same sources. At the ridgetop I was buzzed in through a gate. When I knocked on the door of a ranch house, a muffled voice told me to leave my clothes on the porch. I obeyed, then entered a concrete room that smelled of molasses where in a corner a nude Indian sat shackled to an iron workhorse.

"Where is everyone?" I asked.

He gestured with his head toward a hall with three doors. The first door led to a bathroom and the second to stairs. Behind the third Rudolph stood over a Mexican boy who lay on the floor. He was about 6'6", with a gray beard and leather cross-straps, and the boy was maybe 5'6" with no cross-straps. "Are you Kevin?" Rudolph asked me, sucking on a cigar, looking like maybe he'd just pissed on the boy.

"My name's Hunter. I write for the paper."

"Where'd you put Kevin, fuckface?"

I stepped back from them and took a breath. This behavior showed up often in methheads I spoke to: a crazy idea stuck like a glitch in their minds until it became true. You're a cop. You're fucking my mother. You just shot me. "Kevin stayed home," I said, and in response Rudolph kicked the boy, who pushed himself up. The boy was maybe twenty-four, with a dog collar and bruises—standard fare, I was thinking when I lowered my eyes enough to see the empty place where his balls should have been. Rudolph, watching my reaction, said, "Put that in your paper."

"It was free," said the kid. "Usually it's five."

"Answer him," said Rudolph.

"Why would you let them do this?" I said.

"He's lying," the kid told Rudolph.

"How can a question be a lie?"

"The lie is you'd need to ask."

"Want to smoke?" said Rudolph, which was what I'd hoped for. I guess I nodded too eagerly. The truth about my book is I was a cokehead, what you call "functioning." I don't mean I got high every day, but when I did I used a lot. I'd learned to love it from my wife Cindy, who never divorced me. When she moved to Huntsville, she started dealing so she could afford enough for herself. Sometimes I would drive out there. If we got high together, she and her boyfriend would take me in back with them. She was selling crank, too, and the guys who came for it were country fags from nowhere. "I'll fix you next time," said one stealthily to me as he left. It came to seem that every tough-guy methhead biker was really a fag. One day I was saying so on the phone to a friend from journalism school whose wife, Karen, was an editor. She persuaded me to submit a proposal. I didn't intend for the book to be a brilliant way to hide my addiction from Burl, who believed I was off drugs. I warned him I'd be having some late nights. "Yes," I told Rudolph on the ridge. He put a leash on the boy Zach and led him out front, where the pipe lay by the Indian. For a while after we smoked, nothing happened, and then I guess time fell out of its groove. God knows how many hours passed. There were blackout shades on the windows. On coke you stay soft but now it was like I was wearing a cock over my cock. Both were full of blood, and what I said was, "I'd murder Burl before I'd admit this."

Rudolph countered, "So if he dies, I can cut your balls off?"

I laughed until his eyes stared the funny right out of me. "Let's do it, let's kill him," he said, which seemed like part of the fantasy, so I waited for dirty talk about how I'd become his eunuch. "Is it really what you want?" he asked, and I guess I nodded. It's just thoughts. Thoughts keep us civilized by taking the place of action.

"How would you do it?"

I said I would use his wife's Civil War-era Gatlin gun. I mentioned she was never around because she slept at Sheriff Hahn's. It was only to slow my heartbeat that I spoke at all, because that stuff strips you down to your heart, your limbs, and hunger. If you're writing a book, you see the whole thing at once and think, "This is how it feels to be a shark." You lose sight of it when you come down, but it's enough. I kept the advance a secret from Burl. I went up the mountain one day and found Zach on the floor with a younger boy, both too high to tell me where Rudolph and his slave had gone. The new boy's balls were taped down and the basement was padlocked and Zach said, "You bring the money?"

"I'm just a reporter. Where's Rudolph?"

"He's with Kevin and you know you want it."

Zach reached behind himself for, of all things, a glass of wine. "No I don't," I said, knowing as soon as I spoke that I was wrong. My mind started losing out to the shark parts. Zach saw it too and grinned. When I used to talk to Karen, back before Burl died, she always said how dark my story was, how ugly. "Your vision is bleak," she mused, but when you need things you never call them ugly. I stared at the wound below Zach's cock where five blue stitches stretched toward his taint. What about the rest of his life, I wondered: where would the hormones come from? "I won't have any," he said.

"But how will you get turned on?"

"Are you jealous Rudolph's my master?"

"How'd you hear inside my head?"

"What did you do to him? Where is he?"

"When's the last time you saw him?"

"I've got a knife in my pocket, and I'll use it."

There was nothing around him besides a bare floor, but these words were scarier than if he'd been wearing pants. I stepped back to show I meant no harm. He said, "I slashed your tires, Hunter; you're stuck here." He hadn't moved since I'd arrived. I needed to be writing this down. There was something sick that the drug was doing to him, and the part of me that loved being awake for sunrise, the part that liked the smell of morning frost, wanted to flee. That person wanted the town to take him seriously and liked blaming homophobia for the other part, which kicked in now. It was my third time on meth, the time when it finally "took." At one point I realized my knees were bleeding, which turned me on. Some guys showed up and stayed awhile; I think they were gypsies. Outside we heard yodeling, and I got it in my head that we were in the Alps. Every direction was south because it was all downhill. That was the feeling that kept me coming back up. "I'm meeting the craziest people," I wrote to Karen, and indeed I was. Rarely was Rudolph home, but Zach was always there. He had me beat him up, which I did for a promise that he do it to me in return. I got down on the floor to be kicked in the balls. "I'll knock them off you," he said, but he missed and it hardly even hurt. Do it again. You don't deserve it. Please, I said. Earn it, he said. I planned to. We posted pictures to a site for guys into bruises, and one drove up from Montgomery and was whipping me when Rudolph walked in carrying some grocery bags and asked, "Who are you?"

"Adam," said the man.

"Get out."

He was gone inside of a minute. "We would have asked," I was telling Rudolph as Zach pointed to me and said, "Hunter did it."

"Kevin's dead," Rudolph told me, "and your fingerprints are all over his corpse."

"I've never even met a Kevin."

"Georgia cops talk to Alabama cops."

"I'm sorry we let that guy in."

"I've decided to let you owe me the five hundred," he said to me as the Indian, Paul, walked in with more bags that had a paint smell wafting from them. Paul set them down and went in back, which I've come to see as a turning point. I was a free citizen who could have fled; instead I stayed. If the words spoken next were repeated, if the things we did then were redone, I might recall them. Days passed. There was a ringing sound: a phone. I opened my eyes and saw a plank wall. I was lying on my side on a mat below rafters and a song was playing. Blue eyes crying in the rain. When it quit, I realized I didn't know if I had balls.

I told myself I wasn't on a ridge. I was at home dreaming. Without reaching down, I tried to feel. How could I not know; wouldn't the pain have awoken me? My last memory was going down the mountain for pizza, which I had to pick up from inside, but Burl's niece worked there. "Yeah, that's where the humiliation comes in," said somebody, I don't know who. I can't tell what happened next. Maybe I made it up that the niece worked there. She sure didn't show up at the funeral. Another memory: Rudolph telling me he was named for Hitler. So you're Rudolph Hiter? I asked, in response to which he put his cigar out on my ball.

I reached down to feel that burn. Lo and behold, it was there, stinging, and time still moved and I was intact. As long as I never got high again, it would stay that way. So I stood up and opened the left of two shut doors. It was a bathroom. I stood over the toilet and tried to pee. What dripped out of me was dark yellow, nearly brown. I realized it was hard to breathe. Out of my nostrils I blew strands of dried blood the length of worms, which wasn't the main problem. I looked around for clothes and shoes but found nothing. The other door led to a staircase up. I'd thought I was in an attic, I don't know why. I guess the rafters.

Climbing, I rounded a corner and realized the staircase led straight into the ceiling. The trap door crashed on the floor of the empty living room. The front door stood open wide and the pipe was gone. I heard the spin of tires on gravel and hurried over to see, disappearing around the switchback, a highway patrol car.

If I'd been brave, I'd have pitched an angle on the story when it went national. I'd have sold the rights to my exclusive insider knowledge. Won a Pulitzer. Seen to it that that day marked a nadir. Instead I crouched in terror of anyone's learning I'd been involved. From then on I was afraid, truly ill with fear that people would find out. I never told Karen I knew those guys, nor did she ask. Her silence should have worried me. I've made a lot of bad choices over the years.

The evening after Rudolph and Paul's bail was set, Burl came home, poured himself a pitcher of martinis, flipped the TV to MSNBC, and said, "Can you believe this, right up Curd Bluff?"

"I haven't heard much about it," I said carefully, although I faced the screen.

"Alice is jealous we didn't get it, but thank God."

I didn't answer. Watching me, he added, "I say put them in prison till they die."

"But let the drunk drivers go?"

"Don't you see? The whole country will think that's how we all are."

"Why not blame homophobia?"

"Has homophobia made you cut anybody's balls off?"

Knowing I should keep quiet, I retorted, "You know, if you don't want straight people to judge you for being gay, don't judge the castration killers." He told me it was the dumbest thing I'd ever said. I didn't take that well. I slept on the couch from then until he died. One night while I lay awake CNN was talking about Rudolph. "What I don't get is why *others* paid *him* for it," said a newscaster, joining in a universal repulsion, as if Rudolph were a child molester. The media was surely searching for Zach and the other kid along with the cops, and if enough money was offered, Zach would give me away. It was a wonder Rudolph hadn't done so himself. Maybe he'd forgotten me. That was my main hope while Burl still lived. The day Burl died, I awoke at sunrise from the usual gnawing dread and found that he'd left for work. As the sky grew light, Karen called and asked, "Where's my chapter?"

"Will people think I'm a methhead for writing this book?"

"Are you a methhead?"

"I've used it before."

"I don't even really know what it is."

"It's an amphetamine that makes you depraved."

"This is why we're paying for your book."

"I think I should hang up now."

"I want thirty pages by this Friday."

"Good-bye, Karen."

I paced around the kitchen drinking coffee. Two ladybugs were crawling on the counter, the second following behind the first. They were deaf and dumb and seemed unable to use their wings. The world was bigger for them than for me, which reminded me of how, as a child, I'd conceived of a series of novels about a planet ten thousand times earth's size. This planet wasn't a gas giant but a ball of rock, and on it men required millions of years to map the world. Amphetamines, I realized now, existed so I could write those books. Maybe no one as smart as I had ever used them. I sat down and stared at a blank page awhile and then brewed more coffee. One ladybug remained motionless on the counter, and I imagined dousing it with hot coffee. Immediately I recoiled: what kind of monster was I? If a moral person would consider torturing an insect, thousands of other men were inflicting real harm on each other. Hell would have to be huge to hold them all. It was absurd to think so vast a place existed, I thought, gulping coffee. Imagine one ladybug hurting another. Would it burn in hell? Now imagine a male dog raping a female one, which is how nature makes more dogs: will a devil in hell rule over its soul? Now picture yourself raping a child, I thought, reaching the end of my proof. When we die, we fall asleep. These thoughts were a sheen over another one: someone, somewhere, had some meth I could smoke. I got on-line and started looking. That chat transcript could yet turn up as evidence against me. Everyone was at work. I went to my car. On the way, my windshield killed a butterfly and I saw a horse fucking another horse. At a library carrel I sat for two hours writing nothing, with no one around. I jerked off. Burl died. I chose two books and took them to the desk.

"Hunter," said Thecla, the librarian. "How's Burl?"

"He's doing well."

"I'm still grateful about my DUI. I'll bring a cake."

"Don't go to any trouble."

"Will you two ever adopt? I never wanted kids myself till I imagined how it will feel when my family's dead."

"My family's already mostly dead."

"But I'll bet you at least have cousins," she said, and I did, in Frankfort. I said so. She remembers. This is my alibi. I drove home and found Burl dead. I thought, I did this, I killed him. I seized up. I'd like to think I got stuck that way and have never been the same, but I was always that way. His sister asked me to speak at the funeral and I told her fuck you. I wanted to sit numbly in tears so Curd would see me crying, but all I could do was rock back and forth. For some reason Cindy had gotten it in her head to come. Embracing me, she slipped me a bag of coke. "It's a whole ounce," she said, "I thought you might need it."

"How many grams is an ounce?"

"It's about twenty-eight grams."

That struck me as a lot of grams. To reply "I get to go alone to an empty house" was a mistake, because I'd meant to keep the thought private. I tried hard to feel freaked out about how good it sounded, but I couldn't. There was a Kmart beside the funeral home where I stopped in and bought all of "Lost" and some pizzas. Throughout the night I watched "Lost" and did bumps while a deputy who hates Hahn watched from the road in case Dinah shot me. At noon I began season two. Someone, I don't know who, said, "College was a waste," and I paused the DVD, went to the window, and recalled the words of my advisor: "You want to be a reporter but you're a liar."

My next thought seemed large only in that I was high. Yes, I realized, I'm a liar—not because I tell lies but because I pretend to have a human mind. I had tricked Burl into loving a person who couldn't mourn his death. He'd have been better off with Dinah. I guess that's why I grew so obsessed over her guilt. I sat there dreaming about revenge, paying Cindy to do it someday when Cindy needed cash. It turned me on. I thought, everyone gets hard over this stuff; then I thought, I'm the only monster. I realized I would invite someone over. It had been long enough since Rudolph's arrest that I wasn't scared. I found a sergeant named Victor who was into suffocation, which I'd never tried. I don't remember it much. When he was gone, I began season three. My favorite character was Sun. I fantasized that she was my mother. I wanted her to be crowned queen of Lost Island. During season four Dinah's lawyer showed up, which changed everything, although I only shouted through the door. Afterward it was hard to know what had really happened. As a result I couldn't concentrate on the final episode, which I blamed Tamiquah for. I grew despondent. The coke was nearly gone. It came to seem like Burl's ghost was taunting me. It was saying, "You'll be trapped in that body until you die." When Karen called, I couldn't think of any words. I used "bending over sideways" for "bending over backward." When she asked to see everything I had, I put the phone on mute and did two bumps. I unmuted the phone and said sure, in one week. "This is your last chance," she replied, which made me feel out of breath. Only after we'd hung up did I realize Karen had no idea Burl was gone. Such an obvious excuse, yet it had never occurred to me to use it. I sat there rocking back and forth on the couch where Burl had died, and I knew what I was really afraid of: I would never be a serious person. It's easy to lie to yourself. People who think it's not easy are being too literal about the word *lie*. You don't tell actual lies; you just hide from that area of your brain.

When I made up my mind to quit hiding, the first question was what it would consist of. I sat there thinking until I realized I was sitting where Burl had been shot. With a burst of adrenaline I jumped up and dragged the couch out into the night. My arms were sore by the time I had it outside. The legs got stuck in mud. I had to tumble it over itself to get it to the riverbank. This was the answer, I told myself, pushing it toward the water. I went back inside to look for matches. There was about a gram of coke left, and I gathered it into three gigantic lines. Leaving the lines there, I headed out to set the couch on fire. When it wouldn't catch, it occurred to me that I needed gas. With the garden hose I siphoned some out of Burl's truck into a mug. Three trips it took from that truck to douse the couch. I tossed a lit match from a foot away. The wind was blowing in the direction of the river. As it burned, I did my first line, and then I looked out at the flames and tried to recall why I'd done it. It had seemed like the answer. One crackle of the flames popped like a gunshot, reminding me why I'd acted. I felt ridiculous for believing in symbols. What used to make me smart was knowing symbols meant nothing. The thing I needed to burn was still inside. I fetched that stack of pages, carried them out, and scattered them into the flames. It must have felt exhilarating. A few escaped and floated off; one landed by the shed. I went and picked it up. On it was a list in my handwriting:

1. Making yourself stupid.
2. Blackouts. HIV. Teeth.
3. People who cook it are dangerous.
4. <u>Unhappiness</u>
5. The things it makes you game for.

It seemed these words were proof of thoughts to forget. I didn't recall writing them and I had a hunch that, if they disappeared, I never would. So I carried them to the fire, where they went the way of who knows how many others. My heart muscle stretched wide, sending lactic acid up my throat. I was having an epiphany. No, I only felt like when I'd dragged the couch oustide: my brain had got caught in a wrong heart groove and it would always feel thus when my pulse rose.

I can guess what came next. I put on more clothes and burned down the cabin and took Burl's truck. I seroconverted. There's a flash of memory about Knoxville, which is where I'd met Burl. He'd been a guest speaker in my journalism class, where he talked about the Lillelid murders, which are some famous murders. They were "that way," he said, pointing south, but they'd happened to the northeast. Casually I gestured in the right direction. "Depraved Satanists," he was saying when he stopped mid-sentence, noticing my gesture, and then I moved in with him. Sometimes at bars he let me pick up boys to bring home. "That guy likes you," I'd tell them, pointing at Burl. "Which one?" "Look northeast." "How would I know which way's northeast?" "You just know," and then maybe it would come up later, too, and one night Burl rolled his eyes, as in, "This again," so that I fell out of love. If I'd still loved him last year, I wouldn't have done drugs. I don't blame him but in that small way it's his fault.

My memory picks up at the Alabama line. I felt sure I'd done something terrible in Knoxville; I knew also that I was high, because I wanted to be in pain. I needed to be a eunuch. I didn't have any balls anyway. I guess that's where symbols come from: they were built into the language by the same people who made hell. I sped up and raced toward Rudolph's mountain. It seemed to me someone would be there if I wanted it badly enough, but I had to drive through Curd first, so I bypassed town on Old Stage Road. There were wolves howling from the hills to either side of me warning me of the squeeze of the valley. I floored it. I hit a chipmunk. I hit a dog. I had never believed in threes, but there I was careening toward the bluff when a machine was coming at me, a Toyota truck. It hit me head-on. I flipped over. I realized I was in a truck too, upside down in a ditch.

I climbed out of the window into the night. There was a full moon above me shining on the crumpled hood of the truck I'd hit, whose shape made me chuckle until I realized somebody was inside. That person's blood was spurting out of her like a fountain, the same color as her skin, which looked green. I never mentioned I'm colorblind. They say I'll be dead before I know how others see. If there's such a thing as hell its flames will look green, or what I believe to be green, but it was only the moon doing it; in truth she was black, and screaming, just gurgling in pain.

I approached her window. It took a moment to know the word she spoke was *monster*. She screamed like her voice was the devil pulling me into hell. If I hadn't been so high, I might have run, but it felt good, sort of like the idea of chopping my balls off. I hoped she would slap me, maybe smack me upside the head, because I don't like to be in charge of myself. A lot of the time I wish I were a kid again. "Help me," she cried, bleeding along with the tears. The door had fallen off, so that I could see her femur sticking through her leg. "It was Cara," she cried almost unintelligibly. "She shot your lover."

I really did like being screamed at. If not for all the blood, if not for the bone, I might have gotten turned on by a woman.

"You're all monsters," she shouted, as I remembered what she'd said a few minutes before, when I met her. Now I knew where I'd heard the name before—it was the mother of the black kid who'd been killed.

"Are you related?"

"She's my sister, you faggot"—a word Rudolph had used too, but from this woman it seemed sinister. I changed my mind about the screaming. Things always feel less hot when I start sobering up.

"I guess I'll call 911."

"Fuck you," she cackled satanically, but like I said, I don't believe in Satan; I believe in science. I got out my phone, but the battery was gone. It just wasn't there, and so I stood watching the life cackle itself out of her. When she got quiet, it occurred to me to take her wrist and feel her pulse. It went from thirty to fifteen to zero as I held her. My apologies to Dinah. I feel bad for Cara too. Feeling sorry for the dead is a fallacy, but while Cara is alive I'll remain ashamed.

I walked the three miles up Old Stage Road to River Road. From that corner it was two miles to our cabin. I was limping on the last stretch; it felt like I'd broken my foot. The cabin was a smoldering foundation, and for the first time I could see the river from the road. My book is gone, I thought, staggering toward the shed, where I saw, under a rock, a paper with some numbers:

17. HIV
18. Smell of frost in the mornings.
19. Making yourself stupid.

Now I could remember the fire. At that moment the loss of my book stopped being the biggest story. The story that belonged above the fold was that we were a cancer, all of us: that would be number twenty.

My phone rang, and I took it out and saw a Curd number. What the hell, I thought, answering with a hello.

"It's Henry. Sheriff's looking. There was a confession."

"My battery wasn't here," I said, examining the back of the phone. I couldn't keep up. Maybe this was how it felt to grow old.

"Are you at home? Hunter? Hunter? Are you there?"

I looked to the ashes and the river, trying to choose where to throw my phone as my editor repeated my name. I wanted the river but it was a cliché. Everyone throws phones into water. I got ready to pitch it into the ashes. Just as I was about to send it soaring, I realized the problem: when everything seems like a cliché, what's left is so fucked up it can only be depraved. That's what makes us a cancer. So I believed in that moment. The thought was too condensed for me to remember afterward what it means. Hunter. Hunter. Hunter, he said. Until he hung up, and I threw the phone nowhere, but rather called Cindy to tell her my idea.

The Beauties of this Earth
by Mark Powell

In the first spring after the war, Walt Thomas went home, home to see the old man, and home to rest. He left D.C. before first light, crossed the Beltway and hit I-81 south, coffee and a bottle of Jim Beam between his thighs, his discharge papers in his rucksack. He sipped the coffee and topped it with Beam. By the time he hit the state line, he was thinking of Leigh Ann, but was still sober enough to miss her exit north of Sevierville. He wanted to see the old man first.

Main Street and he caught the first red light by the new Kawasaki dealership. ATVs, motorcycles, jet-skis, three-wheelers. The place was usually populated by men in caps and jeans, guys in Dickies and bib overalls with long goatees flowering down their throats, heads shaved and bolts driven through their noses. Walt had seen one with a series of three or four silver hoops embedded in his eyebrow, looked like a grizzly catfish with a beard of five-pound test lines. The place was quiet this morning, however, and he watched a giant American flag unfold itself in the breeze, then collapse down onto the pole.

Three blocks down, he passed the Otasco the old man had managed for better than forty years. Town had changed in the last decade, Walt could see that. With the rich second-homers laying waste to the mountains, came stores selling lawn sculptures and blown glass ornaments, solar lights to line walkways, paintings that looked like an infant had slung his peas and carrots against the wall. There was a store that sold nothing but flags, a thousand goddamn flags bearings pineapples and watermelons and UT and ETSU logos. The Otasco had closed right after Home Depot opened on the bypass.

There was no diner left, but a place selling humus wraps. There were Mexican restaurants and three pizza joints, but nowhere besides Hardee's to get a decent cup of coffee. A single feed and seed store down near the abandoned railroad tracks. The big fifty pound bags stacked and plastic-wrapped on pallets. Sweet feed and marine pellets. He remembered climbing the loading dock as a boy, standing inside the high hangar-like expanse, going with the old man to buy feed or grass seed.

The old man had been a Marine, joining in January of '42 when he was seventeen years old. By the time he was twenty he had made four amphibious assaults, suffered two Purple Hearts, and earned the Navy Cross. His granny was dead now, and all that was left besides the old man was a cousin living in Charlotte, working for a bank and running for the board of the PTA. Walt had spent his childhood listening to the old man talk about the way they had died along the cliffs on Okinawa. He would drink his Early Times and pass out to dreams of Jesus Christ wading ashore at Guadalcanal. Whisper in his sleep about Tarawa and Siapan, about dead SeaBees and the nights sleeping in the cool insect mud. Every Memorial Day he would drag out a box of photographs, gruff children in Marine fatigues, the blush of a three-day beard on a skinny nineteen year old as he shouldered his rifle across on some faraway moonscape.

The beagles bellowed and twisted around Walt's feet when he stepped out of his truck. The place was empty and he stood in the living room and imagined his granddaddy waking from his dreams. Christ wading ashore through the early mist off Saipan. Rising from musty blankets to walk out onto the porch. It would be early, not yet daylight though moonlight might move cloud shadow across the open fields, the pasture land cropped as close as a shaved skull.

He saw the old man in his porch rocker while along the road a pickup pushed its headlamps so that the world was lit softly—a tree, a parked tractor—a pale footlight spreading a vapor of night fog. The highway ghost-lit and then not.

Okinawa. Them cliffs above Okinawa, son. It got ugly there.

For years Walt had witnessed the old man's solitary offices. It occurred to him that he now understood them.

He was on the porch when the old man came home. The walls were lined with canning, kraut and green beans, corn and chow-chow, and the room smelled of dirt, cool and metallic. It was almost dusk and the old man squinted when he looked at him.

"I figured on you flying down," he said. "Been quicker."

"Hey, Papa."

"Seen your truck pass the store today. You go over and see Leigh Ann?"

Walt shook his head. "Not yet."

The old man sat down and exhaled, motioned at Walt's glass eye.

"Your granny would be glad of it, that it come out like it did. She would have," he said. "But I ain't gonna sit here and lie to you, son."

They ate Hungry Man dinners heated in the microwave then watched the last innings of the Braves-Dodgers.

"I can take you on at the store if you like." The old man cut his country fried steak with his pocket knife. "Could use the help."

"I'm moving on."

"That the plan, is it?"

"That's the plan, yes sir."

"Got you a boy and everything else and you just moving on. Blowing like the breeze."

"I didn't wish it this way," Walt said.

"Didn't nobody," the old man said. "Rest assured, didn't nobody."

In the morning Walt came out of his old room dressed in jeans and Tony Lama boots. The old man sat at the kitchen table and drank coffee. He looked ancient and veined, smaller than Walt remembered.

"Getting on?" he asked.

"Soon enough."

"You really ain't going over to see her?"

"I don't know."

"It might be you a debt."

Walt looked at the garden, the corn high and tasseled, tomato plants staked in wire helixes.

"I ain't give it no thought," he said.

He drove up Picket Post Road to Main Street, past the café ringed with pickups and sedans, past the new Arby's and the antique stores where old women leaned on push-brooms and squinted against the morning sun that was just beginning to peak over the mountains. He took 441 and this time didn't miss the turn.

His house—her house, now—was in a subdivision south of Knoxville, a broad two-story of vinyl siding and new brick. They had hardly moved in before Walt had been deployed, and he saw now that in the intervening months she had done little or nothing in the way of upkeep. The driveway was still gravel, washboarded from over a year of rain and too much hard driving, ruts where tires had spun and slipped betraying her carelessness; betraying those late nights, Walt imagined, drinking margaritas with her boyfriend before driving home buzzed and foggy-headed. The yard was all mud and scattered straw, matted and rotting, up to an apron of dull yellow grass: the sod Walt had laid just days before he shipped out.

He had never understood but did now. Sitting in the driveway and looking at the house that rose from the ground like a tombstone, he understood the house was about *her* future, *her* plans. What happened at Balad had only given her an excuse, cover and commiseration from circles of sympathetic friends drinking Mai Tais in some crowded living room while HBO blared from the tube.

"I don't want the house in Fayetteville," she'd told him over the phone when he was in Walter Reed. They were officially separated by then, divorce in the offing, and he knew she had read a copy of the letter he had left, the one that began *What you see before you is the body of Captain Walter J. Thomas.* He knew, too, that she knew what everyone understood: that at the moment to which his life had narrowed, the cold barrel at his temple, he had flinched.

"Take it," she had told him. "I don't want it. Just leave me the new house. Don't contest anything, and I promise you can see Billy now and then." Walt had stood there in the corridor in his paper gown, watched the one-legged men wheel by, gave little nods as they passed. He had made the down payment with his reenlistment money. "Are you there? Walt?"

"I'm here."

"Well?"

"I don't want the house either."

"Fine then. We'll sell it."

"I want to see my son again, Leigh Ann."

Her sigh like wind singing along high tension lines. "Just don't contest anything then and you can see him. Jesus—" It all seemed to amaze her. "Can you imagine if you actually did contest this? Be smart, Walt. Don't make this any worse."

He pulled beside her beige Civic and cut the engine. Beside him sat a Volvo wagon, a deep hunter green, all-wheel drive, something sensible and middle class. The car belonged to her new boyfriend, Vance something. A school teacher, middle school math, if Walt remembered correctly. She had wasted no time moving from Fayetteville, finding a new job, a new body for the bed, a little heft to impress the mattress, someone to crawl onto when the urge struck.

Walt noticed the Christmas wreath was still up, withered and tacked to the front door, closer now to next Christmas than last. No lights were on in the house, though he imagined Billy was downstairs watching cartoons over a bowl of Cocoa-Puffs. They would have heard him grinding up the drive—he would have to tell her either to get it paved or smooth the goddamn thing out, one or the other—but maybe he could have a few minutes with his son. Last time they had spoken had been on the phone, five weeks ago. His son talking about feeding the beta fish whose tank sat beneath the far window in his first grade classroom. *That's good, son. I'm proud. Now put your mamma on, all right.* She had sold the house in Fayetteville and had a check for him.

"Keep it," he told her.

"All right then. I will."

"Put it away for Billy."

"You don't have to tell me how to raise my child," she said. "Things are good for him right now. We don't have to fuck him up just because we fucked everything else up."

"You, Leigh Ann. I don't know who else you're talking about."

"I gotta go, Walt."

"I just want you to damn well remember who's doing what."

"Walt." This was her school teacher voice, the voice of the weary public servant, put-upon but patient. "You know I'm not the one who stood around while they murdered some poor kid."

He said nothing.

"I'm sorry you made me say that," she said.

Walt walked up the front steps and moved along the windows, cupped his hands to the glass to see inside. No Billy. No one in the living room. The TV was off. No one in the kitchen. By the step sat several ceramic turtles, green and glassy-backed, and he flipped one after another before he found a dull brass key taped to a pale underbelly.

Inside, the house was still as silent prayer. He stood in the foyer and looked up the stairs; dust drifted through a span of light and collected along the wooden balustrade like drifts of snow. He had hardly lived here long enough to know the place, a few long weekends driving over to check on progress, to bitch at the contractor or argue with Leigh Ann for cheaper bathroom fixtures. Hardware it was called, like it was something beside trinkets to impress the kind of people Walt despised, the safe ones, moderately wealthy and healthily fat, the ones who talked about their dental and whole life policies, the ones with model trains or ping-pong tables in their basements, the weekend joggers and internet pussies.

He walked into the kitchen.

The counters were empty, wiped clean and flashing spirals of silvered moisture. Plates and silverware stacked in the sink. A glass held a thimble full of diluted red wine; little tremors feathered the surface. Walt looked out the window to the eight-foot basketball goal that sat unevenly, the ball beyond it, faded orange and marooned in ankle-deep weeds the color of mustard. His breath spread on the window, silver and expanding, then retreated, erased itself like a fingerprint. A little suction cupped thermometer. A potted cactus the size of a child's thumb. He was looking at the vague reflection of his face one moment then her figure the next. She leaned against the door in socks and a long flannel shirt that hung just above her knees.

"I didn't know you still had a key," she said.

He held up the brass key he'd found. "I don't. You should hide this better."

"Mostly I don't count on people snooping around."

"Well, you should. Married to a son of a bitch like me."

Her arms were crossed, and when she exhaled her body seemed to cave, shoulders collapsing forward, breasts sagging so that they rested on her pale forearms. He could see the hairline cracks fissured out from her mouth and eyes.

"What are you doing here, Walt? You want some coffee?"

He turned back to the window.

"Yard looks like shit."

She opened the cabinet and shut it. "Move." She filled the pot with water. "I don't know why you're here. I thought all this was settled and done."

"You don't know why I'm here?"

"That's what I just said."

"That statement makes absolutely no sense to me, Leigh Ann. Absolutely none."

She looked at him, those liquid brown eyes he remembered rolling over him once, their first date, taking a canoe down the Pigeon River in the middle of a terrible drought, the way she'd looked at him after they'd dragged the boat over tiny rocks scattered along the riverbed and were drifting in the warm waning light, the sun sinking slowly over the mountains.

"Jesus Christ, Walt. I wish you'd just get on."

He shook his head. "What is it you want here, Leigh Ann?"

"Please, Walt."

"In this house. With him. Just answer me. Why do you want this?"

She poured the water into the filter. "Why do I want this? Because someone had to. Someone had to make a life while you were off jumping out of airplanes and running all over the world. What can I tell you? That I didn't want my son raised by an absent father living out his adolescent fantasies while squatting in some goddamn third world jungle?"

"I squatted in those jungles for you. Every fucking one of them."

"Keep your voice down, please."

"Why?" He motioned up with his head. "So we won't wake him. What's his name? Vance, isn't it."

"He's trying to stay out of this."

From upstairs came the sound of footsteps, water rushing through pipes.

"Is that him?" Walt's eyes were still cast up at the ceiling.

"Yeah, that's him."

"The new me."

She shook her head. "No," she said. "That's just the point: he's not you." She took two cups from the sink and rinsed them, shook out the water and filled each with coffee.

"You can't get him to do anything about the yard? Sow some grass or something."

"Drink some coffee, Walt," she said. "And then leave."

He took the cup and sniffed it. "He won't come down?"

"He wants to respect my privacy."

"He's afraid of me. Afraid I'll tear his fat head off."

She looked up from the cup she held with both hands. Her sleeves had slid almost to her fingertips. "Would you?"

He turned back to the window and watched the leaves tremble, their undersides translucent and veined. One floated free to drift down, swirling for a moment before coming to rest in the mud yard amid the bits of straw that stirred with the wind, a quiet rustle he imagined but could not hear.

"Billy's at your mother's I take it," he said.

"We stayed out a little bit later than I planned. He was already over there. He's fine."

"Does Vance sleep over when Billy's home?"

"Sometimes. Sometimes, yes."

"Fuck, Leigh Ann."

"You know I still have a life, Walt. I *want* to have a life, at least."

"That's the idea is it, a life."

"Generally. Yeah."

He turned from the window. She had approached him but shrank back now, pressed the small of her back against the island centered in the kitchen. From the window fell clear light, eerily transparent light he felt moving along the bare nape of his neck.

"You know we're still married," he said.

"Walt."

"Technically," he said. "In the eyes of the state of North Carolina we are still technically married, Leigh Ann."

She shook her head slowly and with great attendance. "Oh, Walt," she said. "Poor Walt." She touched his back. "Let me see. Let me see your eye."

He tossed his coffee into the sink and spun on her. A little wave of coffee splashed from her cup onto the hardwood floor. He pushed past her.

"Where are you going, Walt?" She followed him to the door. "Don't go over there, Walt. I told mamma not to let you see him."

"Not to let me see my own son?"

"That's exactly right," she said. "At least—"

"At least what, Leigh Ann?" He was yelling now. "At least fucking what?"

Her voice like that whisper of knowing: "At least not until things are better. At least not until you can explain to him what happened."

He threw his head into his hands. "Fuck," he said. "Fuck, fuck, fuck."

"Walt—"

"Fuck, Leigh Ann."

A voice floated down from upstairs. "Everything OK, honey?"

Walt's eyes flared and Leigh Ann looked at him, shook her head, willed him to silence there in the laddered sun that split the blinds.

"You tell him—"

She cut him off. "Fine. Everything's fine. Come out here." She hustled Walt onto the porch where the Christmas wreath still hung.

"My fucking house, Leigh Ann."

"Please."

"My fucking house."

She pulled her shirt tighter around her. "Please, Walt. Just go."

They stood for a moment. The wind gusted and a shudder of leaves showered across the yard, caught against the gutter and sailed free to cyclone down at their feet.

"Please," she said.

He stood there shaking his head. "Yard looks like shit."

"I know."

"Just get him to sow some grass or something, all right? You want to impress the neighbors and this won't impress anybody."

"I know." She was crying. "I know. Please just go, Walt."

It was late afternoon by the time he got back to the old man's. He took a bottle of J&B and walked onto the porch where moths batted around the porch light. The beagles slept around his feet. He swallowed as much J&B as possible, and then took another drink, and then another.

They had found the boy along a service road beneath a highway overpass in Balad. Seven months into his tour. Walt was riding along with a patrol when the call came. Second Platoon had found the boy crawling around under the bridge pilings and chased him out. Now he was by the river, fifteen or so, the sergeant with his flashlight in his face and the boy down on his knees. He wouldn't stop praying. It was almost one AM, hours after curfew, and Walt could see the pale soles of his bare feet tucked up beneath his legs as he muttered to Allah.

"Said he was headed home, didn't know how late it was." The platoon sergeant shook his head. "It's way too late for that, sir."

"Fucking A," said one of the soldiers.

Walt looked at the soldier who had spoken and saw that his eyes vibrated

"Shut up, Michaels," said the sergeant.

The boy kept praying, prostrate, hands extended and upturned, empty and waiting, as if they might yet be filled with the spirit. Walt could see the rings of hair that grew along the nape of his neck. He followed the boy's motion, the narrow back, the long arms that turned to delicate fingers.

"You find anything under the pilings?" Walt asked.

The sergeant shook his head.

"No, sir. Not yet."

"That's the bridge where them fuckers killed Teddy."

"I said to shut it, Michaels."

Walt smelled the water, the tang of mud and diesel, the surface scummed with foam and trash. The boy kept praying.

"He was all up in under the stanchions climbing around, sir. All up in under. There's only one thing you're doing up there."

"Fucking *hajjis* casing the place."

The sergeant told Michaels to shut up.

Walt washed his hands of it, that's what he said: I wash my hands of this, sergeant. You deal with it. He was halfway back up to the road when he heard the shot. The splash—he never heard the splash. Just kept walking.

At the inquiry, he had sat in his Class A's, creases sharp and medals shining, looked down to see his warped face in the curve of his leathers, smelled the starch in his clothes. Turned over for psychiatric evaluation. Case pending. When they sent him back to his post to collect his things, he took the pistol from behind loose paneling. The letter he had already written and spread before him along with his identity card and driver's license and next of kin contact information. He thought of the boy, fourteen or fifteen, thought of his body caught in the reeds or washed against one of the bridge pilings, raised in a fisherman's net. Then he thought of his wife and of his son.

You know I'm not the one who stood around while they murdered some poor kid.

Then he put the gun to his head.

In the morning Walt woke early, swallowed five BC headache powders, and struck out into the woods toward Sevenmile Creek. He had heard gunshots just before first light and thought someone might have been firing at one of the black bears that rooted their way through garbage cans. The beagles were already running, so he walked alone through shafts of sunlight that fell through the trees and backlit the purple ginger and blue bellflowers that bloomed from the decomposing remains of a nurse log. When he met the creek, he followed it downstream, morning light glimmering along its surface, until he found a small cairn of stones balanced delicately atop a rock in the center of a still pool.

It was there he picked up the first swatches of blood, following them into a laurel thicket where bedded in the cool earth he found a buck lying on its side, its back hip blasted open. A gout of blood had dried, crusting the surrounding fur and turning the dirt wine-dark. The deer breathed heavily and slowly, struggled to raise its head and turn one glassy eye on Walt before lowering it again to exhale into the dust. Walt stepped closer and saw a large Wolf Spider leg its way toward the buck's eye.

In a few years Billy would be as old as the boy in Balad. He watched the spider and thought of those intervening years, stood there until the buck went limp, exhausted. Then he turned for home.

The old man sat at the kitchen table and drank coffee from the metal cup of a Stanley Thermos. Walt sat across from him and put his hands on the table.

"Looks like I might stay maybe a little longer than I expected," he said.

The old man nodded. "I reckoned you'd see her sooner or later."

Walt said nothing.

"You own it now," the old man said. "If that hadn't occurred to you yet it will soon enough."

He stood and staggered his way to the cabinet, and Walt saw then he had been staring down at a wallet-sized sepia portrait of Walt's grandmother. He came back to the table with two glasses and a bottle of twelve-year old Macallan's scotch, poured them each a glass.

"Every time I drink this I start to cry," the old man said. "Thinking about the beauties of this earth."

"The wonders," Walt said.

The old man took a long swallow. "The goddamn wonders, indeed."

Casting Out
by Denton Loving

My brother Jay's troubles had started the previous Saturday with a force of straight line winds that left a two-day trail from Texas to Tennessee. All over Powell Valley, trees of every size had been blown sideways. Giant roots as thick as a man had been ripped apart like strips of licorice. Grace Bailey's trailer moved two inches off its foundation, and every sheet of tin on Mack Jones' barn was yanked up, nail by nail, blown across the Back Valley Road and scattered over his hay field. Two barns and the skeleton of an old house were knocked down completely on Straight Creek.

On Sunday morning, when the torrents of rain were soaked into the earth and the high winds were replaced with a gentle breeze, Jay and I walked through the woods surveying the damage and finding most of the fallen trees had not torn down any fences. There were only a few places where branches lay against the barbed wire or metal clips had broken away from the fence posts. Easy problems to fix.

The roots of some trees were knocked loose, allowing them to sway in the remaining winds. They creaked, giving me an eerie feeling. The noise was like a warning to the other trees in the woods that one of their own was on his last legs.

Jay had looked at every fallen tree, measuring in his head how tall each had been, as well as how big around. He considered what kind of trees had fallen—pines, oaks and sassafras—and guessed at their ages.

"That storm didn't do us no favors," Jay said. The leaves were soft with the rain, less noisy than usual.

"It won't take us long to clean up," I said, trying to cheer him.

By this time, we had walked to the back side of the farm, along the fence line that separated our woods from the back of Aunt Vonda's yard. Daddy owned the woods on every side of Vonda except for the front side that faced Tranquility Lane. She had chosen the name for the little road, which we joked was anything but tranquil since Vonda lived there. Daddy used to own Vonda's property too until she guilted him into selling her a piece of land so she could come back to Tennessee from Ohio. He knew it was a mistake then, and we've all regretted it ever since. The fence surrounding her land, six strands of barbed wire instead of the usual four or five, was more to keep her out than to keep the cows in.

At Vonda's house, the winds had all but pulled up a white poplar that had grown more sideways than should have been allowed. While the loosened roots were on our side of the fence, the majority of the tree hung over Vonda's side. Now that its roots were weakened, it leaned even more. The tree gave off a death rattle as its furrowed bark rubbed and pushed against the tightly stretched strands of barbed wire.

Long before Saturday evening's wind storms, Daddy had gone twice to cut that tree down, and both times Vonda had chased him off. Daddy wasn't exactly afraid of Vonda, but he didn't like to get in the middle of any trouble with her either.

That afternoon, all Jay said was, "I'll have to figure later on some way to deal with that mess."

Without telling Daddy or me, Jay parked his truck on Tranquility Lane the next morning and went to cut down that tree. Daddy was loafing at the Co-op as he did every Monday morning. And Vonda was on her daily run to the Wal-Mart in Middlesboro.

With one slanted cut from his camouflage-colored chain saw, the tree's top end made its journey to the ground with a loud but dull thud and the rustle of limbs and leaves. Released from its burden, what was left of the trunk jerked back and upright as if the ground had reclaimed what had unintentionally been given away. He made quick work of stripping the poplar of its limbs. Then he threw the debris across the fence as fast as he could until there was nothing left on Vonda's side but the tree's long, straight trunk lying like a fallen soldier on the battlefield.

He only stopped when he needed to catch his breath, but Vonda returned before he could have the job finished. Now, I never believed what she said about having second sight, but Jay said she came ripping past her "Jesus Loves You" sign and into her driveway like she already knew he was there. He could see her cussing before he could hear her, even before she could get out of her little red Sunfire that looked too sporty for her seventy-odd years.

Vonda was a little brown paper sack of a woman, full of nothing but bones and spite. She wore a faded red sweatshirt with the hood tight around her head that hid most of her face. Jay could see she was angry, down right pissed off. More mad than he had ever seen her.

"Hell and damnation boy. I'll have your hide and hang it on that fence to dry. I'll slice you straight up the middle like the dirty snake you are," she said. "You rotten heathen. Cutting down my tree as soon as I turn my back."

Jay started to cross through the strands of barbed wire as if standing on the other side would protect him. But Vonda's streak of words seemed to make those six tight strands of wire attack him. His shirt caught on the sharp metal and tore. His hands were scratched and bloody before he realized he couldn't get through the fence. By that time, Vonda was getting closer. She was breathing hard from the constant yelling and the slight incline from her driveway.

"How are you going to put that tree back?" she said between huffs. "I want it back just the way it was."

Vonda never was accused of being the most rational person.

"There ain't no putting it back," he said. "I'm sorry, but it had to be done."

"I'll say what has to be done around here."

"Now, you hold on," Jay said. "That tree was on our side of the fence, and it was damaged. I did you a favor by cutting it down before it tore the fence down."

"Boy, you're gonna split hell wide open with that mouth."

"I was trying to clear it, so you wouldn't have a mess in your yard. But if you don't quit your damn fussing, I'll leave."

"Don't you talk rough to me, boy," she said, as if Jay's foul mouth had given her renewed spirit. "Don't you get in my face. I'll flat take you down. You'll come back a ragged piece of meat. I'm gonna get my gun, and we'll see who's fussing then."

She wobbled down the hill like a crow that won't fly, and then she turned back to face Jay again. "You'll be sorry you cut down that tree. I'll see the rot inside you come out before I'm done."   And then she continued climbing up her steps to fetch her gun.

As wild as Vonda is, it's unlikely she would have actually shot Jay. Even if she had fired, chances are good she would have missed. She once tried to shoot a garden snake, but, aiming several feet too high, she shot through her window and took out her microwave instead. Jay and I had gone to replace her shattered glass, and it took us about the whole time to wheedle the true story out of her. Still, Jay decided not to wait around. He left Tranquility Lane before Vonda could reappear.

Things began going wrong the next day, and it didn't take long for Jay to decide Vonda had aligned the stars against him. There had been a number of small accidents like his toaster catching fire. His TV acted possessed before it completely shorted out. An infestation of Asian ladybugs swarmed in his house.

Daddy didn't take serious notice of anything being wrong until Jay suffered a true brush with death. That was when Ivan, our big yellow bull, found a weak spot in the fence and broke into Dwight Russell's field after a cow in heat. I would have waited him out and let him come back when he was ready, but Jay decided to take the trailer over there to load him up and bring him home. As soon as he got the trailer hitched up, he realized it had a flat. He jacked the trailer up, ready to take the tire off, when the brakes on his truck failed and rolled straight into the barn, dragging the trailer off the jack, and almost hauling Jay with it. It took him the rest of the day to fix his brakes and the flat.

He was already worn out when he finally went to pick up Ivan. Jay pulled up close to Ivan in the middle of Dwight's field and spoke his cow talk to that old Limousine bull. Ivan didn't care to argue about it being time to go home. Not after he smelled that sweet apple in Jay's hand. The bull climbed in the trailer and ate his apple, and Jay shut the door and drove home. It seemed like the first good thing to happen to Jay all week, but that changed when Ivan recognized his surroundings. He must have been excited to climb out into his own field, and in the anticipation, he started to jump, the trailer rocking with him. His hind legs kicked up in the air, and his whole body bucked. Just as Jay unlocked the door to let him out, Ivan's hooves struck the metal wall of the trailer. The sharp, banging noise scared him so bad, that when the door opened, the two-ton bull lost his footing, and he slid the rest of the way out. This caused the trailer door to fly backwards, and Jay, who couldn't let go fast enough, got knocked down pretty good. He laid there in a wet cow pile, trying to catch his breath while Ivan found his land legs and high-tailed it back to the herd.

"You could have gotten yourself killed," Daddy said. "You can't trust no bull. I swear. I can't turn my back on either of you boys for a minute." That was typical bluster for Daddy, but for once Jay had nothing to say back.

On Wednesday morning, Jay was awakened by the sharp yips of a red fox. The sound was so close, and so unusual, Jay ran outside in his underwear to see what was happening. Sure enough, a red fox was chasing his cat Bobby Blue out of the woods and through the orchard.

Bobby Blue was a foundling that had appeared outside of Jay's door soon after Jay moved into Granny's old house. He turned out to be the best cat there ever was. Bobby was a good mouser and good company, but most importantly, he was a work cat. No matter what the job, Bobby would always follow along with the aim to help. Sometimes, of course, he was just in the way, but he thought he was helping. Daddy said he was the smartest cat he had ever seen. What amazed me was how he liked to find a high spot in the evenings and watch the cattle around Jay's house as if they were his and it was his sole duty to protect the herd. He was afraid of nothing, never knowing when something had the better of him, which was almost the case with the fox.

Jay's bare feet ran into the dewy grass without thinking. Unarmed, he yelled at the fox, which paused, looked confused and continued her short, fast barks. Bobby Blue saw his opportunity to escape and ran straight toward Jay and the safety of the back porch. The fox waited, not sure if it was wise to follow or not. Jay went back in the house and grabbed his .22-caliber single shot and a handful of shells. His intent was to shoot just near enough the fox to scare her away. When he stepped outside again, he found the little red beast standing in the same spot. He slid one small shell into the gun barrel and pulled the bolt, locking it in place. That moment, with his feet cold and wet from the grass, Jay forgot how to shoot.

The gun raised fast and steady to where his eye and the sight could meet. He aimed at the ground near the little fox's feet, sure to scare it but not wound it. His finger wrapped itself firmly around the trigger and tightened, but the gun remained silent. He lowered the gun from his face and searched its simple mechanisms, but, somehow, his mind was blank as to why it would not shoot. He tried again, repeating each previous action, yet the rifle and its one single shot were resolute.

He released the bolt and the unfired shell jumped backwards. He pushed it into place and locked the bolt a second time. But again the gun refused to fire. Jay forgot both times to cock the hammer, and even though he looked directly at it, his mind was so befuddled, that important middle step never occurred to him. He could not think to pull the firing pin.

The fox considered all of this with some patience and only an occasional sharp bark. Jay considered it as well. The sun was brighter after this time, and a slight mist was rising from the ground around him and the fox. Jay was suddenly conscious his feet were naked in the dewy grass. He had given up on shooting at the fox. He decided to wave his arms instead, yelling "Get. Get out of here. Go on." Finally, the fox turned and skittered back to the woods. When Jay went again towards the house, he found Bobby Blue waiting on the porch steps, impatient for his breakfast, as if none of this was any concern to him.

The next morning, Jay woke to the sound of the fox's noise again. Stepping onto the porch, he called Bobby Blue, but the cat never appeared, and the fox's barks moved further and deeper into the woods. All day, Bobby's breakfast remained uneaten in his bowl, and by night time, Jay had convinced himself the little red devil must have killed and eaten his cat. The absence of the gray farm cat grew burdensome on Jay, and he could not help but blame Vonda.

After all this continuous trouble, it was hard for me to argue Vonda hadn't set some demon on his back. Even waking up this morning to only a trickle of water pressure seemed like her doing although a busted water line is the kind of event that could happen to anybody.

Daddy and I went to help Jay with his water trouble. The three of us walked back and forth over the line. We tried to find any kind of damp patch of ground, arguing we were too far over one way or another. Once Daddy spotted it, it seemed like the most obvious thing in the world. The ground was soft from the slow release of so much water, and as Jay's mattock went deeper, the dirt turned right muddy before it became a pure puddle.

For a while, there was only the dull, repeated sound of the mattock striking the earth, and then the steady dragging away of the loose dirt. Jay swung down in short, quick thumps, yet not hard enough to cut the water line if he were to hit it by accident.

"Jack, go turn the valve off," Daddy said. The mattock splashed into the mud before Jay's arm would stop. "Looks like we've found it for sure."

I ran down Jay's driveway and across the gravel lane. The gate into the cattle field and the well house door both stood open and waiting. The blue valve turned easy, and I could feel the pressure build in the line, pulsing in my hand like a heart beat, the water waiting to be released again.

By the time I had walked back up to the hole, Jay had dragged most of the mud away from the line. He stood tense then pulled his shoulders down. His back stretched out to relieve the stress. His hair was wooly from what I had figured was another night of restless sleep.

Daddy was already down on his stomach. His hands felt for the puncture in the three-quarter inch plastic as if he were reading Braille.

"Lord God," Daddy said when we heard the sound of a car on the gravel road. Vonda's red Sunfire inched toward the place where we were fixing the water line. Behind her was her man Ligon Fields in his rusted out Ford pickup. Ligon styled himself a preacher, although he was always the first to tell you he had no official training besides what the Lord had given him. He had a regular following, even though he had to sit out from preaching every now and then. For sooner or later, he got caught stealing money or sleeping with a deacon's wife. And once or twice, he'd been arrested for fighting chickens. But Ligon was the kind of man that took such things in stride, laying low for a while and then finding an empty church building, calling in the faithful from his past congregations and starting up again.

Vonda's head turned back and forth from the road in front of her while trying to see us up in the driveway. The car stopped, and she motioned me towards her. I just waved and turned my attention completely to the muddy hole in front of me, pretending I didn't realize she wanted me to come down to her.

"If we ignore them, maybe they'll go away," I said.

Without waiting any time, the Sunfire sputtered up the little incline of Jay's driveway and into the grass as close as she could get to where we worked. Ligon pulled his truck up behind her until their bumpers almost kissed.

"You made me drive all the way up here on this hill, and now I'll have to throw this parking brake."

"Vonda, now's not the best time," Daddy said.

"The Lord don't wait for the time of man," Vonda told us. She climbed out of the car's low seat. "Besides, I'm not looking for you. I'm here to see Jay. I hear he's had enough trouble for a while and we've come to save him from eternal misery."

"Howdy, Ligon," Daddy said from the ground as Ligon stepped closer. "You out saving souls today?" Daddy's hands were still down in the mud, trying to fit in a new piece of plastic line where he had cut out the old piece with the crack. When he looked up, his eyes stuck on a Ziploc bag Ligon carried full of white powder.

"Well, I save when I can," Ligon said, smiling. He was as slim a man as I had ever seen, his skin tough and leathery.

"I reckon there's still a lot out there that needs it."

"The souls are out there all right. But you've got to be like a tom cat and make the calls."

"Well, there ain't no need of making a call here," Jay said. "You two can go on home."

"Lord, now I know you're just trying to vex my spirit," Vonda said. "And here I am come to help you."

"I don't want no more help from you. That's what got me in this mess to begin with." Jay's face started to color.

"Hush up boy. I brought Ligon up here to end your suffering."

"With what? A bag of sugar?"

"This ain't sugar," Ligon answered in a tone suggesting Jay should know better. "This is salt of the earth. Salt from which we all come. And from which we shall all return."

"Sugar or salt, you can put it away. I'm not going in for none of your voodoo."

Vonda grabbed for the bag as Ligon's arms went straight up. For a moment, I thought he was going to hit Jay, but Ligon opened his palm and laid it on Jay's forehead, his long fingers extended around Jay's skull in a death grip. "You listen to me, boy. An evil spirit has ridden an ill wind and sat down on your soul, and I'm here to get him out whether you want me to or not. Now close your eyes and pray, dammit."

Vonda's hand reached into the snowy powder and then flew out to scatter the salt in a circle around their feet. She threw and threw while Ligon began praying aloud.

"Devil, I rebuke ye in the name of the Lord," he started, but he progressed into such a fast, high-pitched whine, the words all jumbled together so that only God could understand them fully. I thought maybe this was what it meant to speak in tongues. The whole time Vonda's wrinkled little fingers went in and out of the salt, flicking the crystals onto Jay's and Ligon's feet, while her own legs danced in a circle around them.

I couldn't tell what effect this was having on Jay, although it surprised me he remained standing in the middle of this mess, with Ligon's hand pushing firmly down on his head and Vonda pelting him with salt.

Daddy's hands had finally stopped moving in the freshly dug hole. His entire body became still, watching the proceedings.

I was mesmerized, sure flames would leap up from the ground at any moment. Everything in my head seemed to run together. I felt like I was walking in darkness, feeling my way forward with one foot before the other. I was afraid of falling down. And in my mind's eye, I saw Vonda throwing handfuls of pure fire from her magic bag and onto Jay. I went to step forward, but I felt overpowered by the sudden darkness. It seemed to overtake everything around me until I wasn't sure which way to go. I moved forward, but I don't remember ever being so afraid to fall. My heart beat to the rhythm of Ligon's voice, which grasped for breath as his face and neck grew redder.

Out of nowhere, that fox began to bark. The noise called me back from my imaginings, and I looked across the road and into the field. Down by the creek, I saw a gray streak followed by a red flash of fire. That crazy little fox was chasing Bobby Blue, barking like a regular dog, but at a higher, eerier octave.

Ligon paused in his prayer. Vonda stopped her dance. Jay took the opportunity to step away from Ligon's reach, and even Daddy stood up to get a better look across the field.

Bobby Blue jumped across the creek and then paused to see if the fox was still following.

"Come on, Bobby," Jay yelled. "Come here."

The fox sat across the water and stared boldly up the path Bobby made through the cattle field, his lithe body swimming gracefully through the spring grass.

Jay moved further away from us and closer to the cat. "Where have you been?" he asked from the other side of his yard. Jay sat down in the grass to pet Bobby's blue gray back. Neither of the two paid the fox any more attention, and at some moment when I wasn't looking, that fox disappeared.

"Well, I guess that's the end of that," Daddy said as he lowered himself back down to the ground.

"And I guess we better hit the road," Ligon said, making long strides back to his truck and looking to the sky. It was hard to tell if he felt insulted or just recognized when his job was finished. "Looks like more rain's coming," he said, mostly to himself as he walked away.

"Might do it," Daddy answered, but not loud enough that Ligon or Vonda either one would hear. Bent down, his hands tightened the hose clamps he had already secured around the line. "It might do it."

"You all go home with us," Vonda said as she walked back to her car. The half-empty bag of salt hung limply by her side. "I've got a good mess of beans cooked." There was nothing but sweetness in her voice. She opened the car door but stopped before getting in.

"We better get this water running again," I said. "But thanks anyway."

Daddy and I watched their vehicles back slowly down the hill and make their way out of the lane, driving by Jay and his cat.

"What in the world?" was all I could say to Daddy.

With his eye moving from Ligon's truck to Vonda's red car, Daddy said, almost to himself, "Those two beat more than you can stick a bucket under. But at least they've got conviction. You've got to give them that." His hands were muddy, and he rubbed them together to remove the moisture.

I was unsure of what we had witnessed that day, even of what I had felt happen to myself. I didn't expect Daddy believed much of Ligon's show, but it was hard to even talk about it.

"If he feels better is all that counts," Daddy finally said.

Jay never said for sure what he thought about that visit from Ligon and Vonda, but that day I watched him lie in the grass, so relaxed he reminded me of what he looked like as a little boy. Bobby Blue climbed over his chest until their heads rubbed against each other. That was the first time in a long while I heard laughter from Jay.

Mary, the Cleaning Lady
by Scott McClanahan

When I was a little boy, I used to stay with this woman named Mary. We used to go around Rainelle cleaning houses for people. It was just after my Mom had gone back to work, and she used to carry me into Mary's house before the sun came up. I'd be about half asleep and wrapped in a blanket, and since it was still dark outside she put me on Mary's couch. Then after she left, I would watch cartoons on the television and then fall back to sleep dreaming a cartoon dream where I was a cartoon too. And then one day I woke up and it was time to go cleaning. I remember one morning Mary said, "Whelp, you ready to help me gather up all my cleaning stuff and get going?"

I helped her gather it all up and put it beside the door just like she always did. "And if you're real good today and you don't get afraid then maybe we'll stop by the bus station and get you an ice cream cone."

She smiled and then she said, "I promise it'll go by fast today." Mary was always right too. I knew Mary was someone who could control time.

Since she was offering me an ice cream cone to eat, I knew what today was.

It was Wednesday.

Wednesday was the day I dreaded because that's the day we cleaned the monster's house. Now on most days we cleaned nice people's houses—like on Monday we cleaned the house of the little old lady with the shriveled up arm who always tried stuffing my pockets full of whatnots and Hershey kisses.

On Tuesdays and Fridays we went into Middletown and the welfare apartments and cleaned the house of a woman who had a goiter. I used to dream about popping it with a pin, and wondering if it would deflate like a balloon after I popped it. The woman with the goiter always smiled at me.

But every other Wednesday we were always cleaning the monster's house, and Mary always bought me ice cream afterwards because it was so scary.

Even now I was dreading it. Even with the ice cream cone thrown in, even with Mary promising me she would speed up time so it wouldn't take that long. So we took off that morning walking through the back alleys of Rainelle, past old shacks built when they were working for Meadow River Lumber company back in the 1930s. And I carried Mary's bucket and mop and held her hand, and Mary carried all of her cleaning things with her other hand.

And then she told me about Rainelle.

She told me about how it used to be called Slabtown, and how the new town was built overtop of the old town. She told me if you only dug deep enough there was a whole other town that no one knew about, and was covered up by us all.

She said they even found an old wagon when they built a house 20 years back—houses, streets, covered by these streets, covered by Rainelle.

We walked a bit more.

I imagined this other lumber town Rainelle covered by Rainelle. I imagined people still living in that town like it was a 100 years earlier and nothing had happened. (I imagined even animals walking upright and living like people live in pants and shirts and walking with walking sticks. It was just like in the cartoons).

Mary said, "Now when we get there you can just sit on the porch and play with your cars, but if you get scared of him and he starts carrying on and trying to fight—you just go outside. You don't have to stay, alright."

So I shook my head because I knew what kind of monster he was and I had a whole pocketful of matchbox cars to keep me busy.

I was just wanting to zip and zap and race and crash and bash them all together.

I wouldn't even have to think about the monster if I was playing hard enough.

So I held Mary's hand. We turned the corner around the alley and there it was.

It was the monster's house. It was all gray looking and falling down. The paint was chipping off from where it hadn't been painted in a couple of years. There was an old rusty truck in the front yard with weeds growing up around it.

So we clomped up onto the screen-id in front porch and Mary knocked.

No one answered.

She put her head inside and knocked again.

No one answered.

She put her head in more and shouted, "I'm here. It's Mary. I'm here to clean for you." She was real careful saying this, even though they took the monster's pistol away a couple of months before.

"I'm here to clean up your toilets and sweep your floor."

And then it was quiet.

And then we heard it.

It was a groan groaning grrrrrrrrrrrrrrrrrrrrrrr like a giant rumbling stomach.

We went inside and I kneeled down on the shut-in porch and started playing with my toys.

I imagined the monster's face and the monster's claws. I imagined the monster's smell and the monster's teeth. I imagined the monster eating me, consuming my flesh.

Mary walked into the big room and started talking and getting ready to clean the bathroom with her bucket and her mop.

I sat and took my cars and jumped my cars on the cracked linoleum of the fenced-in porch.

I took one of the hot rods and ran it over the crack in the floor.

Then I jumped it—bam.

I took another one and jumped it too. I let them crash into one another—playing death—bam. But after only about five minutes of this, I was so bored I couldn't take it anymore. I got up and sat in this old dry rotten chair for awhile, and then I got up and walked around the porch.

But then I had an idea.

I wanted to see the monster for myself. I was tired of imagining what he looked like.

After weeks of coming here I'd never seen the monster's face.

So I tiptoed over to where the door was.

And then I looked inside.

I stopped and breathed deep.

Then I looked again.

IT WAS HIM.

But now I could see.

It wasn't a monster. It wasn't a monster at all.

It was just an old man.

He was in a medical bed.

He was all propped up and he had diapers on and a ratty looking t-shirt. He was sitting up. His skull looked like a skeleton skull. He was so skinny he looked like he had a second spine running down the length of his skull. His mouth was open, black and wide and greenish looking and he didn't have any teeth in and he was touching his arm and ripping at his chest, whining, "Worms. Worms."

Above him was a clock and it was ticking tick tock tick tock.

And then I saw him and he saw me.

I was scared.

So he started shouting dirty words at me like, "Ah shit. You little fucking shit."

Then Mary was back in the room, trying to calm him down. "Now you quit talking filthy like that."

He just kept on. "O god. O god. WORMS. O fucking worms."

So Mary turned towards me and said, "Scott why you go ahead and go outside. We'll be done in a just a minute."

But I couldn't move.

I was so scared. I stood watching him.

Mary bent over him, whispering, "Shhhhh. Shhhhhh."

He moaned, "O god, kill me."

And then Mary told me to leave again.

I slowly started backing up and listened to the old man moaning, "O god. O god."

So Mary looked at me like she meant it this time.

Leave.

So I went outside. I gathered up all of my cars, and I went and sat down on the broken concrete steps.

I listened to his moaning and I listened to him groaning, "O god. O god."

And then I heard Mary running the sweeper.

And then the sweeper wasn't sweeping anymore.

And then I heard a whisper, "O god, kill me. O god, let me die."

And then I heard Mary saying, "Now daddy you quit talking like that. You just quiet down."

And then he was quiet.

I thought to myself—Daddy?

What?

Mary cleaned for what would have been about 10 or 15 minutes, but since she told me earlier it would only be a minute, it really only felt like a minute. The minute was up and she came outside. She was smiling. She handed me her bucket and we started walking and holding hands.

She said like nothing had even happened, "Well, I guess we need to get this boy an ice cream cone. He did such a good job today. I told you the time would fly by." And then I grinned and Mary grew quiet.

We walked for a long time in silence.

Mary said, "I'm sorry you had to see that. I'm real sorry."

I said, "Mary, is that man really your daddy?"

Mary shook her head "Yes."

I asked, "Well, why was he saying all of those bad things?"

We just kept walking and then Mary said, "O he won't be long for this world now. His mind's just gone and eaten up. And the funny thing is he would be so ashamed of himself if he knew he was saying those things. He'd be so ashamed."

So I asked, "Was he a good man, Mary?"

Then she chuckled again and then she grew quiet again. "Of course, he was a good man. He was my daddy."

We walked to the Terminal Drug where the Greyhound bus used to stop in Rainelle. Mary ordered two small vanilla cones for us. We went outside and sat on the sidewalk beneath the old rusty bus sign. "Ride Greyhound—Rates available from anywhere in the continental U.S."

But there wouldn't be any of that today. There would only be two of us licking our ice cream cones and knowing there were good things in this world too.

It was hard to believe, but there were.

There were good things like ice cream cones, and trying to keep houses clean, and your mother bringing you to Mary's house wrapped in a blanket, so you could watch cartoons and dream your cartoon dreams.

Gravity
by Jarrid Deaton

The Given Growth Kentucky Parade is the highlight of the year for all the front porch sitters and sidewalk strollers in this town. Every year is the same. The Mayor pulls himself up into the passenger seat of the antique 1949 American La France fire truck, while the fire chief steers the sad old beast, and they lurch from the city proper down the short road that leads to the county line with high school band kids and bored coal miners and housewives sore-kneeing their way behind in the wake of the motor's sputter and smoke.

The unbroken weeds reach to my hips as I stand just over the hill near the side of the road where the parade will pass by. Waiting for the rumbling of the engine and the blaring of brass, I keep my eyes on the horizon for the hundred ghost shadows that will slither over the small rise just seconds before everything comes into view.

The Mayor is why I'm here. It's been thirteen years since I've looked him in the eyes. Thirteen years since I felt sick seeing his rusty beard and broad, thick face. My mom had to look at that mess for as long as he's been Mayor. My mom answered phones and typed city council meeting minutes until it became her career because he kept getting re-elected. My mom, feeling the scratch of that rusty beard on her thighs during those sun-dying evenings when my father taught a night class in history at the local community college because that's the direction it all went.

Three years old and I'm in the parade. Mom says we rode on the back of the truck. Me in her arms and Dad in Frankfort interviewing for a teaching job he wouldn't get. That's the only time the parade had me in its line. From my memory, I always said no. It was my world, not theirs. Mom said the Mayor would offer to let me ride in the truck, blow the horn, wave out the window. I remember those offers. I would just shake my head and go back to whatever I was controlling. Back to where my name was secret and known just to me. Dad always called the parade stupid. Growth, he would say. What a joke. The last time this town grew, he would say, was when we got a Wal-Mart ten years ago. Dad saw the parade as a communal acceptance of mediocrity shaped by fear. Half the town, it seemed, would march to the edge of escape only to get scared of the outer world and retreat back to the womb of Given. It was an almost-birth before the baby changed its mind. Dad and I got out. Then Dad got out again. He got out of it for good. But he didn't leave when he wanted. He still had one thing to do.

Six years old and I'm sitting on the tiled floor of city hall. Mom's legs are beside me. She's typing. The office is another world. I'm in from school and already my name is gone. I'm not Devon. I'm Cobra Commander, I'm Megatron, and I'm carnivorous dinosaurs. Her fingers still on the keys, Mom asks if I want to see Grandma today. Your father, she says, he's teaching tonight. Housework, she says. You can stay with Grandma while I get some housework done. I'm okaying everything, my mind on my universe. Claws scuttle over the fake plant near the desk, track marks in the dust that settles on the leaves. The Mayor's black boots click-thump-click next to my hand as he talks to Mom. He puts his finger against her closed lips and laughs a deep well laugh while a velociraptor eyes his boot tip. Before it lunges, plastic fangs bared, he steps back and looks at me. Planning attacks, I see, the Mayor says, and winks. I half smile and turn away again. My dinosaur retreats back into the fake jungle of dusty desk plants.

The Mayor has been a fixture in Given since before he even thought about seeking acceptance from the population. Dad used to tell me how the Mayor was the big running back for the high school football team. He seemed like the kind of guy who would go away to college, come back, maybe start selling insurance, but the Mayor did much more than that. He played college football for Alabama and things looked all stars and hopes and bright futures for Given's heralded son, but a low tackle ripped his knee from the bone and that was that. Dad always said this was the part where the Mayor should have been hooked on pain killers, maybe signed up on disability, or took a couple of shitty, low-paying jobs, and then, a few years down the road, mixed some bourbon with those pain killers and that would have been that. Instead, the Mayor hit the world of local politics wide open. The first thing he did was run for city council. Then, the next year, he was all smiles and words when he announced he was running for Mayor. This is after Donald Severn, the mayor of Given in 1977, resigned to head back to his farm and care for his not-long-for-this-world wife. With a slight limp and ambition coming off him in heat-haze waves, the Mayor won over ninety percent of the vote. Even Dad voted for him the first, second, and third time. That's how things started. When I think about it, I realize that Dad and the Mayor could have been big buddies before the Mayor's great planet of hubris and masculinity caught my mother in its gravitational pull and jerked her out of our orbit.

Eleven years old and the living room explodes with yells and screams and threats. The Mayor's boots click on the hardwood floors and Mom cries wild from down in her throat. It's just turning to an evening-orange outside when Dad pulls up. He left his night class with a take-home test and came home early. He'd known for over a year, he told me later. He just didn't want to see it. Didn't want it to swirl into reality because his eyes focused on the actual scene. The door and Dad swing into the house at the same time and he's whirlwind angry and yelling. Outside, he screams. The whole room becomes sound with insults and broken vows echoing from one wall to the next. Opening my door, I'm Devon again. I'm in the real world and I want more than anything to get back out. The Mayor grabs the phone and dials numbers fast. Get over here, he says, and lets the receiver swing to the floor. Then they're in the yard. Arms in the air, they all scream, their voices raw, and then scream some more. Mom slumps to the ground against a shrub. The back of it goes through her hair and she freezes, staying that way. She stops yelling and starts sobbing. I'm on the porch and nobody looks back. The fire chief drives up to the curb and stops. Dad takes a swing at the Mayor and connects with his mouth. The sound is like a basketball bouncing on a wet sidewalk. The Mayor goes backwards into the tree in the middle of the yard. Still standing, he cocks his head the way some people do to make their neck pop. Dad starts at him again but the fire chief has him by the shoulders, then the arms, and pulls him away. The Mayor does nothing but walk by Dad who pulls and pushes and snaps his teeth like an animal trying to get untangled from an old farm fence rimmed with barbed wire. The fire chief holds tight and the Mayor slow-steps over to his sedan, eases out of the driveway, and is gone.

The one thing my father made sure to tell me every day was how he wanted to watch the Mayor fall. Thirteen years ago and he remembered how his punch didn't do the job. The Mayor standing square jawed then staggering, his back against that tree. My mother screaming like a train had plowed through the yard. Dad was you bastarding and assholeing and piece-of-shitting while the Mayor headed for his black sedan. Dad got an offer to leave without having charges pressed if he didn't come back to Given, ever. He took it. I went with him.

The entire time I lived with him after we moved, Dad said he didn't feel anything anymore. There's nothing, he said, nothing that changed his mood from day to day. All he wanted was to send the

Mayor to the ground. The best place would be right back in the yard of our old home. The grass all destroyed with wild onions because Dad is the only one who really knew how to care for it. That's where he wanted the Mayor to fall. Mom, maybe she starts down the steps to come to his side but the board gives and she falls. The steps are cobbled shoddy because Dad didn't do it. The wood is crooked and sick. The cracks like wrinkles, knots like tumors, the house has gone over to illness.

That's what Dad wanted. But, he said, it would really be okay if it happened anywhere else.

My memories of our family before that day are fragmented and ruined like jagged puzzle pieces left outside in both storm and sun. I can't think of togetherness without the Mayor popping up for a cameo in all of my childhood hopes and dreams that I want to revisit. I try and think about my first Little League game. My dad coaching third base and flashing signs that really meant nothing. It was all for show. I remember him helping me get my stirrups lined up to go over my socks, then lacing my rubber-cleated shoes. My mother watches from the stands in my memory and she smiles, first at me, then at Dad. But then I always notice the Mayor, shaking hands with the parents and shoving a chilidog in his mouth. The sun catches his wiry red hair, making him the center of attention. The memory version of me flails weakly at three straight balls that hit the dirt before even crossing the plate. That's not even how it happened. Dad told me I got a double in my first at bat. The Mayor somehow ruined this memory. The bastard is good at that. I can only imagine what went on in my dad's mind after the great explosion. His memory bank was probably sealed forever save for a picture of the Mayor's smiling face with his arm around my mother. That's all he had to focus on. That image, that pain, that obsession stayed with him all the way to the end.

I would call Mom from time to time, and Dad said he didn't care. Said it was probably good to keep in contact. She only mentioned the Mayor once. It was when I called her on my sixteenth birthday, and she told me they were getting married. Most times when I talked to her, I could tell that she was worried about me. Not just me in my current state as a teenager at the time, but me in the future. She always asked about school and if I had a girlfriend. Six times I told her yes. One of those times I was telling the truth. The only girl I had an actual relationship with was when I was eighteen. We dated for a little less than two months before I forced her away. I couldn't trust her. It didn't matter how many times she proved herself to me. On nights when she wanted to go out with her friends while I was off doing something else, I was a nervous wreck. I would rage and rail against her, accusations thrown like phantom punches, and she would cry. I hope I can find an end to this. I want to live and love like I think people are meant to do before things get mashed up and hateful. I don't blame Mom, though. Not all the way. She was just as ragged and torn as I am when she made her big mistake. Things were never that great with Dad. I know that. There were late night shouts and Dad coming home at odd hours smelling like beer and cigar smoke. Even though I sided with him, have all these great memories of him that are tainted by Mom and the Mayor, I know that part of it was his fault. As for me, I don't think I can get things going in the right direction until Dad's wish gets taken care of. My mind taken up with too much of one thing, it has no room for the happiness and comfort that people look for. Not yet.

Now I'm waiting here in these weeds for the arrival of the man who sent my family in splinters out of our home and into the wildness of the yard. This family, the one that went to the beach when I was nine, all of us together with the sand sticking to us, saltwater stinging our eyes, if only this snapshot was the one that I could keep. Dad with a book on sharks that he bought overpriced at some little tourist hut where we stopped for chips and drinks. Mom with multiple beach hats and a desire to learn how to peel and cook shrimp, and me wandering the beach looking for both living and dead things to emerge silvery and full of teeth from the ocean. All of us there, no jobs pulling my parents in different directions at different times, everything free and amazing. The horizon was without boundaries, the open water extending to places that I didn't know about, but knew I could reach if I wanted to. I remember returning to these hills and mountains in Kentucky and feeling closed off, trapped again. We never went back to the beach. Two years later and I left home with my father. The mountains smaller around Lexington, but still blocking my sight, I felt like I was stuck in the past while still hoping to make it to the future.

Today is my official return to it all. Around a year ago I drove into Given and followed all the old back roads that I used to bump my bicycle along when I was a kid. The old, dirty roads are cut ragged with trenches from logging trucks and four-wheelers. The kind of roads you hit when you want to drive at your own pace or if you just don't want to be seen. These roads run behind all the old homesteads that sit deep between the mountains near the outskirts of the city. My Toyota truck bounced just like I remember my bike bouncing as I sent dust flying in the air with every stop and turn. I drove past our home and noticed that the grass was cut short, the hedges neatly trimmed. The house had a new coat of white paint and there were no leaves clogging the gutters. An old friend of my mother, Dana Cooley, told my father just a month before he died that the Mayor was always out in the yard doing some kind of chore. She told him that Mom seemed happy and that she always talked about me. About how I was going to come and visit when I found the time. Mom always wanted to know when was I coming to see her. I didn't have to stay for long, she said, just a visit. I would be coming sometime soon, I told her. Be on the lookout, I said.

After we left Given, Dad rented a small apartment in Lexington. We lived there until he paid for me to go to college. I'm there for two years. I was History, Art, Psychology and English. Two years of college, then he dies. He had been teaching high school just outside of Lexington since we moved. A janitor found him curled in the corner of the bathroom, cold-eyed and wheeze-breathing, his head flat against the floor like he was listening for a heartbeat coming from the cool tile. The doctors said it was a brain aneurysm. Dad was in the hospital for three days and never spoke a word. The last night, he reached for a small cup of ice beside the bed and knocked it to the floor. It was the last thing he ever touched. I was in the room when he lifted his head from the pillow and turned his body toward the stand where the cup was. I asked did he need help but he kept turning at the hip and stretching his arm, wired up to beeping machines. I imagine he wanted to touch the ice, cold in his hand or in his mouth. All he got to feel was the lip of the cup, his dried mouth brushing the awkwardness of the chemicals that held it together. Then he was gone.

Dad's nothing but gray-black flakes in an urn, and all I can think about is making the Mayor hit the ground. Right now he's a moving statue. He's the whole city made flesh and nothing ever comes back to slice at him, eat away at him. To show him that in the end we're all heading in the same direction. That's all Dad wanted, and he died before getting his second chance. There's no round two. Even by points the Mayor would've won without throwing a punch. It was rigged, judges in his pocket. But here I am beside the ditch and the marching music floats closer. Here I am ready to leg it up the side of the hill and stand in the center of the road. The horn of the fire truck blows loud and it comes flashing lights over the dip in the road. The red machine may be doing three miles an hour. The long sweating line of Given's residents moving even slower with sun headaches. The band blares a public property marching anthem, and I dig my boots in and scale the hill. With the county line to my back, I stand and wait. A confused army with full bellies of fried fish and moderate regret move in my direction. The Mayor in the lead, his hand out the window and waving at nothing but trees and road-kill, the horn blows again. Some of the kids give up walking, their parents scooping them up. Their arms hanging heavy with their children, they keep going. Not too far now. Then the truck will change direction and they'll head back to town.

As the fire chief turns the truck toward the graveled extension on the side of the road, I see the Mayor look in my direction. They aren't the only two in the cab. Beside the Mayor is my mother. Her eyes go wide and she is talking fast. I stand about fifty feet from where the truck growls and screams as it starts to circle around. The Mayor says something to the fire chief and the truck comes to a stop in mid-turn. The Mayor turns to me again and fixes his eyes on my form. I can almost see the dirty back roads of memories in his brain leading to the core where my mother files papers and answers the phone, and there I am in the floor next to the fake plant that will exist forever. He half-stands in the seat and starts to get out of the truck. I pull my fingers tight, and my knuckles ache with the sudden pressure. My mother puts her hand on his shoulder, says wait, but he keeps going. I imagine catching him flush with an uppercut, his whole body shutting down from the impact, the mediocre army of Given gasping as their giant falls to the ground like a normal man. A weak man. Moving out of the truck, he keeps his eyes on me, worried. His boot heel catches on one of the shining silver steps and his bad knee buckles. He tries to grab the door to hold himself but his balance is lost. Gravity does its textbook thing and pulls him tumbling toward the dusty asphalt like it would anything else, and he breathes hard and red-faced. A crowd rushes to his side, but he thrashes and curses, his arms shove at them as he struggles to stand. As they back away from the uncoiled anger of the Mayor, he falls again with all his weight landing against the front tire of the truck. My mother kneels beside him as I walk toward the crumpled form of my father's nightmare. She looks up at me and says, please, please, Devon, don't do this. She's wearing bright red lipstick that I've never seen her use. All through my youth, my mother refused to wear any makeup except for the occasional blush. Now her lips shine red and I want to turn away. She must sense that something's wrong because she wipes at the lipstick with the back of her hand, but it just smears across her mouth in a wet slash.

The music of the band fades and the marching residents of Given show their backs to the county line and limp to town on tired legs as the Mayor closes his eyes and asks my mother for a cup of water.

As she starts to press the button and release water from the cooler on the side of the truck, I come up to her and take the Styrofoam cup from her hands. I fill it to the top and walk around the front bumper. I hear the engine tick and feel the heat escaping from the hood. The Mayor's eyes are still closed as he leans against the tire with both hands clasped around his ruined knee. I sit beside him and put the cup to his lips. My mother leans against the truck with her broken lips parted and the redness now spread across her teeth. The Mayor tilts his head back and drinks without opening his eyes.

Worth
by Valerie Nieman

He saw the young guy coming slantwise down the bank, and knew that he'd sit down next to him.

Doyle Strawser didn't like people fishing close by. He didn't mind the men themselves, their talk, even kids with their jittering around. It was the nearness of their lines to his in the water.

The man paused, looked out over the lake.

He set his bucket down but kept the fishing rods in his hand. The lake, recently thawed, was gray as steel where paint had worn away from steady handling.

"Mind if I set up here?"

"Free country," Doyle answered, then opened his hand out toward the water.

He'd seen this guy in his orange hunting coat, fishing too close to the sucking current of the overflow. When he went up to the car, the guy had shifted position. Now he'd come the rest of the way around the lake. He must have seen the fish Doyle just caught, the sudden wet pop as it twisted to the surface.

"Any luck?" The young guy swung out a line baited with a mealworm and yellow marshmallow.

"Some."

The second rod had a limp night crawler on the hook. Doyle didn't say anything about his choices. The man cast it out farther, and the egg sinker took it down fast, about three feet to the left of Doyle's bait.

He fished trout pond style, a small orange-and-yellow bobber clipped loose on the line between the tip and the first guide to indicate strikes. He fiddled with the bobbers until they hung pretty deep below the rods, swinging lightly in the breeze.

Doyle dabbled his fingers in the lake and wiped them dry on his twill pants. He took a can of Copenhagen out of his vest pocket and pinched up a wad of tobacco, watching the young guy work at propping up his poles. Instead of using forked sticks or spiral metal holders he tried to balance them with piles of rocks. Slapdash.

"Not too bad of a day," Doyle observed.

The rocks slithered and one of the rods clattered down. Bent over, his face turned away, the young guy said, "Beats sitting around the house."

He settled the rod back on its perch and sat down, bracing his heels against the rip-rap.

Out of work, Doyle thought. Not any welfare bum, not with hair trimmed neat at the back of his neck, his cheeks raw after a morning shave. Probably one of the guys laid off from Hedwick Mine, no hope for him when ones with 20 years or more were let go.

One of the red-and-white bobbers that marked his own lines dipped a bit. It might have been the wind, the way it seemed to slide lower, but Doyle looked at the dimple where his line went into the water and saw it move toward shore.

He lifted the rod carefully from its holder, brought in the slack by easy turns.

The line rested still in the water.

A sudden run toward deep water and the bobber slapped against the rod; Doyle jerked back and the rod bent at the stop of the fish.

Doyle worked the fish in, estimating by the manner of the strike and the resistance that it was a rainbow, decent size. He reached in and lipped the fish as it rolled in the shallows. The hook was buried deep in its gullet, and he twisted it free with a sound of gristle breaking and whiff of garlic from the scented bait. He hefted it, a bit more than a pound and a half, gleaming with water and self-mucus, soft pink along the midline shading to steel blue and up into deep green at the top of the back.

He smacked the trout's head against a stone spattered black with dried blood. The jaws opened, shut, and he hit it again. The first was a flat cracking sound, the second a dull thud. The pearly gill covers flared, quivering, and the freckled tail curled and then stretched flat. Doyle slid the trout into the bread bag he carried, beside two smaller fish, their golden eyes filmed. The young guy watched so avidly that Doyle felt guilty.

Doyle unclipped the bobber, rebaited the hook with a ball of yellow Power Bait and a red garlic marshmallow. He offered the jars to the fellow, who said thanks, but didn't reel in to replace his baits.

Out on the lake the ganders spread their wings out and stretched their necks close to the gray water, moaning. The females flew up and settled. Too far south, too early, the light too low in the sky. The ganders swam toward them.

Doyle spit into a hole between the head-sized rocks that lined the steep bank, on the side away from the young guy.

Two men in an aluminum boat trolled around the island, the electric motor silent but the movement flighting up the restless geese and ducks. The men were bent over as if they had to row, humped against the chill on the water.

The young guy picked up one rod, alerted by a bobber that trembled and jumped then went still. A sudden, sharp strike and he hooked the fish, not much weight from the look. Still, he brought it in carefully, workmanlike. It was a brook trout, belly fins sharply marked in white and orange.

"Never many of those in the stock truck," Doyle said. The brookie was slender, something close to wild.

The young guy dipped his hand in the water and grasped the fish gently around the body. Doyle had seen farmers like that, tender with animals though they were headed for slaughter. He extracted the small gold hook, then slid the fish back into the lake. Doyle must have made a sound, not realizing, because the man turned toward him. Doyle tucked his face down into his beard and watched his lines.

Tossing the fish back like it had no worth! There he'd been thinking about giving him fish, putting himself out to help him. Thinking maybe he was hungry, or had kids.

Doyle felt restless all of a sudden. He pushed himself to his feet and went up the bank. The dry strings of crown vetch planted over the rip-rap caught at the lugs of his boots. He straddled across the guard rail, legs stiff from sitting, and went behind the car to piss.

He opened the passenger door and got out the thermos of coffee, light from his earlier visits. As he poured into the plastic cap, he watched the young guy lie back gingerly into the slope. Out of work and fishing instead of looking for a job, but then he likely had unemployment. Fishing filled the days better, he supposed, than sitting like some did outside the feed store, flexing hands stiff from lack of things to do, settling deeply into the benches. Better than sitting in an apartment, looking at the stories on television and wondering how long it would take someone to notice his absence.

Doyle saw the clouds layering, contemplated calling it a day. Then he went back down, his feet careful against the irregular teeth of the rocks, and settled into his place.

"Think you had a nibble."

He said "Huh" and looked at the still lines in the water, the current toward the outflow making a soft V from each line.

"They put a good many in here?"

Doyle nodded. "Half a truckload from Bowden on Tuesday."

A thick tongue of fish, a stream like molten steel, fish and water poured out. Something to see. He remembered once when the lake had been all but frozen, a January stocking, trout dumped down the icy boat ramp, sliding and twisting their way to a patch of open water.

"They used to stock careful, diff'rent places around." Doyle pointed. "The little bay, the other side of the island, back at the inlet. Now they just dump them." Hundreds of them, thousands, surely thousands. They weighed them at the hatchery by the pound, not the fish, so many pounds to this lake or that stream.

A red-winged blackbird lighted on a cattail stem, flaunted its epaulets and screamed, "Oh you cheat!"

"Mostly rainbows," Doyle said, catching back the end of a thought. "They used to stock brown trout. I remember catching one."

That was when he was a kid. His uncles fished, not his father, and he went with them to streams over east where there wasn't any coal, any mine water to ruin them. Later he didn't fish at all, working all the daylight through at his father's store.

"They raise some yet," the young guy said, "mostly fingerlings to stock up in the mountains."

"Don't get up there with these legs. I just fish the lake. Pretty nice rainbows they put in, and a few brookies." His mouth clamped shut on that word, thinking of the shame of a fish slipped back into the water.

"You here when they stocked Tuesday?" There was a faint tinge of disapproval in the man's voice.

"There's fish enough in the lake if you know to catch 'em. No sense following a truck anyway—they feed them trout full before they leave the hatchery."

Doyle looked over at the young guy, who stared past his lines to a lake that might be a hundred miles long, so distant was his focus.

"What's your name?"

"Gene."

"Doyle Strawser." He stuck out his hand and the young guy gave him his, cold and dry, a firm grip.

"Harold Strawser Feed and Seed."

"Yeah. That's me."

He'd been named Doyle after his mother's people, but his father was held in such esteem, a farmer of champion cattle and clean fields, that Doyle was known as Harold Strawser's boy. Not Harlan, the oldest, who farmed the valley spread their father had farmed. Not the younger kids who'd scattered to find new faces in larger towns. Doyle was the second son—the one behind the counter when he was hardly old enough to see over it, learning the trade of the feed and supply store that his father's prosperity built.

People called him Harold's boy right to his face.

He came to hate it over the years, the way his father did things, the way the store was arranged, and he not allowed to change a thing. Finally when the store was his alone, Doyle found that he'd adjusted. He didn't see the need to repaint the sign, to change things. When Harlan came in for calf starter he would bang his shin on the pallet of mineralized salt blocks, as he had for years, and just laugh.

Doyle used to believe that he was needed at the store every day. He had a suspicion that when he left, the store just disappeared. Then with the troubles at home, he'd started going away fishing, days at a time, and found that things went right along. The workers always had a vague look of surprise when he came back, as though he had some purpose they'd forgotten.

The young guy stood, stretched his back. "Not having much luck here," he said.

Doyle glanced down at the jars of proper bait he'd offered, but didn't say anything.

"Think I'll move on." The fellow wound up his lines and lifted his bucket, rattled his way up the bank.

Doyle stretched his legs out, pleased at not having to keep himself to a narrow spot. It was a relief to have him gone, to be done with the effort of carrying a conversation like rocks from one place to another.

He stuck his hands in his pockets and waited for a bite. When he'd about given up, his eyes half-closed against the wind and his nose dripping, a bobber tap-tapped against the rod and he set the hook. A small fish, 10, 11 inches. But it made four in the bag, and with the temperature dropping and wind shifting it was a wonder to get that one.

Doyle levered himself up from the bank. He climbed to the road, leaning into the slope, balancing himself between his fishing bucket in his left hand, his rods in the other.

He set his rods against the green fender of his car, had to catch them as they skittered away, too cold-fingered to feel where they would hold when he set them up again. Finally he got them aright.

He was draining the stale ends of coffee from his cup when the young guy walked over.

"Thought you gave up, Gene."

He shrugged and looked down at the bread bag moving with the last reflexes of the fourth trout.

"Got your limit there?"

Doyle lifted the bag. Four trout, that best one close to 20 inches, showed like gunmetal through the red and yellow printing of the Kettering's wrapper.

"You have pretty good luck."

"Good enough for today."

"You didn't stash a couple more, under the rocks?" He looked at Doyle slantwise, his thin mouth turned up at the corners, his blue eyes sly.

Doyle laughed, knowing better. "There's guys do that, but not me. Not sticking my hands down in those rocks. There's rats live in the rocks."

The fellow shook his head slowly.

"You're sure this is it, just the four." And Doyle, who had been suspecting, was sure when the voice changed, so that when the man brought out his ID—Conservation Officer Gene Titchnell, West Virginia DNR—it came as no surprise.

"You seen me catch 'em," he protested, rattling the tackle and stringer in his bucket, sure the warden had seen no more than those four fish.

The conservation officer stood for a moment, Doyle looking right back at him. Then he moved around the car, reached up under the wheel-well into the frame, brought out a fish and slapped it down on the hood.

"Five."

The vibration was enough to send the rods sliding, and Doyle, startled, lunged for them. Dark snuff-spit burst from his open mouth and onto his beard. He wiped the back of his hand across his mouth, rolling the wet tobacco from his lips.

Titchnell walked back along the other side of the car. He leaned down, looked, reached back under the leaf springs.

"Six." A trout caught first thing that morning hit the metal with a hard swack, its nearly dry skin sticking immediately.

Doyle took off his auction barn hat, worn and creased with daily handling, and ran it around and around in his fingers and then put it back on.

The officer checked the other rear wheel—nothing—and then asked him to open the car. Doyle did and stood aside, stiff with knowing that the men all up and down the bank were watching.

Some seemed not to look, but their eyes were bright under the bills of their caps. Others, interested in the spectacle, came up to their cars to get coffee, or to sit inside with the heaters running and watch.

He knew these men who fished Michael Run Lake, pretty much as well as he did the lake itself, the high earthen wall that kept it in, the brushy shallows and the deep hole. "Harold's boy," he could all but hear them say, "Harold's boy got hisself pinched."

Doyle pushed his chilblained hands into the pockets of his red hunting vest—held together with a pin, the zipper broken since fall. In the one side he had a carton of mealworms that he hadn't even opened, planning to take them home and add to the rest.

"Eleven," the warden said, the five trout stuffed into another plastic sack under the passenger seat.

If he lost his license, Doyle thought, watching Titchnell pick over his car, there wouldn't be any need for the mealworms. He had saved them in a five-gallon bucket, fed them bran he ordered special, and waited for them to turn into the black bugs that would breed more mealworms. Hundreds, thousands, without any need of the bait shop.

Titchnell checked the empty glove compartment.

When he pulled down the visor, a small brookie hung for a moment, glued to the bare metal roof, then slid right down into that bean-counter's face.

Doyle kept from laughing. In the shuddering loose mirror on the open door, he saw himself, tobacco stain on the white that had become the better part of his beard.

"Twelve."

The warden poked around the car. Doyle watched a commotion out on the lake, as two ganders flushed a female from the water. They honked but she was gone, circling to land well away.

The ganders beat their wings until their bodies lifted from the water, but they did not fly. The female cruised closer and they cried out to her. Doyle couldn't help but think of his own wife and her loud pleasuring. He mistrusted that, how Emily took such pleasure from him even after the kids and all.

She had her ways, not what people might think. Set in them. Finally he couldn't take her controlling his life, 28 years of her guiding him this way and that like a horse trained to fancy gaits. Gentle as a rein on the neck but there, always there. Last fall, the night of the first real snow, he left. She had the house with three years' worth of wood racked up, and the new Jeep and all the things that were hers in the house, that she had settled in their places and he supposed were there yet, undisturbed by his going.

"Twelve," said Titchnell, deadpan, "is three times the limit."

Doyle studied the trout laid out on the weather-chalked hood of the car. He was shamed by the sight of the stiff fish, the white spots where their skin had dried, the gummy flatness of their eyes. When he had pulled them from the lake they were pretty as anything, rainbows shimmering on their flanks, dark freckles scattered over, the fine pointed teeth in the jaw and the rasp of the tongue. It was God's bounty, the perfection of plenty, and he was meant to have them. He had devoted himself to this, in the cold and the rain, bringing this beauty up to the light.

Close to the island, the ganders crooned and flattened themselves to the lake surface. The geese turned away. They didn't pay any more attention than they did to the fisherman who cast and cast, the blade of his spinner turning slowly as it arced down, until it splayed on the water and sank. He reeled and cast, reeled and cast.

Doyle knew them, Pete who liked the spinners, Shorty, Gandy, Jim who used gypsy oil on his bait. They all hid fish. Fish they'd earned, fish their taxes paid for, not somebody out of Pennsylvania or Maryland. Some got their limit and took it home, coming and going four, five times a day when the stocking was on—there every day, hauling in the white-fleshed trout, fat with the indigestible bait they swallowed, corn, Velveeta, salmon eggs dyed green and red.

"I videotaped you from the van," Titchnell said, pointing out the painted-over telephone company van that had been parked along the guardrail when he got there, like something a man might live in were he down on his luck. Doyle supposed he should be impressed by the efficiency of the operation, but he thought it shameless. Sneaking, spying. A woman's look-through-the-curtains way of doing things.

"What were you thinking, Doyle?"

He despised this familiarity, as though it was allowed after an hour's fishing beside each other. Doyle stared across the lake into the brush willows on the far bank. A plastic bag, caught in the branches, shuddered in the wind and fell limp.

The warden was like the men who came into the store, the ones who called him Harold's boy, Harold's boy, and thought nothing of it. Thought of it as praise.

"Your license?"

Doyle got out his wallet. As the warden wrote down the numbers, he spoke up. "The address ain't right. Pine Street. 318-A Pine Street."

Titchnell glanced up, then crossed out the Rural Route address and wrote in the new one. He turned the license over to check for stamps.

They were all there, trout stamp and conservation stamp and all. There was a difference in refusing to obey the law and accepting what skill and the water gave—like in the Bible, a net so full that it couldn't be brought into the boat.

The conservation officer scratched away on his pad of citations.

The trout were his due, earned by his expertise and loyalty, his special ability demonstrated, the fish coming to him as his right. In the freezer of Doyle's apartment refrigerator, they were stacked in foil and plastic wrap like ears of corn.

"I could confiscate your tackle and car, but I won't," Titchnell said.

Doyle stared down at his boots, at the dry vine trailing from the laces. So that's what the warden thought, then, *poor old man.* Doyle blinked at the heat in his eyes and didn't dare to look at him.

Titchnell handed him the citation. Then he took a black garbage bag out of his coat pocket and bagged up all the trout, slipping them into its mouth like so many bits of litter. Doyle supposed that was what they were, now.

He got into the car and started it. The engine shuddered in its odd pattern.

He drove slowly along the gravel road that circled the lake. This hollow was once a bottomland farm, the fields stretching back from Michael Run, until the flood control people saw the great bowl the land made here and raised the dam to fill it up.

The car smelled like fish, like always, and Doyle felt as though he was just getting here. The sky was gray as morning and he was empty-handed.

Bait
by Richard Hague

When LaWanda Heever walked into the Sheep's Head bar on the river road outside New Richmond, Ohio, everybody turned toward her. She was done up in her finest Friday night outfit and loaded down with enough jewelry to sink a barge. Over her fire-colored hair she wore a semicircular crown of rhinestones alternating with plastic pearls. From her earlobes hung gilded lanterns the size of wooden bobbers. On her right wrist a charm bracelet glinted and flashed, displaying a silver-plated snapping turtle, a miniature towboat, a crucifix with a tiny red garnet at its axis, a delicate heart pierced with what appeared to be a harpoon, and a bronzed #6 Kirby fish hook with the barb clipped off. Her fingers were laden with huge synthetic gemstones, all of them big enough to choke a shad. And as usual she had soaked herself in scent. Making her way across the bar, she left behind her a persistent fogbank reeking of lilies, cinnamon, and minnows.

Her regular table, small and cramped, stood next to the glass doors opening to the river. She sat down with a clash and jingle, raised a forearm in the direction of the bar, and sang out, "Sharkey, honey, bring me my beer!"

Sharkey, owner and bartender of the Sheep's Head, was an eelish fellow, tall, thin, with loose leathery skin like a hagfish's. His teeth jostled from his gums at all angles, stained amber from the Pall Malls he chain-smoked. But he had long ago ceased worrying about being pretty, for he was a family man. His wife Betty was a broad, short woman with a temper and voice like a kingfisher's. His two sons, though just eleven and nine, were already surly and into kung-fu. In answer to LaWanda's shout, Sharkey smiled sourly and drew a beer.

LaWanda loved Sharkey, had for going on a year now. She cared nothing for his wife and children—they were no more to her than flies. When the thought of them lit momentarily on the oil-stained shores of her conscience, she shook her head and they were gone. LaWanda's single idea was to steal Sharkey away, to carry him off down the river to Cincinnati, where they could disappear forever and start a new life.

She often dreamed of what it would be like. In precious detail, she imagined the bait shop they'd open on the river—all the neat rows of Eagle Claw hooks in plastic bags; the colorful Pfluegers and Rapalas and Big O's; the green gurgling depth of the minnow tubs; the humid smell of the worm cooler. And oh, the characters who would come in— pretty young boys skipping school in the spring to fish for shad and perch, old black men with their musical stories of catfish, handsome drifters whose sullen expressions she might brighten with her friendliness, even a little flirting...

But no, Sharkey was her one and only. She wouldn't need anyone else, not down there in Cincinnati. Life would be good with him as her old man.

Sharkey made his way to LaWanda's table. The closer he got, the more nervous he became, his eyes lowering, his narrow shoulders hunching even more, so that he grew so slim LaWanda almost had to look twice to see him.

"Honey, how you doing?" she said as he set the mug on the table. "It's a fine night out, Sharkey. Warm and foggy and secret. I bet you there's a whole fleet of cars up there at the end of town where them kids go to park. How's your Buick running?"

"All right, all right, LaWanda," Sharkey mumbled, hands hunting his pockets. "That'll be fifty-five cent, or you want me to run you a bill?"

"I want you to run me down the river," LaWanda said, grabbing one of Sharkey's orphan hands.

"How's business?" he asked, pulling back. His eyes would not linger on LaWanda, but jumped from the doors overlooking the river, to the phone booth in the corner, to his own hands, now clasped like root tangles before him.

"Wonderful, wonderful, couldn't be better," LaWanda lied. "Sold me five dozen minnows today. Bass is biting up White Oak Creek. Some fella from Cincinnati, had a mustache and smoked a pipe."

LaWanda looked off dreamily.

"I might of asked was he going out with anybody or not, but I didn't think of it till he was out the door. He was pretty, Sharkey. Real pretty."

"Uh huh," Sharkey said absently. A call from the other end of the bar rescued him.

She'd tried everything: jealousy, begging, joking, even once a businesslike approach in which she had cornered him long enough on a slow night to lay out an intricate financial plan designed to convince him of the rightness of a merger between them and an assault on the beer and bait market in Cincinnati.

Nothing had worked. Sharkey refused her advances, but never, to LaWanda's mind, in a final sort of way. She had the feeling that he wanted to be convinced, and that his unwillingness was a weak dam of sticks that might be broken down if only the current of her persuasion built enough power.

She drank her beer and stared out over the river. There was no moon that night. The water lay silky black between shores, sheer and dark as a negligee. She wanted to wrap herself and Sharkey together in its softness, and to slide, like lovers down a bed, into happiness and success.

She'd never had much of that with men. She didn't blame them, though. Circumstances had always gotten in the way—marriage, infections of wanderlust, the bitterness that some men carried like a birthmark not their fault. She had known dozens of men, young and old, and had liked so many. But always, there had risen some darkness, some uncrossable channel between them that even love had been unable to bridge. Years ago, especially, men had entered her life with a kind of innocence, a physical straightforwardness that had left her with memory after memory of naked flesh streaming with river water. But if, even then, there had been no lasting, at least there had been an abundance of laughter, that connection. Coming back to the bait shop after long nights of fishing, they had joked over coffee with her, and had awakened in the hot afternoons in her house high above the river to tell stories that had kept her chuckling into dark. Some had stayed as long as a year, finding jobs in Utopia or Higginsport, or across the river in Augusta or Maysville. And when they had at last gone away, there had been a sweetness that lingered to make the sorrow at least memorable, even somehow good.

But then the circumstances had changed. No longer were wives, and an urge to move on, and that strange inherited bitterness the obstacles between her and men. Age had something to do with it. For several years, the only ones to come into the bait shop were much older than she, or much younger. And it was the younger ones who troubled her. Many of them had been wounded in the war. They limped, or breathed through two holes in their faces, noses blown off and still incompletely repaired. She remembered how drinking affected some: the nightmares, the ugly words when they woke beside her, the vacant, rambling, terrible stories they told in painful bits and pieces. She remembered the smell of marijuana in her place that lingered long after they'd left, and the sour haunted emptiness that would not heal.

Circumstances had changed. LaWanda sat drinking in the corner, but the faces of men moved before her in the smoke and dimness, a river of mixed and inconclusive pasts. She pulled herself away from it with difficulty and rose to the surface, watching Sharkey hobble back and forth along the bar, the bright reflection of his face in the mirrored bottles like a moon trapped in glass.

When he brought her fourth beer, Sharkey asked LaWanda again if she'd pay the bill out. With the warmth of the beer inside her, LaWanda imagined that Sharkey's face had somehow softened, his brown eyes grown liquid as stones in an eddy, his shy smile delicate as the curve of a perch's fin. LaWanda couldn't help it, she grabbed him around the buttocks and pulled him against her side. Sharkey stumbled back, groaning. Somebody at the bar hooted. "Go get 'em, Sharkey! Hoo boy!"

"Now dammit, LaWanda," Sharkey whined. "I got me a wife and two kids. What'll people think, you grabbing me like that?"

"Who cares?" LaWanda said. "Me and you, Sharkey, we got something between us. Listen. The bait business is good. Leave off this dive and go down to Cincinnati with me. We could make it big."

Sharkey backed off, grew stern. "I'm cutting you off, LaWanda. There ain't nothing else I can do. You been coming in here every Friday, making a spectacle. I got my reputation. My kids need braces. My johnboat's lying busted in the yard. What you talking about, Cincinnati? You crazy? *I'm a married man.*"

"To hell with that," LaWanda grumbled, rattling her bracelets. "Bring me another beer."

"I won't," Sharkey said. His hands fumbled again at his pockets.

"By God," LaWanda said, glaring at him. "You bring me a beer, you sorry snakeskin, or I'll make you wish I was gone."

"That wouldn't take much," Sharkey muttered. "No."

LaWanda heaved herself up from the table. "I ought to beat hell out of you," she said, shoving herself so close to Sharkey that her bosom pressed the spare flesh of his chest. "I ought to kick your ass."

A man at the next table stood suddenly and walked over. Gingerly he parted the two, saying, "Now, come on folks. This ain't no way to spend a night out."

LaWanda stared straight ahead. As yet, the other man did not exist for her. The space between herself and the bartender seethed with a murky current. That touch against Sharkey, though born of anger, had quickened something in her. It was the closest they'd ever been.

Sharkey stood at the end of the stranger's arm, eyes leaping. He said something then fled toward the bar. The trouble swirling in LaWanda did not cease, but with Sharkey's flight, simply moved a couple of feet closer and engulfed the stranger like floodwater.

He was an odd, tall, somehow drowning-looking man with a narrow nose, green flecked eyes, tiny teeth. His jacket was damp and smelled of the river. Slipperiness washed off him like the silt off a muddy stone. But LaWanda's anger had begun to ebb, and she allowed him to take her arm and sit her back down at the table.

"Listen, honey," he said as she settled her bracelets and earrings and smoothed her hair. "There's no reason to get worked up. Relax." He patted her hand, his damp fingertips lingering over the hunks of glass in her rings. "Me and you'll just set here and talk awhile, and have us another beer."

Sharkey brought two mugs. The stranger paid. "That's the last for the lady," Sharkey said grimly. "She don't get anymore."

The stranger smiled, clutched LaWanda's hands abruptly. "Let's get out of here," he said. "I know this place up in Higginsport."

LaWanda whipped her hands out of his. But her bracelet caught on the edge of the table, jerked her short, and she shouted. Holding her right hand up before her, she saw the plated fish hook sunken deep into her palm. Wincing, she pulled it out, thankful she'd clipped its barb. Still, a drop of blood welled up from the puncture, vivid and round as a tear.

The stranger made to pull a hanky from his pocket, but before he could, LaWanda was on her feet. She stormed across the bar, jewelry clinking like suddenly rustled chains, and pushed Sharkey aside at the door. As she slammed it behind her, she could hear men hooting and the ripple of snickering applause.

She stood over the minnow tub in her shop. Green with algae, it glowed beneath the fluorescent light, swirls of glare troubling its surface near the aerator. In its depth, LaWanda could see the schooling minnows, their backs a silvery gray, their bellies, as they turned, soft and moon-silver. They sped from one end of the tub to the other, always veering at the last moment, boxed in, helpless to escape. The wound in her palm throbbed. She thought of Sharkey, the beery breath of him, the way cigarette smoke clung to him like an ashy ghost.

"I ain't no better off than these minnows," she said aloud. "I've been using myself as bait. Telling that Sharkey we could run off—I'd as soon run off with a hornet. And that stranger. He wasn't no more than a carp, a scavenger. So what am I?"

LaWanda sighed. She gripped the edge of the minnow tub and leaned, trying to see her face in the rush and gurgle of the water. Nothing. Bits of light and dark, ribbons, shreds, a fever-confusion of paleness and fire.

The next morning, LaWanda woke early. Her head and heart were clearer. She felt ready for a fight. She dressed quickly, leaped into her car, and drove straight over to Sharkey's. He and his family lived in an old brick river house, long and narrow, with stone arches over the windows and three worn granite steps rising to the porch. The place had been painted years ago, but now strips of weathered blue hung from it like exhausted bunting.

Sharkey's wife answered the door. Behind her in the living room, the two boys battled one another, lunging with fists clenched before them, flailing at each other's head. Betty stared, her face frozen in disgust.

"Sharkey here?" LaWanda asked. "I want to talk to that sorry bastard husband of yours."

"He ain't here," Betty growled. "And even if he was, why you think he'd want to see some hussy drunk?"

"Because he knows what's good for him," LaWanda said. "He knows he's got a life to live."

"He's done lived it already," Betty said, her face reddening. "It's finished, far as you and him is concerned." She tried to close the door, but LaWanda leaned inward, and the door halted as if a boulder had fallen against it. "Get back!" Betty snapped. "I'll call the sheriff."

"You do that, honey," LaWanda said. "Do that. And while you're at it, you can call out the National Guard, too. You'll need it. I'm about full up with all this."

LaWanda stepped back and let the door slam shut. She walked back to the street and got in her car. She drove back down into town, cruising Main slowly, keeping an eye out for Sharkey. They'd have it out, right on the street if that's the way he wanted it. She was tired of hanging around the Sheep's Head, cajoling, wasting time. She was tired of dipping minnows for a living. She was tired of waiting for life to walk through the door of her shop, the little bell above it ringing like the winner's gong on a game show.

No. Either Sharkey would go with her, right now, or that'd be it for him. His loss. Let him rot in that house by the river with that Betty of his and them two hoodlum boys.

She saw him step out of the drugstore and head down the street, away from her. He walked with a limp, much more noticeable outside than in the bar. LaWanda watched, some sudden dread clutching her.

Sharkey stopped, lit a cigarette, and coughed. His hands curled for a moment like a chicken's feet before him. The bony slats of his shoulders rocked and warped. He leaned over, suffering.

LaWanda couldn't help it, she moaned. The thought that she'd wanted to run away with him chilled her. "That man don't need me," she thought. "He don't need me nor want me. He couldn't even *take* a woman like me. I'm too big for him, too coarse, too *live*. He'd break like a stick."

LaWanda shook her head, and tears fogged her eyes for a moment. "What he needs," she said aloud, "is a goddamn hospital. That's all—some peace and quiet to die in." And she remembered Betty's words: "He's done lived it already. It's finished," and she shivered with the knowing. Sharkey was another wrecked one. Another emptiness she'd suffer.

Her car had slowed almost to a stop now. Sharkey stepped off the curb, half a block ahead, and crossed the street. He looked her way, blinded by the low morning sun. His face was puckered, the skin hanging loose from his jowls, his hair meager and pale as a possum's. He shambled across, stepped awkwardly up onto the sidewalk, and disappeared into the Sheep's Head.

"So that's that?" LaWanda wondered, amazed at how life had its way and, luckily for her, spared her this one more time. Amazed at how easily misfortune had swerved aside, how lightly the trouble that had gripped her now let go.

She stalled the car and rummaged in her purse for a tissue. Then she gathered herself, the traffic pulling around her, folks staring in. She didn't give a damn. What did they know? She'd come through a thing, she'd lasted it out.

A pickup slowed, coming her way. Just above the grill, a bumper sticker had been plastered across the front of the hood. **Life's a bitch**, it read, **And then you die.** LaWanda stiffened.

"No sir," she said, firmly.

And when the truck pulled abreast of her, she could see its driver, a boy no more that sixteen, shirt off, his lean hairless arm slung out the open window.

"Hey!" LaWanda cried, pointing toward the front of his truck. "Not me! Not me, you sorry cowlick," and she pounded her horn. Over the blare and the astonished look of the boy she blew him a kiss the size of her life—all of it—and tossed her thick orange hair, heavy and rich as a veil on the back of her neck. Then she started the car and gunned it, straight ahead.

The Coal Thief
by Alex Taylor

Under the oak trees there was the smell of tobacco smoke and damp bark and dirt. The early winter light sifting through the branches showed a world stiff and still, the bank of gravel ballast just beyond the trees and then the train rails shining in the cold. Still miles distant, the morning freight blew its whistle. Soon it would breast the curve and roll past the tangle of briars where Luke hid with his uncle Ransom, but for now the train was still covered by the trees, and its wail fled away through the thin misting of snow, lost and gone.

Luke watched the rails glinting blue against the pale ground and wished for it to be night again, the fields honed with frost and he and Auncie beside the coal stove while the wind crawled through the grass beyond the door. But it would be hours before the gray light rolled away again. Now, the creosote shone on the crossties and the snow thickened in the wind, glinting like powdered glass. The train blew, closer, and Luke pushed his hands under his arms to warm them.

"Watch you don't slip when you catch it. The rungs will have ice on them," said Ransom.

Crouched beside Luke in the dead leaves and pine needles, he drew on a cigarette. The smoke pooled around his face and then blew away.

"How much do we need?" Luke asked.

"As much as you can kick off the cars." Ransom took the cigarette from his mouth, studied the wet gray end of it, and then pushed it back between his lips. "Make sure you jump before it gets to the top of the hill. It'll be carrying the mail on the down slope and you'll never make it if you wait 'til then."

He pulled an empty feedsack from his coat and held it out to Luke.

"Here. I figured you'd forget so I brought an extra."

Luke tucked the sack into his coat pocket, ashamed he had forgotten, that he was only a boy and that Ransom was right about him.

He heard the drivers churning now, the train bawling down the track like something scalded, the black smoke looming above the trees. He tried to remember everything Ransom had told him about catching trains. *The ways to get by in this world—ease into it, don't grab too fast, but let it pick you up. Don't think.* He sifted through these old lessons like a primer, but when the engine appeared down the track, dark and heavy as a rain cloud, he was afraid again. Far down in his chest, his ribs shivered from the bucking of the rails, and snow scuttled across his neck. The sound of the train drew into him, slow and deep. Blowing on his hands, he stood to meet it.

Don't resist. Don't think about your daddy.

Luke wiped the snow from his eyelashes and followed Ransom out of the briars.

Don't think.

But he did.

He thought of other times, of years wilting into the ground cover of memory. This winter, he was only twelve, but his life felt halved already, portioned by the years before and after his father had been killed falling from a coal car. There hadn't been much left, only enough to fill a box of poplar wood too small for any man to lie down in. Any whole man.

Now he watched the train booming down the rails. Wind drew snow off the coal piled high in the cars and the engine wheezed, slowing as it came up the grade. His toes felt numb at the end of his boots, and he kicked the ground to herd the blood back into his legs. There in the cold, he felt empty, as if he were no more than his ragged coat and shirt, no more than clothes draped over a cross of sticks to spook crows from a cornfield.

He felt like he might blow away.

He dug through his pockets and found the stale biscuit Auncie had given him that morning. She'd said he would get hungry and made him take it. He ate it now, the crumbs falling over his chin, and he tried to remember the lie he'd told her about where he was going, but his mind was cold and empty. All he recalled was the black dust at the bottom of the coal bucket and Auncie's blue hands reaching for him, her telling him how he didn't have to go, how she could make fire from anything, damp kindling and dress fabric, anything.

But he had gone. Because Auncie couldn't make fire from anything. She was aged, her body bent from long years of trouble, and she could tend to no fire. Nights in the house, she let the stove go cold and had to wake Luke to light it again. She was withery in these frigid months. Her mind slowed and left her dull and wandering, unable at times to even have sense enough to put socks on.

Following Ransom through the dim morning, Luke had looked back at the house settled between the persimmon trees with not a sliver of smoke rising from its chimney, and he was glad to be out in the world where the cold was no surprise. Stealing the coal was nothing. Bringing it home in a feedsack was nothing. But Auncie's hands on his coat and hearing himself lie to her while she sat in the icy kitchen—that was the hard part. Even now, Luke thought, she's got no idea. She's got no idea how cold it's going to get tonight.

The biscuit was hard and stale but good. It made him angry to taste it; to think of Auncie always good and always alone in the house made him angry as well. He was only a boy, but that thought didn't help. Coal buckets went empty and houses turned cold for boys just as they did for men and old women. There weren't any favors. There were no favors, so why shouldn't he lie to Auncie and go out in the white morning to steal coal and laugh at the thought of warm fire, of closed rooms where steamy things cooked, of the cold shut away behind a door?

He reached down and took a handful of snow from the ground, eating it slowly to wash the biscuit down. Ransom put a hand on his shoulder and pointed to the train.

"Pick up your legs when you run for it," he said. "Just reach out. She'll pick you up like a mailsack if you let her."

The train moaned again and then was flowing past them, stretching out through the trees like a shed skin. The air rushing from it was hot enough to chap Luke's cheeks, and the smell of burnt coal rose pungent and sour. Luke's heart cowered in his chest, the noise of the train pushing it deep inside him, but when Ransom began to run he followed, his boots slipping in the loose gravel. The crossties jerked under the rails and the track spikes rang out, but he was there, reaching for the icy car ladder.

And then the train took him up.

Below him, the wheels gnawed over the rails, but he held on, climbing until he reached the top of the car. Snow whirled over the coal, streaking the sky and hiding the trees behind a gauzy veil. The wind pricked his face. If he squinted, he could make out Ransom working several cars ahead, kicking the coal from the train, but the snow shifted and everything blurred.

He was very cold now. His hands ached, the knuckles showing like knots of blue rope. He sat to work in order to warm himself. He pushed his hands through the stoker coal, pushing it over the edge of the car, his hands black from the soot as the heat of the work began to draw up into his arms.

But now the train was gathering speed. The wind slapped Luke's ears, and he looked over the coal cars barreling on through the snow. He knew he'd stayed on too long and was afraid. Already the engine had crested the hilltop, drawing the rest of the train after it like the trail of a black robe.

The speed shook him. He hadn't paid attention and now the time for a safe jump was past. He looked for Ransom, but the cars ahead were empty.

He's done got off, he thought. *He's done left me.*

The pale ground was only a blur below him and when the train wailed, he stumbled, falling backward into the coal. The bricks scraped his neck and the sky above him was slate gray. Briefly, he thought of riding the train out, but he knew he couldn't do that.

He would have to jump.

It was witch-cold on top of the freight car, and the train was taking him on through white fields and winter-darkened trees, its engine burning, and he would have to jump.

Luke pulled himself up from the coal and went to the ladder. He climbed down. The ice on the rungs melted under his fingers. Below, the ground was a white river, rapid and flowing. All around, the wind swelled and the snow and coal cinders nicked his cheeks. All that was left for him to do was let go and he did. He let go and pushed himself away from the train, sprawling down into the hard gravel of the road bank, his body shuddering when it hit the ground. There was a thunder of wheels, and wind struck the oaks just below him, the air splashing everywhere. One of his legs throbbed. Blood was in his mouth. But he heard the trees clattering and the train bleeding away through the country and he stood up because he could.

He thought suddenly of the tightrope walkers he'd seen at the circus, people that ran across wires without falling. It was something he wanted to learn. Alone in his bed the night of his father's funeral he tried to cry, but his mind wandered again to the circus, the thing he wanted to join. The moon was a cupped white hand in the window ready to scoop up his tears, but they wouldn't come. He recalled his father's breath soured with bourbon and the jingling of brass fasteners on his overalls, his whiskers scratching Luke's cheeks when he kissed him goodnight, but none of that seemed enough to cry over, and he thought of the circus again, the smell of manure and sawdust, the strange, bearded men in bright clothes that never lost their balance above the crowd of faces. He thought of what it would be like to die from falling. He wondered if it would feel like moonlight spilling on a cold wooden floor while winter lay adrift in the world.

Now his head filled with a dim pulsing. His lips were wet and he touched them, and his fingers came away bloody, but he was there, all in one piece. He almost laughed at what he'd done.

"Before you do anything, you better cry for your daddy some first." That's what Auncie had told him when he said he wanted to be an acrobat. But he couldn't cry. Not when there were men in the world unafraid of high drafty heights.

Ransom came walking up through the snow. His feedsack was full of coal already and he lurched from the weight of it.

"Thought maybe you'd decided to ride that cannonball out of the county," he said.

"I jumped," said Luke, smiling. "I waited too long, but I jumped anyway."

Ransom nodded, his face grave and wearied from staring through the snow. Flecks of coal dust clung to his lips. He took a freshly rolled cigarette from his pocket and ducked away from the wind to light it. When it was going good, he passed it to Luke.

"Next time you'll keep your eyes peeled," he said.

Luke only held the cigarette, its end glowing like a jewel. There was no need to smoke. Holding it and smelling the sour reek of the tobacco was enough.

"Come on," said Ransom.

They went back down the tracks to where the coal lay spilled on the ground. Snow fell down the collar of Luke's coat, but his leg hurt and the cigarette fumed in his hand, and all of that pain and smoke seemed to warm him. Far away, the train squalled again and even that noise, distant and hidden by the trees, was full of heat and burning things.

Luke began filling his sack. He worked until he was panting, a glaze of sweat on his lip, his nose running.

"Ain't this a heap?" he said. His voice was beaming, but there was no answer. Luke turned and saw Ransom staring down the tracks, his face shaken and sad, his smudged gray lips drawn in against his dark teeth.

"Luke," he whispered.

A man was walking up the tracks toward them. He wore a long wool coat and a two-piece suit of tweed under that, and the light shivered against his polished boots. There was no hat on his head and the snow dotted the sleek hair greased back over his scalp in a dark frozen wave, and he seemed unbelievable, a trick of the flakes and frigid shadows.

"Who is it?" asked Luke.

"Hush," said Ransom. "He'll tell us who he is."

The man stopped a few yards from them. He stood in the middle of the tracks and his mustache was damp with snow under his nose. He was very tall and had a face like carved soap. He kept his hands in his pockets.

"Morning, boys," he said, nodding.

Ransom shifted the bag of coal to his right hand. "Morning."

The man took his hands from his pockets and Luke saw he wore a pair of leather gloves, the fresh grain shining in the snowy wet air.

"Looks to me like y'all been at some hard work." The man pointed to the bags of coal.

"We ain't broke a sweat just yet," said Ransom.

"No. Too chilly for that today, I reckon."

A strong silence crawled out of the trees. Snow whispered over the ground, but there was no other sound. In that quiet, Luke studied the tall man standing between the tracks and thought it strange there were men like this in the world who dressed everyday in tailored suits and fresh slacks. This man was tall and the wool jacket lay clumped over his shoulders and there was a strong smell of bathwater on him.

"Do you know who I am?" the man asked.

Ransom shook his head. "Never seen you before in my life," he said.

The man grinned. "No," he said. "And you may never see me again after today. But I bet you can guess where it is I came from."

Ransom spat and wiped his mouth with the back of his hand. "I'd be guessing," he said. "But I'd say you got a badge and a gun on you somewheres."

The man drew the wool coat back. Under his arm, the handle of a revolver poked out of a holster. There was an embossed piece of metal pinned to his chest. When the man saw they had both gotten a look, he let the coat fall to place again.

"The Paducah line is my boss," he said. Then he nodded at Luke. "Who's the boy?"

"Nobody," said Ransom. "He ain't nothing. Just a boy."

"He's not yours?"

"No. I don't know him."

"Well. You don't know many people now do you?"

Ransom didn't say anything. He wouldn't look at Luke, but stared off through the trees where the snow had spilled. His face wasn't flushed from the cold anymore, but worn and colorless, and it made Luke afraid to see the power the man in the wool coat had over his uncle, as if stitched sleeves and raggedy jackets were no match for ironed-smooth trousers.

"Hey, son," said the man, smiling at Luke. "Where'd you come from?"

Luke felt his hands begin to shake. He hid them in his pockets and tried to speak, but his voice was feathery dust in his throat.

"Nowhere," he sputtered. "I ain't nobody."

The man put his hands on his hips and stared at him. "Nobody," he said. "Nobody from nowhere. Sure. I know you. Well, let me tell you. There's a law for folk that don't have no name same for ones that do. Kicking coal off a train ain't legal for nobody."

The man reached in his coat and took out two pairs of handcuffs. The metal clicked and glinted and looked very cold.

"Once you get these on, maybe you'll remember who you are," said the man.

He stepped forward, but Ransom dropped his bag of coal and the man stopped, his eyes peering bluntly through the snow at the two figures before him.

"Just put them on me," said Ransom. "You ain't got to cuff him. He's only a boy."

The man paused, holding the cuffs out. His mouth was open and Luke saw the pale tongue moving between his teeth.

"He was big enough to steal that coal, so I reckon he's big enough to wear these cuffs," the man said.

"No. He ain't that big. Look at him," said Ransom.

Luke felt the man watching him. His neck was fevered and sweat crawled down his ribs and he had to look away through the trees rising on the hill where the snow curled in the wind like the feathers of a burst bird. Somehow, he thought of Auncie, alone in the cold house. He saw her hands scattering over the coal stove, her fingers pressed to its belly as if she could midwife some ghost of heat from it, but when he tried he could squeeze those thoughts out of his mind and see only the snow clotting over the tracks, and his heart rushed through his chest, a thickness that made his mouth dry.

"What could he do to you?" said Ransom.

"It ain't what he could do. It's what the both of you could do together."

"You put those cuffs on him and you'll never live it down."

"What's that mean?"

"Means I was in the war and did plenty of things I'm not proud of. But I never once chained up a boy. I was never that scared the whole time I was over there."

The man's lips tightened. He threw a pair of cuffs into the snow then put the others in his coat.

"Pick those up then and put them on yourself," he said to Ransom.

Ransom squatted and clicked the cuffs over his wrists. His hands had turned a vivid red in the cold and they shivered, but his face was still with flakes of snow lingering on his cheeks. When he stood up again, the man went to him and clamped the cuffs tighter until the skin shone bloodless around the metal.

"How those feel to you?" the man asked.

"Well, if they fit any better, I just don't think I could stand it," said Ransom.

"I don't reckon they'll help you remember your name, will they?"

"No sir, tight metal and broken wrists usually don't serve my memory."

The man wiped the snow from his mustache and spat, but the wind rose and blew the phlegm against his coat and he raked it away, wiping the glove against his trousers when he was finished.

"Well," he said. "We'll find out who the both of you are once we get to county lockup." He pointed to Luke. "You get to tote the coal since you ain't wearing no cuffs. The Paducah company will be wanting it back."

Luke picked up the sacks of coal. They were heavy and his arms ached, but he hurried anyway, lurching and struggling as if it were the weight of water from a deep well he carried.

"Y'all walk in front of me here," said the man. He pointed to the tracks, but neither Luke or Ransom moved. "Come on," said the man. "It's cold enough to freeze your balls off out here."

"Where you'd park your car?" Ransom asked.

The man grunted and buttoned the front of his coat. "That don't really matter. We'll get there."

"Could get there faster if we cut through the woods," said Ransom. "I bet you're parked on the Percyville Trace. I know a real quick way through the trees that'll get us over there."

The man looked through the snow at the levee of black trees, the flakes thickening as they fell through the empty branches to cover the ground, blotting out all traces of travel. His breath crawled in and out of him and his face was blank.

"If you know a quicker way, then show me," he said, finally. "I hate being cold worse than anything."

Ransom grinned and looked at the man. "If I show you this shortcut, what is it that you're going to do for me?"

The man raked the snow from his coat sleeves. He stared at Ransom. His eyes were blank and cold. "I don't make deals with trash," he said.

"Then I guess we're just going to have to get back to the car the long way."

"I guess so."

"We're going to have to take our time and get real cold in the going there." Ransom chuckled. "What's the coldest you ever been, Mister?"

The man said nothing. Snow had crept into the creases of his coat and slid into his collar. His face pulsed redly under the thick dark mustache he wore, the phlegm running from his nose beginning to crust on the whiskers. He pulled a silver watch from the fob pocket of his vest, checked the time, then snapped the hasp lid and grunted.

"If you can show me a shortcut," he said, "I'll see to it they go light on you and nothing won't happen to the boy. That's the best I can deal. You understand?"

Ransom nodded. "I understand real well," he said. "I know how bad it is to be cold in a strange place you ain't never been before."

Then they all straggled down the gravel bank, Ransom going first with Luke and the man in the wool jacket following him into the forest.

The ground rose steadily under them, building into a hill, and they walked in silence, their breath gathering in thick clouds. In the trees there was no wind, but they could hear it drawing through the open spaces they had left, the loose air gasping through fields and over the tracks, but where they were the snow and gray light fell listless and faint as hair. The woods were smothered in cold.

Luke could hear the man walking just behind him, his boots scratching through the frost, but he stared at Ransom's shoulders bulging against his tight black coat and did not look back. The feedsacks rubbed blisters on his hands, but he went on. The pain was easy, hidden by the cold he felt, and these woods were something he knew. His father had hunted squirrels here with him and he knew the way the trees grew, white oaks on the eastern hillsides and loblolly pine on the west. In the fall, he could find ginseng sprouting among the moss of the northern slope. In the cool places where the shade was heavy. He could find lots of things. When he looked now, he saw them all again, the ginseng and goldenseal and mayapple shooting up through the black soil, the earth surrendering its hidden life, all of it waiting to bloom again once the cold was gone. There was no need to be afraid. The coal was not heavy and the blisters on his hands didn't hurt.

They came to the top of the hill, and Ransom called for them to stop. Luke dropped the sacks of coal and they slumped against his legs. He pushed his hands in his pockets, wriggling his fingers to warm them.

"I think I took a wrong turn somewhere," said Ransom. "You can't get to the Percyville Trace this way."

Ransom breathed slow and the man in the tweed suit paced on ahead, his face turning back and forth as he looked among the trees. When he turned to them again, he didn't say anything, but his eyes were full of a hardness that hadn't been there before.

"I thought you said you knew a quicker way," he said.

Ransom shrugged. "Thought that I did," he said. "But it's hard to tell rightly where you are in these trees sometimes. You can get lost real simply."

The man in the wool coat wiped at his running nose and grunted. The brass cuffbuttons at the ends of his sleeves flickered like candlefire.

"Let's head up this way," he said bluntly.

Ransom and Luke followed him down the slope, the powdered snow wetting their pant legs and their breath heaving loose inside them. After a time, the man stopped, put his hands on his hips, and stood looking about as if searching for something dropped or lost.

"Can't get to the Percyville Trace going this way neither," said Ransom, smiling. "I knew it from the start."

The man pulled at his mustache. "If you knew you should've said something before now," he said.

"Well, I seen you was bound and determined to get yourself lost so I didn't speak up. Myself, I only been lost in the woods once before today and didn't want to give advice to a feller that was clearly an expert on that kind of business."

The man's eyes flared. "Tell me where to go," he said.

"Well, I would. But it's kindly hard for me to point with my hands cuffed like this."

The man spat and shook his head. He turned away from them and looked off through the trees again. Luke could hear him whispering to himself, a sound quiet and frigid as the snow falling through the oak boughs, and it made him glad to think of the man lost in the trees he had always known.

"Listen here," said the man, turning to face them again. "You're gonna tell me how to get back to the Percyville Trace."

"Well," said Ransom. "Way you talk might make us think you didn't enjoy our company. What's the hurry?"

"I ain't standing out here in the cold all day with you two."

"Looks to me like you ain't got much say in that no more," said Ransom.

The man grunted. He paced off through the trees, squinting at the snow and light, and then stopped.

"Now these woods are an odd thing for somebody ain't never been in them before now." Ransom began to talk slowly. "You go in them thinking you can tell your way around, but the trees got a way of making you lost. You could be close enough to spit on whatever it is you're looking for and never know it's in here."

Ransom squatted in the snow. He looked up through the trees, then brought his hands to his face and breathed through his fingers.

Then he looked at Luke hunched inside his jacket and he nodded at the sacks of coal lying at the boy's feet.

"My daddy brought me in here when I wasn't eight years old," Ransom continued. "Walked me through the trees and then left me. This was in the summertime. I didn't have no water with me and by the time I finally found my way out I guess I'd drunk the sweat out of somebody's boots I was so thirsty. Don't you know I looked a sight, too. Covered in ticks and briar scrapes."

Ransom stared at Luke while he talked. Every little bit he nodded at the sacks of coal and Luke couldn't think what that might mean, what he wanted him to do, but he felt the cold leaking out of him and heat rolled in his belly.

"Course my daddy weren't mean for doing that. It's an odd business raising a boy. That's all. You got to give them a chance at standing by theirself in the world. And there ain't no shame in making it hard on them neither. I think about that day when I was lost out here and it was so hot the birds had stopped talking and the woods were so empty it was like I was the only thing living in the world. Day like that will teach a boy some things."

The man in the wool jacket came back through the snow. Ransom stood up, and they glared at each other, the man's face shivering and blotched, Ransom's eyes calm and still.

"Think I've heard enough," said the man. "Now show me how to get back to the Percyville Trace."

Ransom shook his head. "I ain't showing you a damn thing," he said.

The man pulled the revolver from his coat and pointed it at Ransom.

"You going to shoot us, Mister?" Luke asked.

The man did not look away from Ransom. "I'm gonna take y'all out these woods is what I'm gonna do." He jerked the barrel toward the trees. "Lead us on," he said to Ransom.

Ransom didn't move. He stared at the blue gun barrel, the breath trickling over his lips. His face was still calm as if what he watched was no more than the dawn breaking loosely and dim over the fields and trees, the man with the gun only a piece of quivering shadow the light would soon take.

"Get to walking," said the man.

Ransom jerked his head once, then again.

He ain't going to do it, Luke thought. *He's going to get us killed.*

The man's breath was faster now, whistling through the spaces in his teeth, and the blood had come to his face, the blotches melding together so his cheeks glowed the color of hot iron.

Luke knew he was going to shoot them both. Out here in the snow, in these forest depths, no one would hear. The sound would be muffled by the thinly trickling snow, and the thought made Luke very hot inside his jacket. He felt the wind frisking his clothes, sliding down his collar.

"You going to shoot us?" he asked again.

The man kept his eyes and the revolver pointed at Ransom. His hand was shaking now, but he didn't try to hide it.

"You're gonna take me out of this place," he said.

"No," said Ransom. "I ain't neither."

The man's face went blank. The color fled from his cheeks. He stepped forward and swung the pistol, bringing the butt down hard on Ransom's neck, the sound dull and thick. Ransom crumpled to the ground, his eyes shut tight. The man stood over him, his back turned to Luke. He was raising the pistol again, but would use the business end of it this time. Then Ransom rolled onto his back, his face a fierce tear, his eyes jagged streaks as he looked at Luke.

"The coal!" Ransom shouted. "Get him with the coal!"

Luke was startled by his voice, so full of fear and blunt pain.

But the man in the wool coat was turning to him now, slowly, the edge of his pale face glinting like a shard of moonlight, and Luke did not have time to be afraid anymore. He jerked up a sack of coal and swung it hard. It hit the man in the chest and he sprawled backward into the snow, his mouth open as if this were all a mild surprise. Luke hit him again with the coal, in the belly this time, and the sack burst, spilling coal chunks over the snow.

The man grunted and rolled onto his stomach. He was trying to stand up, but Ransom tackled him from behind, and they twisted together, throwing snow into the air, their faces slurring while they fought.

The gun, thought Luke. *He's still got the gun, and he ain't dropped it.*

Watching them struggle, he was afraid again. The fear had come surging back through him after the coal sack burst, and now he stood rigid, looking on the pair of men fighting in the snow as if it were something eventual that couldn't be helped. He was cold all over and when the shot came, it was a sound as dull and forceless as an ax striking ice. There was no echo. There was only the grunt of the gun, thick and clumsy. The two men were both lying still now, piled together, but Luke saw the blood sprayed over the snow, its heat melting holes in the frost.

Slowly, he moved forward. His head felt stiff and his eyes watered from the cold, but he went to them.

This is me walking a high wire, he thought. *This is the thing you see before you die from falling.*

Ransom was dead. His ruined face was wet with blood, the eyes wide just below the bullet hole. The man in the wool jacket rolled from underneath his body. He pointed the revolver at him, but Luke kept coming. He was cold and afraid and he stood over Ransom's body, the slack mouth and pale lips like the face of a man waiting for a long drink.

"You both tried to kill me," gasped the man in the wool jacket. He staggered up from the snow and kept his gun on Luke. He was breathing heavy now and the front of his suit was slick with blood.

Luke squatted beside his uncle Ransom. Far off, the moan of another train drifted to him through the trees. The wind came crouching up through the brambles and thorns, slinking over the snow. Luke looked at the sky twisted and caught in the oak branches. He thought of Auncie stirring some cold pan of beans, shuffling from the empty coal stove to the window to watch for him, waiting for him to come and warm the home, to make things well with fire.

"You goddamn hillbillies," said the man. His lip was bleeding and he spat redness onto the snowy ground. He wiped his face with his gloves. Then he picked up a handful of snow and held it to his lip, the water dribbling off his chin. "You both tried to kill me," he said again.

Luke stood up fully. Ransom was dead now. Ransom was dead and his father was dead and Auncie was waiting lonely and freezing in the tiny house and he was here in the snow, his fingers going numb with cold.

"Mister," he said. "Do they got some nice warm beds at that jail in town?"

The man shook his head, the swoop of shining black hair blowing frayed over his brow. The blood on his coat and trousers looked like woodstain and he kept touching it, wiping its wetness with his gloved fingers.

"We got to get out of these goddamn woods," he said. "I can't hardly feel my toes anymore."

The man's face had turned a bleak cindery gray. His lips looked as if they'd been painted with billiard chalk and his hands shook as he pointed off through the trees.

"C'mon. Show me," he said. "Show me where to go."

Luke looked at Ransom's body where it lay in the frost like strewn water. "I can't take us out of here," he said. "I don't know the way to go."

The man in the coat flew at him, grabbing his collar and yanking him close so that his breath clawed at Luke's eyeballs, cold and barbarous. "You little shit," he said. "You little goddamn shit. You know the way and you're going to tell me." The man held the revolver under Luke's chin. The barrel felt sharp and icy against his skin. Slowly, the man raised his free hand and pointed at Ransom. "You don't show me the way out of here and I'll blow you're head off same as I did to him."

Luke felt the blood rushing through him, molten and thick.

He will do it, Luke thought. *He will kill me out here same as stomping a mouse.*

"Okay," he said. "Let me go. I think I know the way back to the tracks. Let me go and I'll see if I can get us there."

The man's grip slackened and his hands fell away from Luke's collar.

He straightened the front of his jacket for him and a grin grew under his mustache, his spacey white teeth coming out of the dark whiskers like stars.

"That's a good boy," he said. He waved the pistol at the trees. "Lead me on."

Luke nodded. He went to the one unbroken sack of coal and picked it up, hefting it over his shoulder.

"What the hell are you doing with that?" the man asked.

"Taking it with me," said Luke. "You said the Paducah Line wanted it back."

The man grunted. "You goddamn crazy hillbillies," he said. "I don't see why they don't put the whole damn bunch of y'all in a cage somewhere. You'd eat each other alive and then nobody would have to worry with you no more."

"Sure," said Luke, nodding. "Okay. Sure. Let's get going then. On over this way. That's the right way to go."

He hobbled off through the thickest part of the trees. The man followed, his boots whispering through the fine morning-fallen snow. Luke went on and he did not look back at Ransom lying dead in the frost, his blood cooling in the snow. He did not look back because he did not have to. All he needed was right in front of him. It was the closed frozen woods, the trees rearing black against the white sky like cracks in porcelain, the snow so thick now that it had hidden their footprints, the swelling hills and deep hollows where things could be lost so simply that no one would ever even think to look for them again. It was the coal riding his back. That was all anyone could need. And he could go on for just a little while longer through the cold, leading the man in the wool coat over the snow-covered lands that were strange to men of his kind, men who wore gloves of grainy leather and smelled of sudsy baths. Luke could go with him in the pale blanched world, both of them getting cold, cold, cold until the man would stop, his slow breath crawling out between the blue lips, the breath slow and slowly crawling until it was all still and nothing but quiet remained. Then Luke could go on home to Auncie and make big fires in the stove with the coal and warm himself under blankets and be not afraid.

He could do this because it was all there was left for him to do.

Walking in the snow with the man trailing behind him, Luke remembered the acrobats again. Those were men unafraid. Odd fellows borne aloft on high wires like the angels Auncie sang hymns about. And the main part of walking a wire was waiting. Waiting for the exact perfect moment when all was balanced and you could put your foot down and go on again.

"We're going the right way," Luke said over his shoulder. "We're not far now."

He heard the man grunt, but there was no other sound. The snow had stopped and all was quiet.

Luke went on through it. His hands were cold and bare, but he was going to the place where he was needed, and a great surge of joy sprang in him so that he stepped up onto a fallen oak log and walked along it, treading softly, one arm out for balance.

"Goddamn crazy hillbillies," he heard the man say.

But Luke did not turn to look and he did not fall. Already he knew the man's breath was slowing, the cold making him stone. Soon the man would lie down in the snow and his heart would grow quiet. Luke knew he could wait for it to happen. Walking along the oak log, he knew he could wait for a long time. A long cold time.

Real Good Man
by Mindy Beth Miller

Paul jumped back in his sock feet to avoid the jagged pieces of glass that skidded past him as the vase shattered to bits on the linoleum floor. Desta turned her back to him and returned to scrubbing a sticky kettle in the sink. She shook her head, rubbed a curled finger under each eye. It hurt him to see her doing that, so he punched the wall with a tight fist. A flowered plaque fell to the floor and cracked down the middle. He spat a curse over it.

"You think I walked up to him and said some kind of smart shit, don't you?" Paul said.

"Don't keep this a-going," Desta said. She clanged the kettle into the drainer and leaned her forehead into her hand.

"Say it to me, if you think you're so damn big," he said, gripping the edge of the counter in his hands. His throat tingled like a whole handful of splinters were stuck in it. It was the way he'd felt as a boy, right before he took the bite of his daddy's mining belt.

Desta dropped her hand and eased back against the counter. She stared out into the yard without speaking, a dishrag dangling in her grasp. After a moment, she said, "I can't stay with a man who puts his pride ahead of his own family." She tilted her head and raised her eyebrows, adding, "I won't."

Paul scratched his fingers through his hair, hard. "What do you think I've been doing?" he hollered. "I ain't done nothing but work my guts out to give you all this." He held his arms out wide before letting them smack down onto his sides like a tree collapsing.

"This makes the second time," Desta said. "How are we gonna make it if you ain't fit to hold down one measly, stinking little job?"

Those words—*fit* and *little*—raked against his heart. He knew Desta was worried, that she feared losing the house and the car, not being able to give a good life to their children. But she should have thought better than to say such things to him. He hadn't done anything wrong to lose either one of his jobs. He was just the easiest to let go. He was always the man on the bottom rung of the ladder, the one with the least experience. Paul had never raised his hand to her, but if she had been a man standing there, he would have busted her mouth. They cussed and went on for fifteen minutes, throwing up past failings to each other and blaming the other for any and all wrecked hopes. Their raised voices penetrated the stillness just outside the house, setting the dogs to barking.

"What if the boys were here?" Desta asked. "To hear you talking like that?"

"I don't give a damn."

"I know you don't."

"Look," Paul said. His hands were clutching at the air, like he was about to make something appear. "I'll fix this. I'll go talk right to Weston Carroll. We went to grade school together. He'll listen to me."

Desta rolled her eyes and slapped the dishrag into the sink.

He watched her march into the living room, hands on her hips. This was her way of showing him how frustrated she was, and as much as it upset him, it caused a strange little thrill to run through him, too. Her toughness and hard nature were things that he loved about Desta. She never budged in an argument, and most often, ended up getting her way. He followed her and stood where he could see her face, a face lined with both heartbreak and resolve. When she glanced up at him, he noticed that she didn't look at him the way she used to. There wasn't a trace of belief in her eyes. She used to lift her chin when she looked at him, full of admiration. A sigh seeped out of her that drained her face of its youthfulness. She lay a hand on the couch and dropped her head, reminding him of a rose crushed beneath his step.

"You'll see what I can do," Paul said, not much higher than a whisper.

Desta smacked her lips and nodded. "Let's see you do it then," she said.

That hollow stare of hers said it all: she thought he was a fool. He didn't want to believe that she saw him that way. He rested his hand on the back of his neck, the act of a man-child who doesn't know what else to do. He felt as though he'd been unlucky his whole life. There'd been chances that slipped by the way, promises that people forgot about. He moved his hand from his neck to his work shirt, smoothing out the front. He studied the lettering on his chest: REDFOX COAL COMPANY. Just last week, Desta had been proud that he drove a rock truck up on the job.

"How about I just blow my damn brains out and get it over with?" he said.

Desta gawked at him. "Are you stupid?" she said.

Paul yanked his .22 off of the rack on the wall and stepped out onto the front porch. Desta was on his heels, grabbing at his arms, pleading with him. He scanned his piece of property and gritted his teeth at the sight of a few sheets of tin shed from the roof. The gleam on the metal stabbed his eyes. And he fixed his gaze upon the pickup truck, given to him by his brother, speckled orange from rust. All of Low Gap, the whole world, seemed settled into a kind of breathless expectation. He ripped his arm away from Desta and raised the rifle. He shot three times toward the sky above the mountains—at the brilliant blue, at God, at nothing. A thundercloud of birds scarred the sky, and their sudden lifting caused a whole stand of poplars to sway as if struck across the face.

His arms tingled from the blasts. He liked the feeling it gave him. He craved it, lusted after it—the feeling of power he got from watching the swaying of the trees.

Paul sat near the darkened window, phone in hand. It had taken him hours to get through, but now Weston Carroll had to take an urgent call from a bank in Lexington. *Just like always*, he thought, jockeying for position in line or even stepping to the side so one more significant could pass on by. He sucked in one Salem after another, squashing out each one in the green palm of the ashtray with growing fierceness.

He figured that Weston just wanted him to hang up, but he stayed on the line.

"Yeah," Paul said, surprised to hear a voice on the other side. He scooted forward on the couch. "I was just wondering if there was some chance of me getting my job back."

Weston was quiet for a time.

"You know me, Wes," Paul said. "I'll do good by you. I won't let you down."

He looked out into the yard: Desta and the boys stood around a little fire, roasting marshmallows. The orange light shimmered on their clothes and skin. They were smiling. He half-listened to Weston's matter-of-fact, overused response. He tore his eyes from them and pressed the phone into his jaw. He opened and shut his mouth, waiting for the chance to speak. Everything around him was aglow with moonlight. His shadow looked like a pool of soot. Weston still hadn't hushed, so he rubbed his sweaty temple with the tip of his thumb. Cigarette smoke twirled above his head.

"Oh," he said, shocked by the question. He laughed through a closed mouth. "I know times is hard."

Weston had one last thing to say.

Paul felt his face harden. He sat up straight and searched the wall for an answer.

"Will I be all right?" he said to Weston. He repeated the question, and then, slammed the phone down. He leaned back on the couch and covered his eyes with his hand.

He shot up onto his feet and stomped out into the blackness. Desta yelled for him, but he didn't stop or turn around. His eyes stung, and he didn't want her to see them. His heavy breathing felt as though it would split his chest, and if he'd been alone, he would have screamed at the mountains. Gravels crunched so loud under his boots that he imagined them thudding against his brain. He wanted to hit something, anything, so he swatted the back of his hand at the lightning bugs around him. He reeled in a circle as he walked, striking a few, missing more. Then, he stopped and watched them—they were like dazzling pinpricks of light from another world.

He revved up the old pickup and squealed his tires on the holler road. After his talk with Weston, he felt powerless, unable, so he drove down into town to try and forget about it. He pretended, like a child, that he was headed right into something. That he would slam into it somewhere, sometime soon, and knock it to the ground. The night was thick with fog. It was the time of night when the mountains lived, when they breathed and relieved themselves from the heat of the day. Something about it seemed magical to him, eerie. It was like the earth somehow hid its secrets from him behind a gauzy curtain.

Parked by the sidewalk, far from any streetlights, Paul watched as, every once in a while, a light popped on in one of the townhouses up on the hill. He sat with his head against the glass, taking long drinks from a can of Old Milwaukee, and wondered about the people who lived in that house. He'd never felt more alone.

The engine was off, but "Tulsa Time" was playing on the radio. His legs were stretched across the seat, and every time a flickering line of light from the headlights of a passing car invaded the cab, he closed his eyes until it had gone. He took one last, long drink of the beer and crushed it in his hand. He righted himself and put his fingers on the keys that were still stuck in the ignition, but changed his mind. There was a cutout newspaper article above the sun visor, one he'd placed there months ago, which he snatched down and held close to his face. It was all about Weston Carroll. Paul rubbed his prickly jaw and laughed.

He dug his Bic cigarette lighter out of his pocket and set fire to the paper. He leaned his head to one side and admired the curling edge. A spark dripped onto his crotch. He swatted the seat and his jeans and flung the burning paper out the door. The seat covering had a charred hole in it, so he smacked both hands on the steering wheel.

"Damn it to hell," Paul said.

He shoved the creaking truck door open. When he'd switched off the radio and gotten out of the truck, he slammed the door shut and kicked the front tire. Then, he just walked up the road, almost staggering at first. He wasn't drunk, but his head felt like it was closed off in a box. Main Street was empty. Nothing but crumbling brick buildings, empty places with KEEP OUT NO TRESPASSING scrawled on the windows in white paint, and deep potholes. It was a dead place. An old coal town gone bust. He could have charged down the middle of the street, wild and screaming, and no one would have given a damn.

He felt like he would lose it in the silence.

But there was a light on at Odds & Ends, a tiny antique shop.

When he got close enough, he leaned his shoulder against a light pole and looked at the store. The owner of the place, Hester Morgan, a man called Hess by just about everybody, sat outside in a wicker chair. He was killing time, it seemed, or hoping that a late-night straggler would drop in. Paul crossed the street and lit a Salem. A bunch of junk was out on the sidewalk—glass lanterns, eyeless and nearly hairless dolls, some old farming tools, yellowed romance novels, and even a toilet. He raised his hand to the old man.

"Evening," Hess said. The gray stubble around his mouth was stained with tobacco juice. "Set down awhile, boy. You don't look to be buying nothing."

"Ain't used to this, I guess," Paul said. He plopped down on the doorstep, which was a little uncomfortable for his long legs. "Nowhere to go, nothing to do."

"Damn straight," Hess said while swatting away a mosquito with his baseball cap. "Life treating you hard, is it?"

Paul shrugged. "Poor man ain't got a shot."

Hess nodded, then looked up and smiled at him. "Hillbilly Palace is still open," he said.

Paul drew on his cigarette, blowing smoke from his nose. He flicked some ashes away and shook his head. He stared at a blond woman pacing up and down the bridge that spanned the river, which was illuminated in a pulsating orange light. Her shorts were unbuttoned and unzipped. She was barefooted. The sight of her made him angry. He stared up at the black, silent sky.

"Trouble with your woman at home?" said Hess.

"Trouble's everywhere," Paul said and flipped the still-smoking butt out into the street.

"Heard that." The old man crossed his legs and spat a brown string of saliva into a pop bottle. "I sit here every day," he said, thoughtful, "and watch people go up and down this road. They'll stop, look at what I've got setting out on the street or peek through the window. I can tell what they're thinking. They think that maybe they ought to buy a little cheap something from that old man, but they reckon it's all just rusted and nasty and secondhand. Beneath them. They glance at me like they're real sorry when they don't buy anything."

"You don't believe em?" Paul said.

"People just flat don't care," Hess said, holding out his hand. "Their world is not your world. They don't see you in it." His voice grew louder, like he'd been dying to tell this to someone for a long time. "I could be standing in this building one day, ready to hang myself from the rafters, and people would still walk on by with somewhere else to go."

Paul watched a car slow down on the bridge and pick up the barefooted woman. It sped away. He wondered, *What will happen to her?* He straightened his back and thought about the things Hess had just said. Not all people were uncaring, heartless. He was different. There was something within him that he hesitated to call special, but it was something deep and good. He was a real good man, this he believed. But he wanted to be more. What he wanted more than anything else in the world was to be somebody important.

"People protect themselves by being ignorant," Hess said. "To them, you're just some sad little shit who got screwed over."

Paul looked down at his hands. It was so dark that he couldn't see them completely. When he stretched them out, his fingers were lit up in a pale slat of light. It scared him sometimes, what his hands couldn't do. Or what he hoped they could do, but couldn't. He and Hess sat there in the dark, neither of them saying a word. The street smelled equally of greasy food and gasoline. It seemed to him that they both fastened their eyes on the railroad, on an old coal train that never went anywhere.

The early morning light caused Paul to rub his eyes from time to time, but he drove on, determined to keep pace with the SUV in front of him. He did not tell Desta where he was going. He doubted that she'd agree with his plans. She would most likely misunderstand his intentions. He only wanted to speak with Weston face-to-face. He figured it best to talk to the man, to explain everything and reason with him. Give the man a chance to do the right thing. When the moment presented itself, he would be ready. So, he followed Weston down every road he took, every turn he made.

It didn't seem as if Weston noticed he was being followed. Paul didn't care if he happened to be discovered anyway. He wanted Weston to know about his presence. He figured that Weston would pull over at some point, step out of his vehicle and demand an explanation. A better opportunity to tell his side of things might never present itself.

He trailed Weston for a long time, driving through neighborhoods that he knew nothing about. They ended up in Woodland Park for awhile, a place of big houses and people who'd made their money in the coal industry. Paul recalled going there as a child to look at Christmas lights. Weston visited with a family there, so Paul pulled into a shaded area near someone's driveway. A place he wasn't likely to be seen. He sat there, waiting, listening to the radio and drinking coffee from a Styrofoam cup.

"I am the master of broken things," he remembered saying to Desta last summer, half-jokingly. He could get anything back up and running—junkyard-bound cars, spent air conditioners, leaking washers, crappy vacuum cleaners. He could do it all, so it didn't seem impossible to him that he could find some way to convince Weston Carroll to rehire him on the spot.

When Weston emerged from the house a few moments later, another man was with him. Paul sank down in the seat and adjusted his shirt collar so that it covered part of his face. He didn't want to have to confront Weston in the presence of this other man, a man who would be free to talk about the desperate nature of his situation. The two men shook hands and laughed.

"I'll get that for you right away," the man said to Weston. His voice was loud and carried out over the street. "You come back anytime."

Paul gritted his teeth— everything was so easy for his old boss. People were lined up to help him, to find a way to please him. He could snap his fingers, say the word, and it was all taken care of.

Weston drove to the end of the road and turned. Paul waited, letting him get on ahead. He knew the way, so it wouldn't be hard to keep up. He still wore his old work shirt that bore the name of Weston's coal company. He smiled, thinking that this was his job now.

Like a hunt, he thought. Some men actually did make money doing stuff like that. One of his favorite things was deer hunting. A true man's game. He didn't mind being drenched in deer piss so as not to give himself away or having only the cover of leaves on a cold winter's night, waiting for his moment. The biggest he ever got was a ten-point buck. Such a majestic animal and a thrill to kill it. He'd hauled it home in the back of his truck. Had even taken pictures with it. The smell of the hunt—the blood and sweat and musk—saturated the cab of his truck for days afterward. Sometimes he never washed out the blood.

He was curious now, sucked in. He wanted to know details about this man's life. The idea that he could be a witness to some kind of crooked activity in which Weston was involved, even catch him in the act, made him feel that what he was doing was right and proper. He waited for Weston outside of Hardee's, parking where he could see him eating and talking to some other men. He ended up going through the drive-thru and ordering the same thing Weston was eating: a Hot Ham 'N' Cheese. He tossed it out after a few bites.

The last few stops yielded nothing of interest. Weston spent an hour at a lawyer's office. Paul later felt as though he wasted an hour and a half outside The Pavilion, hanging around until Weston returned to his vehicle all red and sweaty from the gym. He took some satisfaction in the fact that Weston Carroll, while a tall man, was not an impressive figure. He was in the few remaining years of a comb-over and had a ring of flabby fat bulging from his waist that only made his skinny legs look skinnier.

"Tough week, Wes?" a pretty brunette said from across the parking lot.

"Honey, that's every week," Weston said.

Paul's top lip curled. "You bastard," he said, under his breath.

He didn't feel like trailing Weston any longer after that. He suddenly felt as if he'd been reduced to tagging along after him, brought down lower than he'd ever been. Perhaps Weston knew what was happening all along and had led him around to all of these places on purpose. Maybe he'd had a good laugh about it. Paul shook his head and slammed his foot on the accelerator.

He raced along the curvy mountain roads, cursing when he hit a bump or break in the pavement. He decided to go to Weston's house and wait outside, which would force the man to speak with him about all this. The house was easy enough to find—it dwarfed everything else on its street. Paul stepped out of the truck and gave his hair a quick comb. That house was a wonder. Bright yellow lights lit up the house's exterior in the darkening day, enhancing its bigness. People drove at a crawl past the place just to admire it.

There was a walkway leading up to the house, so he took it. Just to get closer. He studied the house and the wide stretch of property. The lawn looked as though it was being maintained by a landscaping crew. This was not a man who had known hard time, yet Paul spied a few cracks in the white columns. Someone had also recently poured a new rectangular slab of concrete, which hadn't been angled properly. Paul guessed that Weston had screwed that up himself. In any case, the whole place, in all of its immensity, was a sight to see. He shoved his hands into his pockets and sighed, feeling like a speck on the face of the sun.

He looked up and down the road. Still no sign of Weston. He figured that Desta and the boys would be missing him by now. Before turning to go, he saw a pair of shoes by the front door. That was such an odd thing to him. He never imagined a rich man leaving his shoes outside. He never did such a thing himself, afraid that dogs would carry them away. He picked up the shoes—a pair of shiny, black Oxfords—and turned them from side to side. He checked the size of the shoes and nodded.

On the walk back to the truck, Paul kept looking down at the shoes that swung from his fingers. It was a quiet Sunday evening, so he didn't think anyone had seen him take them. Besides, it was careless to leave them out in the open like that. He planned to wear them often, as if he'd be taking Weston with him, to where real hard times existed.

He sat in the cab and placed the shoes in the passenger seat. He wished he could feel like Weston must feel with all of those things, at least once. Like he was more than a man.

Paul and Desta made a pallet on the ground that night and watched in breathless wonder as the stars flickered into view. Back when times were easier, they used to do this whenever they had the chance. There was really no other way to view the dome of the sky in Low Gap—the mountains swallowed up most of it. Desta loved to watch the night sky, and Paul liked to watch her face. She pointed out the few constellations she knew, the Milky Way, and the planet Venus. He believed that Desta could have accomplished so much in her life. She amazed him. He often worried that his loving her had held her back.

"Lay aside what's bothering you," Desta said, "and just look up there. Nobody can be sad for long when they're looking at that."

Her hair was soft as moss against his face. He held her tighter and felt the warmth of her breasts pressed into his side.

"I'm sorry I throwed that fit yesterday," Desta said. "I just want everything to be all right."

"It will be," Paul said and kissed her forehead.

"I want it to be," she said. She rose up on her elbow and brushed her hand over his face, which was still unshaven. Her hand smelled like Clorox. "Look at you. You look like somebody who ain't got a thing to live for."

He avoided looking into her eyes. "I've just got a lot on my mind," he said.

"I called a few more places for you," she said. "There ain't a thing open anywhere, seems like."

"Just got to keep trying. Maybe I'll get a lucky break somehow."

"Where've you been sneaking off to?" Desta said. She looked him over, casting a lingering stare at his feet. "And where'd you get them shoes? I know they ain't yours."

Paul sat up and leaned back on his hands. "I got em from Hess Morgan up in town," he said. He stared at the ground. "I have to get out and do something, Desta. I feel like I'm nothing when I'm just setting."

She placed her hand on his cheek and said, "We're going to get through this."

He didn't say anything back to her.

"I thought you said you was going to talk to Weston," she said in a soft voice.

"I've been trying to get up with him," Paul said, nodding his head while he looked at her. "He's a man that you've got to catch at the right time."

"And when is the right time?" Desta said. "You wait too long and that'll be all she wrote."

"I'm going to find him tomorrow, all right?"

"Do you want me to come with you?"

He sighed and just gaped at her. "No," Paul said. "You kill me, you know that? I reckon I can talk to the man by myself."

"Well, I'm going with you tomorrow," Desta said, "just to make sure you do."

Paul threw up his hands. He wanted to tell her to shut up, but couldn't deny that he needed her. Sometimes he wished he could be more like her. She never shrank to a challenge and faced everything head-on.

"We can't make it like this," she said. "You moping around. Me taking care of the boys." She placed her hand on his chest. "I need to believe in you again."

Paul grabbed her hand and held it. "Don't you know that I want to give you everything?" He swallowed hard. "I need to know something, Desta. Could I ever do anything to make you leave me?"

Desta looked at him for a moment or two. "Not likely," she said and smiled. Paul smiled back, but he didn't believe her. Then, she looked away from him and up into the sky. She was made for more than this, for more than scraping to make a living. He had to get his job back somehow, he reckoned, if for no other reason than to feel her trust him again.

Paul stared up at the stars again, too. Desta's strong shoulder was against his. With her by his side, he could be anything. So long as he had her. His Desta. His destiny.

"Watch at them two," Desta said, pointing at the boys who stood down by the creek. They split the still water with fistfuls of gravel. She laughed out loud with every splash and covered her mouth with her hand.

Paul cracked a smile and jogged down the little hill to where they were. He wrestled each of them to his waist and hugged them, messing their blond hair with his fingers. The soap on their skin filled the air.

"Couple of rough little outfits," he said. The boys tugged on his arms and begged him to carry them on his back, one at a time, across the shallow creek. As he snatched up the first boy, Paul forgot about the things he couldn't give them and focused on the things he could—a strong back, a gentle hand, a memory or two that would last.

Desta sat real close to him in the cab of the truck, and every time he switched gears, his hand would brush against her knee. She giggled and rubbed her hand up and down his arm. It felt like old times. The boys were staying with Desta's sister, so they were free for awhile to be a little bit mischievous with each other. Whenever people in Low Gap spied two people sitting close like that, they said they were courting. He smiled at the idea of courting his wife. She used to be a firecracker back before they were married and for sometime afterwards. It seemed to him that right now, for just a little while today, that girl had returned.

"That's his SUV yonder," Paul said.

They pulled in at ERLEEN'S—a general store and country kitchen.

"You go on in and look around," Paul said. "I'll set out here and wait for Weston."

Desta squeezed his hand. "I'll give you all time to talk," she said.

He told her to buy whatever she thought they needed and that he would be parked at the side of the store, waiting on her, whenever she came back out. He did not tell her about the .22 behind the seat.

Desta marched into the store with that determined step of hers. He admired her confidence. Nothing ever held her back. She wouldn't let it. She knew what it was like to crawl and scratch through life yet come out of it ten times smarter, stronger. Because of this, he could never tell her his deepest secret: he knew she was stronger than he'd ever be. It wasn't meant to be that way.

Weston Carroll exited the store with a paper bag in tow. He was accompanied by the same man Paul had seen him with the day before in Woodland Park.

Paul remained in the truck. He felt his heart beat faster. The two men talked and cracked up about something. Paul's hands sweated against the steering wheel. He didn't dare remove the .22 just yet. As he sat there, rehearsing the whole thing in his mind, people walked all around his truck and into the store. He thought about how none of them could even imagine what he was about to do.

He tucked in the tail of his REDFOX COAL work shirt and stepped out of the truck. His shoes—Weston's shoes—clicked against the pavement. They were far too shiny to be his, Paul knew. They didn't match his rugged wear at all, but not one soul seemed to notice. He leaned against the door on the passenger side and waited his turn.

"Hey, Weston," Paul said, loud enough for Weston to hear him.

Weston looked at him and squinted like he didn't know him.

"Reckon we can talk?" Paul said. His hands felt funny, so he pushed them into his pockets and jiggled the little bit of change he had.

"What's this about?" Weston said, striding over to the truck. He held up one of his car keys. "I have to be gone from here in about five minutes."

"Won't take that long," Paul said. He opened the truck door and pushed the seat forward. When he turned back, Weston was checking his watch. "I'm in bad need of a job right now," Paul said. "I've mentioned it to you a time or two."

Weston shook his head as if to say he didn't remember.

"I'm willing to do something small until I can work my way back up," Paul said.

"Look, I'm sorry," Weston said, waving his hands around in an exaggerated motion while still holding tight to his keys and paper bag, "but there are no jobs right now. I had to lay off a whole bunch of people, not just you."

Paul could see Desta in the store. She was talking to the lady at the counter.

"Listen," Weston said. He glanced from side to side as some people walked past them. "There's no need to embarrass yourself. Go on home and think about things. I'm sure there's some other places that could take you on right now."

"I've tried everything else," Paul said.

He reached into the truck and pulled the .22 from its hiding place.

"Aw, shit," Weston said, backing up.

Paul pointed the rifle at Weston's mouth. "Well, how about it now?" Paul said. "There bound to be something you can offer me."

"Now, calm down, fella," Weston said.

People stood at the store's windows, pointing at Paul. Some of them ran towards the other side of the store. He saw Desta come out into the parking lot. She stood stock-still on the cement steps. A gallon of milk slipped from her hand and exploded on the pavement.

"Lower the rifle," Weston said, eyes large, "so we can talk about this sensible."

With every step that Weston took backwards, Paul took another step toward him. He locked the butt of the rifle against his shoulder. He felt like he could make something big happen. Weston lifted his hands just a bit before bumping into his SUV. Paul saw streaks of sweat running down his face.

Paul nodded once and said, "Don't feel too nice, does it?"

Just as those words shot from his mouth, something hard smacked him on the side of the head. He felt as if the day had been switched off, as if the world spun in reverse beneath his feet, pulling him into darkness. He was startled by the feel of his knees smacking onto the ground. But then everything sped up again and the darkness retreated, turning into a dull light that brightened into the day and he was looking up at Weston's friend, holding a plank of wood.

"Paul," he heard Desta hollering, as if she was standing far away from him on some high hill. He saw her jump from the steps. He could hear how much she loved him in the way she cried out his name. He knew that now and sighed.

He tried to stand back up, but his slick-bottomed shoes caused him to keep slipping on the pavement. Blood trickled across his eye. He pressed his hand to it and then stared at the stains on his fingers. He slapped the ground, looking for his rifle, but couldn't find it.

"Are you all right?" Desta said, beside him now. She dabbed a wad of paper napkins to his stinging eye. She was crying.

He held her wrists and then the sides of her arms. She was there with him. She hadn't left him.

"Crazy bastard never had the thing loaded," Weston's friend said, checking the chamber.

Paul scooted back against the side of the truck and released a puff of air from his lips. Desta cleaned away the streams of blood that squirted down his face. He looked at her and then down at his hands. They frightened him, what they could do. But he felt fine with what they could not.

Upheaval
by Chris Holbrook

The cab of the truck feels hot already, and already Haskell can feel the film of coal and dirt gomming his skin. Clouds of dust rise high enough to pebble his windshield, so thick the roadway edge is barely seeable. He wonders who it is driving the spray truck and why they're not doing their job.

As he passes the raw coal bins, he meets George Turner flying toward him on his road grader, the machine bouncing so high on its tires that Haskell feels a gut-clench of fear. He thinks to himself, That's too fast. He's going too fast. He touches his own brakes as if to slow George Turner's grader and battles the urge to cut his wheels toward the road edge.

A shrill ringing begins deep in Haskell's left ear, like the whir of a worn bearing. He can see George Turner's face—the beard stubble on his jaw line, the thumb-smudge of coal black beside his nose. It surprises Haskell how near George looks. He braces his arms for the hit, grits his teeth as the ringing grows more worrisome. Almost before he knows it then, and with no more a calamity of dust and motion than a hard wind might have caused, the grader is by and gone, not even near to tagging him, not really. The ringing in Haskell's left ear fades, becomes a little pin-prick of sound near the hinge of his jaw, so slight he can almost ignore it.

Lord have mercy, he tells himself. His headache has begun to throb more strongly, and he feels a weakness in his hands, as if he's gone too long without eating. He pops two aspirin and swigs from his water jug. It had been a solid chunk of ice when he'd taken it from his freezer that morning, but the ice is melted away now, the water almost warm. I'm as nervous as a cat, he tells himself. He drinks deeply, chasing the bitter taste of aspirin, letting the water fill and calm his stomach.

If I just get through this day, he tells himself. If I just get through this day. He presses the water jug to his forehead, feels its surface moisture seep into his temples. He sees the spray truck then, parked at the road edge next to the Peterbilt that Albert Long drives. It is Jim Stidham's boy, the one they call Tad, standing at the rear bumper, fighting to coil up a hose. As he passes nearer, Haskell sees the Peterbilt begin to back toward the rear bumper of the spray truck. He thinks, Surely that boy's got sense enough to look around him. But Tad keeps on coiling the hose, neither moving nor looking up. Haskell thinks, Surely he can hear the backing alarm.

He tries to catch himself before he leans out the truck window and yells like a fool. He tries to tell himself that what he thinks he is about to see happen—Tad Stidham getting pinched between the truck bumpers, getting crushed, getting killed and mangled—is no more about to happen than he'd been about to collide with George Turner's grader. It's just him, him in his nervousness looking for the worst to happen.

He leans out the truck window then and bangs the door with the flat of his hand and yells, "Ho! Look out there! Ho!" Tad Stidham startles so suddenly that he almost trips himself on the hose. For a moment he looks wildly around. He looks at the Peterbilt that has stopped backing a good ten yards away and is now pulling forward onto the haul road. He looks at Haskell going by in his big rock truck.

Haskell sees the expression of the boy's face change from startlement to anger, and he knows by that what the boy must be thinking—that Haskell's called warning has been just to scare him, has been just to make a joke of him again because he is low man on the totem.

The boy flings the hose to the ground and shouts something at Haskell. And though he can't hear the words, Haskell knows he's been cussed. He feels a touch of anger himself then. He doesn't cuss other men. He is angry still when he passes the walking dragline and turns his truck to get in line for reloading.

He watches the boom of the dragline swing out, a football field long. It is hard to think how big a piece of equipment a dragline really is, hard to see without some other smaller piece of machinery standing near for comparison.

He watches the bucket rake into the overburden. Tremors rise up through the tires and frame of his truck and up through his boot soles and legs like all the ground beneath and around him is being upheaved. It is hypnotizing. One haul, a hundred tons. He feels his mind ease some as he waits, knowing he has a good ten minutes or more of sitting idle.

The morning breeze has died, and though the air has grown less humid with the noontime heat, it feels even muggier now. Most of the men sit or half-lie on the ground or on the tailgates of their pickups as if to move even enough to eat is more an effort than it is worth. Others pace on restless legs, and some stand and kneel at intervals, seeming to find no ease in either position. Once and again a man will speak to say how hot and miserable it is. They sit quiet otherwise and sullen in a way not common to any.

Haskell sits next to Joe Calhoun on the tailgate of Joe's pickup. The old man's left hand is wrapped around from wrist to fingertips with a white handkerchief. He holds the hand away from himself as if neither to see it nor let it be seen. It bothers Haskell not knowing how he's come to harm himself—Joe the oldest man on the site, the least careless, the least likely to mistake himself around machinery.

Josh Owens and Bill Bates sit nearby, facing each other across a cable spool upended for a card table. They focus on their play with heads lowered, hardly speaking but to bid or pass or call trumps, their behavior so out of keeping with their normal foolery that Haskell feels his own humor made bleaker by their company.

Haskell wipes his shirttail into his eyes, clearing sweat and fine grit from the corners. His vision clears for a moment then becomes hazy again. He bites his sandwich, and even that seems mucked, the bread made soggy by the steamy air, the baloney flavored less by the taste of mustard than the scent of diesel fuel on his hands. He pitches the rind of his sandwich toward the ditch line and takes a drink of water to rinse his mouth of the tainted aftertaste.

When he looks again at Joe, the old man's face, dark as it is with sun and weather-burn, seems almost sickly. He is about to give over and ask Joe if he's all right, when a sudden, unexpected uproar commences among the card players. Haskell looks to see Bill Bates standing over Josh Owens, Bill flinging his cards in disgust upon their make-do table.

"That's enough," Bill is saying. "By God, that's enough of that." The sides of his neck and his ears have become suddenly blotched with red, and the skin of his face where it shows through the mask of coal-black has flushed red.

"Now, I don't mean nothing," Josh says, standing as well.

"You don't never mean nothing."

Haskell has half-risen to step between the two, when Joe Calhoun mutters something almost beneath hearing. Haskell leans toward the old man, straining to catch his words. "What?" he asks. "What is it?"

For a moment longer Joe sits completely still, his face pained and angry-looking. Suddenly then, he turns to Haskell and speaks in a strong, loud voice. "I said a man's got to watch. Watch himself and everybody around him. That's just the fact of the matter."

Joe stands and strides over to Bill and Josh. Without speaking he gathers up their cards in his good hand and walks on. After a few paces more he stops and turns, staring upward toward the job site. Josh and Bill stand facing each other a moment more, then stalk off in different directions.

For awhile then Haskell sits studying the big insulated cable running from the generator house to the dragline. He tries to think how many volts it carries. 60,000? 80,000? It is a firing offense for a man just to walk near that cable. He can still feel the motion of the rock truck in his legs and arms, and from time to time he reaches to the pickup's bed wall, feeling the need to brace himself against something solid. He rises and walks over to where Joe Calhoun still stands, still staring toward the job site.

"Got to be on your guard," Joe says. "All the time."

"You'd think a man could get some little break," Haskell replies. "Some little peace of mind."

The other men begin to rouse themselves then. Those who are still pacing stop and stand staring a last few moments into the distance beyond the near ridges. On the leveled hillside above them the dragline works on and the two payloaders work on to keep filled the outgoing coal trucks. As they start up the hill-path toward their machines the men raise their eyes to watch the boom of the dragline swing about, the huge bucket darkening the earth askance of its path. Haskell feels a slight chill at the back of his neck as the ground where they walk becomes shadowed. His head begins to throb more strongly.

Half-an-hour before quitting time Haskell hears it, a sound so faint as to be imagined, just barely out of kilter with the regular uproar of haulage—of backing alarms and rumbling wheels and buckets and blades and whirring auger bits—a lone, flat-sounding boom like close-by thunder, like something near in distance, heavy and solid, coming hard to ground—followed by slow-growing quiet.

He guides his truck off the haul road, parks it on the level, then goes to stand with the crowd of men on the incline above the overturned coal truck. The boy is just being lifted from the crushed-in cab.

Who is it?

That Prater boy. That Dwight.

Got away from him, huh?

The most of the coal load still lies within the side-turned truck bed, though spilled blocks strew the hillside from the road edge downward, marking the path of the wreck. Hydraulic fluid has begun to drip from a burst reservoir, a reddish stain forming as from a living wound within the litter of broken glass and metal and other odd rubbish.

Is he killed?
I don't believe he's killed.
He ain't killed?
No, he ain't killed I don't believe.
In the half-hour before the ambulance arrives the men pace along the road edge and barely speak, each straining to hear first the oncoming siren. When the vehicle is spotted finally they all wave their arms and whistle and call out, guiding it to them. They step aside as the paramedics descend to the wreck, but then crowd forward as the stretcher with the injured boy is hauled up. They reach, lifting, jostling, getting their hands in.

The Prater boy's teeth are gritted. His head and neck are held rigid in a brace. He must roll his eyes wildly to see about him. As he is lifted into the back of the ambulance, he raises an arm.

He's a tough one, somebody calls out.

The rear doors of the ambulance close. Hands pat the sides of the vehicle in signal. Somebody yells, ho! For awhile then no one speaks. There is near silence across the job site. The dozers and rock trucks, the payloaders and road graders all are hushed. Even the dragline has yet to be restarted.

In the dearth of machine noise, a soft roar can be heard, as of gathering wind. A bank of clouds crosses the sun, darkening and cooling. On the near ridgelines, the stands of fir and hickory, of beech and sassafras begin to sway. Before long the wind is passing among the men, a cooling wash of air scented with coming rain. Then several voices start in together.

I seen a boy one time open a gas main with his dozer blade. Burned him and the dozer both up.

That day Arthur Sexton and Sonny Everidge hit one another head on.

You don't know what's like to happen.

They move about restlessly now, no longer tired out. They nudge one another with elbows, clap hands on one another's shoulders, jostling and play horsing, a sudden wildness come upon them.

Sonny broke both his arms, his collar bone, three ribs, his ankle, fractured his skull. They say that Sexton never had a mark on him. Not a bruise.

You got to watch yourself.

Old boy I worked with at Delphi.

Their talk carries loudly into the stillness, their voices echoing strangely in and about the cutbanks and spill dumps and coal bins.

Told how a deer come leaping off a highwall.

Who was it to blame? That Everidge boy and that Sexton?

Watch yourself and everything around you.

Crushed in the cab of a man's pickup.

Joe Calhoun stands holding the wrist of his injured hand, staring into his bandaged palm as if to answer for himself some puzzlement. From time to time he looks up and shakes his head and laughs aloud.

It's just something that happened is all.

You got to watch. All the time.

I don't remember if he was supposed to been in it or not.

One by one then they hush, their high-sounding laughter falling still, their unruly moods dampening. Finally they all stand quiet again in consideration of the wreckage. They stand as if praying, as if thinking together a single thought.

Bill Bates and Josh Owens are first to quit the assembly. They head off together down the hill path. But for Bill's height and Josh's width they could pass one for the other, their clothes covered from cap to boot toe with grease and oil, their faces and hands blacked with coal dust. They walk near side by side, conversing in friendly-seeming terms.

The second shift comes on, and slowly the work noises start up again. As he leaves the job site with the other men, Haskell feels his own day-long pall of nervousness and worry begin to fade, his mood uplifted by passing talk of knife brands, of heat and dust, of weekends planned fishing.

Dory is there when he comes through the back door into the kitchen, where she always is when he comes in of an evening, still wearing the red Food Town smock that is the first and last garment he sees her in each day. She reaches to take the thermos and dinner bucket without speaking, without looking at him even.

He feels the calmness of the day's end begin to go out of him. He feels in its place a spark of anger coming on, over what he can't name. I've not been home five minutes, he wants to say. Not even in the door, hardly. Not even got my shoes off, hardly. But he gets no chance to speak.

The boy starts in, the way he always does, his talk a breathless gabble of noise out of which confusion Haskell hears plainly no more than, Dad. Hey, Dad. Dad. Haskell stares Dory down, his look as purposeful as he can make it. Can you do something? Now? Can you?

She tilts her head back, shaking it slowly, rolling her eyes toward the far wall as she reaches for Robbie.

Haskell passes through the kitchen with the boy still clamoring after him. He pauses just long enough in the hallway to watch Dory kneel before Robbie, to watch her place her hands on his shoulders and speak to him in a stern almost harsh manner that still yet settles the boy enough to hush him.

Before he goes on he notices the small bandage on her thumb. It is worn and dirty, as if it has been there for days. He notices too the dark streaks of grime on her smock, the spots of grease, the blue pricing ink staining her fingers. A bobby pin has fallen loose so that her hair on one side hangs lankly across her face. Her shoulders slump in a way that is not tiredness only, and it occurs to him that she would have gotten home hardly before he did.

He blinks and shakes his head as if to rid himself of some unseemly spectacle, of some bad odor or vexatious thought. He'd like to tell her how bad his legs hurt, how bad his back hurts. He'd like to tell her what a day he's had. I've not been home five minutes, he'd like to say.

He drops his clothes in a pile on the bathroom floor and runs water into the tub until it is hot almost to steaming. Chill bumps rise upon his shoulders as he settles himself in. He feels the sting of bug bites on his legs, of cuts and scrapes on his hands and arms and sunburn on his neck. When the water begins to cool, he drains it off and runs more in, keeping the bath as hot as he can stand it. I don't see what she's got to complain about, he thinks.

The space where the oil filter fits, beside the water pump and the A/C condenser, is so close Haskell can barely get a hand in to grip the wrench handle. Then too the filter is on so tight hand strength alone will not break it loose. He will need to get leverage with his arms, his back, and there is scant room to maneuver.

He can feel Robbie crowding in at his elbow, see his shadow across the motor. Each time Haskell moves it seems he bumps into the boy. He has to watch Robbie from the corner of his eye, try to see that he doesn't cause himself harm. He's said to him, how many times, in the kindest, most patient way he knows how. "Robbie, son, there's so many ways to get hurt around a car engine. So many ways to get hurt working with tools."

But the boy is mindful of nothing Haskell tells him. He crowds in, his hands fiddling without cease—upon a hose coupling, a cable, a belt. He pulls tools from the box—pliers, a magnetic screwdriver—turning them over and over in his hands, all the while chattering about twenty-eleven different things—some animal he has seen, some cartoon show, some wrong done him by his buddies at school.

Haskell can feel the anger rising in his chest, the adrenaline surging into his arms, his hands. Just one good, hard jerk, he thinks. One good, hard pull, and it'll break loose. The loop of the oil wrench squeezes so tightly that the filter's soft metal casing begins to crimp, though the thread does not give. He wants to pull the wrench off and fling it into the creek. He wants to take a hammer to the filter, to the whole damn motor. Break the shittin' thing to pieces.

From the corner of his eye he sees Robbie playing with a socket wrench, ratcheting it over and over. It is a battle to keep from yelling at the boy. He takes a deep breath, then another, and after a moment he is able to cease his effort. He lets go the wrench handle, takes the cup of coffee he'd left cooling on the car fender and steps off a little ways.

When he's had his breather and his sup of coffee and is calm again, he says to Robbie, "You ever see such a tight sumbuck?"

In the moment after his father speaks to him, Robbie becomes quiet and still. He gives a hesitant grin and shakes his head.

"We'll get her," Haskell says. He props a foot upon the bumper this time, leaning further in, rocking down upon the wrench. The filter's casing crimps even more, like a beer can being crushed, but the wrench does move, or at least Haskell thinks it does. He rises on the bumper, bearing down with as much pressure and might as he can muster. Of a sudden the wrench slips loose, and Haskell heads off balance into the motor. He throws his left hand up to catch himself, bangs it hard against something sharp—a bolt, a lip of metal.

It comes out of him then. He strikes the oil wrench against the filter, against the generator, the head cover, the breather lid, flailing with it as he pushes himself upright. He throws the wrench hard to the ground, holding his skinned knuckles to the side. As the first surge of pain runs through him he curses, feeling sorry for it even at the time, but spewing forth nonetheless.

"Goddamnit," he says to Robbie, "Goddamnit, I said to leave them tools alone."

He is several minutes getting calm enough to pick up the oil wrench and return to his task. "It's always something," he says to himself. "Can't do the least thing without it being something, always something." He takes another breath before he speaks to Robbie. "Try not to get in my way," he says, his voice as level as he can make it. "Just try not to get in my way is all."

He leans over the motor, fits the loop of the wrench onto the filter again. He gives a pull, and this time the filter moves. He pulls the wrench as far as the tight space will allow, getting a half-turn before coming up against the generator. He slips the wrench off, replaces it, pulls. The filter turns easily now. In less than a minute Haskell has it free. "We got her," he says. He holds up the filter, dripping oil from the open end, spattering it almost gleefully, like a drunk man spilling his cup. "We got her, Robbie."

But the boy is not there anymore. Haskell walks around the car and then the yard, calling the boy's name. He is nowhere, as far as Haskell can tell, within sight or hearing. Haskell is about to go into the house and look for the boy there when he glimpses Robbie's face at the edge of the living room window just before the curtain falls to.

When he's emptied the thick oil from the old filter into a plastic jug, Haskell finds his nine-sixteenth box-end wrench, gets down on his back and scoots beneath the car to reach the oil pan. As he loosens the plug, he tells himself that it's better anyway for the boy not to be fooling around the car while he's working on it. He tells himself there's so many ways to get hurt around a car engine. So many ways to come to harm.

They all sit quiet through their supper together, Dory hardly raising her eyes from her plate except to glance toward the window or the wall clock. Robbie is quiet, though Haskell is half-afraid to move lest he give the boy some unintended upset. He begins to wish more and more strongly for conversation, a joke, anything to cover a little the irksome sound of forks scraping against plates, of chewing and swallowing, but there is nothing he himself can think to say.

By the time Dory rises to clear the table, Haskell has begun to feel the first mild throb of his daylong headache coming back on him. Listening to Dory clang away at the plates and bowls, it occurs to him to ask if that noise is necessary, to ask if that noise is in some way for his benefit.

"Sit down here and rest a minute," he says instead. She continues to move as if she has not heard him, and for some reason (he is not sure why) he feels it foolish to repeat himself. He feels a tug on his arm and hears vaguely the sound of Robbie's voice saying something again and again. He blinks his eyes open, though he'd not been aware even that he'd had them closed. Dory is sitting across from him at the table again, watching him.

Haskell feels a growing urge to strike something—the wall, the table. He can see himself upending the table, kicking his chair across the room. Something, anything just to make known what he thinks of the situation.

He speaks without knowing he is about to. "You'd think a man could have just a little peace of mind when he comes home of an evening," he says. "You'd think a man could look forward to a little rest in his own home."

"You can rest," she says.

"Ain't no peace of mind around this place."

Dory leans closer to Robbie until she is almost hovering over the boy, hovering as if to pull him from harm. A splotch of light from the overhead bulb reflects from the white cloth covering the table. It brings shadows to the underside of her face, deepening the creases about her mouth, her eyes. She has become years older looking by that light— her skin blotched and unhealthy looking, her cheeks and eyes sunk in so that the outline of bone can be seen, the sockets and hinges. Haskell watches the mechanism of her jaw as she opens her mouth to speak.

"You can rest," she says. "Nobody's stopping you from resting."

It occurs to him to ask what she means by that, but he says nothing. In his oncoming gloom he has begun to think again about Dwight Prater wrecking his coal truck, about the sound it had made going over, about the way the boy had looked being pulled from his truck cab, him shaking so hard from shock you could hear his teeth chatter from as far up as the roadway. He thinks again of his own near mishap, what he believes was a near mishap, with George Turner's grader, and he feels again the urge to touch his hand against something solid, to steady himself against the fitful dizziness and upset he feels come upon him again, against the tiredness.

He looks at Robbie. The boy is staring at the bare tabletop, his face stiff, a flush of redness on his cheek and neck. Dory places her hand upon Robbie's shoulder, and he seems at once to calm.

Haskell rises and walks out of the kitchen. He stands on the back porch a long while, feeling the comfort of the moist night air.

When he finally feels some at ease again, he turns and looks through the screen door into the kitchen. Dory and Robbie are still seated at the table, their heads close, speaking so softly together that Haskell can barely hear the sound of their voices. He thinks how he'd like to tell her about Dwight Prater wrecking his truck, about him almost colliding with George Turner's grader. He reaches his hand to the door, pauses, then walks off the porch into the dark of the yard.

On his first haul Haskell watches his truck's rear end in the side mirror, lining it with the berm as he backs toward the highwall edge. His eyes and skin feel gritty. His feet and knees and his lower back all ache as if they'd not been rested even a single night. His neck feels tight, and already there is a dull pressure in his temples that throbs with each shriek of the truck's backing alarm. He feels his shirt pocket for the aspirin tin, then suddenly the muscles in his back and legs and arms all clench at once and he hits his service brakes. He leans out the window and looks hard at the ground before the berm.

The truck's engine throbs through his chest, and for a moment it is as if his heartbeat rises and falls with the idle speed. He tastes diesel at the back of his throat, feels the sting of it high in his nostrils. His head swims like he is drunk. He fumbles for the seat belt catch, and then he realizes if it was going to go it would have gone already. He sucks deep breaths. It was not the ground giving way, he'd seen. It was heat shimmers. Or it was the shadow of a cloud passing. Or it was light on his mirror.

For awhile he watches Joe Calhoun working his D-9 on the adjacent hill-seam, the dozer's blade cutting into the overburden, loosing boulders and small trees toward the valley floor. It seems a marvel almost the way the huge dozer clings to the contour of the hillside, the way the tracks sidle and shift on the near-vertical incline.

He watches as Joe Calhoun goes about leveling a large beech, first ditching the ground on the downslope and then above. In a short time the tree begins to topple of its own weight, its branches catching and snapping against the still-standing timber, its roots tearing slowly free of the ground. Joe Calhoun moves the dozer to and fro, nudging with the blade in a gentle-seeming way.

Haskell has run a dozer himself. It is as familiar as any piece of machinery on the site, but he watches it now like a man seeing something he never has before. He feels strangely like he is about to see something or know something he never has, that all he has to do is sit still long enough and watch close enough and it will come to him.

But as the beech begins to skid down the hill slope, its broken limbs shinning whitely in the bright sun, clods of black dirt dripping from its tangle of upturned roots, he feels again the sensation of loose soil sliding beneath his wheels. He presses his foot even harder onto the brake pedal.

From the corner of his eye he sees Ray Sturgill sitting in his truck, waiting his time to dump. Haskell wonders how long a while he's been sitting idle just watching another man work, if it's long enough for Ray to have thought something.

He lets off his service brakes and continues backing until he feels his wheels touch the berm. Then he puts the transmission into neutral, sets the park brake and pulls the dump lever. At the same time he guns the engine. Dust rises with the clamor of falling material from his truck bed. He can feel the truck's back end jarring, and for a moment he feels dizzy again. He clenches his hands tight on the steering wheel and raises his foot above the brake pedal. But then the bed empties out and the rear end is still again and he is not slipping off the highwall edge but sitting stable.

He lowers the bed, puts the truck in gear and lets off the park brake. The adrenaline fades out of him as he pulls back onto the haul road. He begins to worry then that he's forgotten something important or overlooked something important he should have seen. He runs through his morning safety checks—belts, brake linings and pads, wheel cylinders, hydraulic lines. There is nothing he can think of that he's missed.

Total Immersion
by Silas House

After Liz tells her, Charma doesn't say anything for a long moment. She is sitting on the couch, smoking a cigarette with one hand and patting the baby's back with the other. "Saved?" she says, as if completely baffled. The word comes out in one great plume of smoke. The baby is sprawled out asleep across the top of her legs. "Tell me you're kidding, Mother."

Liz balances on the edge of her chair and pulls off her panty hose. Her big toe has broken through, just as always. "Why would I kid over such a thing, Charma? You don't kid over stuff to do with the Lord— that's dangerous."

Charma laughs. Her laugh is clear and pretty. Men melt for it. "You are the worst sinner I know, Mother. People actually refer to you as 'The Whore of Black Banks.'" Charma laughs some more. She shakes her head, carelessly flicks her cigarette toward the ashtray.

"Just that one woman," Liz says. She pulls her legs up under herself and rubs her feet.

"Because you were having an affair with her husband!" Charma plays with the baby's thin hair. He is four months old and his scent has spread across the whole room. The whole house smells like Johnson's baby bath. "You're *still* having an affair with him. How are you going to handle that, now that you've took up going to church?"

Liz looks out the window, even though it is covered by sheers so thick they can't be seen through. The sunlight is very bright there, causing them to glow. They look electric and alive. "I guess I'll just have to quit him."

"Yeah right," Charma says. She is always saying this, and she has a certain way of emphasizing "right" that drives Liz crazy. Liz feels like jumping up from the chair and leaning across the coffee table to smack her daughter's face.

"When hell freezes over, you'll quit him." Charma picks up the remote and aims it at the television, a signal that she is finished with this conversation.

"It'd be nice to come home from church and have somebody be tickled that I got saved," Liz says. "Most daughters would love for their mothers to join church."

"I would, too, if I didn't think it was just another one of your phases."

Liz gets up and goes to her room. She moved in with Charma four months ago when her landlord kicked her out. She has a good-paying job at the yarn factory, but she has never been able to save money. She blows her paycheck every weekend because she can't be with her boyfriend, Bruce, then. He has to be with his wife, Lanie, who wears a 1980s hairdo—she even has bangs—and saucer-sized dabs of rouge. So Liz spends her money at the honky-tonks and has people over for grill-outs on Sundays. She buys family packs of ribeyes and baking potatoes. Plus she has that big debt to the collection agency, and they take a chunk of that out of her check. She wouldn't live with Charma if she had anywhere else to go. They get along fine as long as they never see one another.

Her room is small and dark. There are clothes all over the floor and the remnants of last night's supper—a combo from Long John Silver's— are strewn out on the nightstand. She sits down at her vanity table and looks in the mirror. She is finally starting to show her fifty years. People have never been able to guess how old she is. She was thirty before she ever got carded at the liquor store. But now her face is lined with her mistakes. Her eyes seem drawn at the corners, and her mouth is starting to pinch and grow smaller.

She always thought she would feel different when she got saved. But she doesn't. She always imagined that she would feel so clean—inside and out—and that a light would radiate from her face. She had thought it would feel as if God had reached down and grabbed her beneath the ribs to pack her around as if she was floating, her feet dangling just over the floor.

She has thought about going to church for the last year or so. She knows this is the only way she can ever get away from Bruce. He is a force of nature. Black wavy hair and blue eyes and a tender voice that whispers when he is trying to charm her. His breath is always hot and sweet. He keeps a Cert in his mouth all the time, even when he is smoking. He goes on trips to the riverboats in Cincinnati where he and his wife gamble. He plays the tables but Lanie only offers herself to the slot machines. She is too conservative to risk playing 21. On these trips, Bruce sneaks into the fancy shops on the riverboats and buys Liz expensive outfits with his winnings. He brings them to her in plastic covers like you get at the drycleaners. She can never understand how he sneaks these things past Lanie.

She and Bruce cannot go to public places like the riverboats or the racetrack or even the Shoney's right here in town. They can only go to secret places. They spend a lot of time on the lake in Bruce's bass boat. It is red and has what Bruce calls a "meadowflake" finish. The meadowflakes glisten in the sun. They fish for a while and then Bruce always says he finds it incredibly sexy that Liz is willing to bait her own hook and take her own fish off the line. She loves catching bluegills, she loves the way he looks at her when she reels one in. She knows how much he loves that little squeal she lets curl from her mouth, knows how excited he gets by seeing her bent over the side of the boat to slide the fish into their basket. After they have fished for a few minutes he speaks to her in that low, breathy way and she always finds herself lying back on the scratchy boat-carpet. With his weight upon her, sometimes she can feel the water moving beneath them—even through all of that fiberglass—and it is like being in a dream. It is like floating.

All this will have to change. She will *not* go to church and have an affair. She was raised to know better than that, anyway. When she rededicated her life today, her sister, Avalene, who had forced her to go to church with her, said this: "Liz, you was always the biggest sinner ever was. And most of the time the biggest sinners make the biggest Christians."

Avalene is right. Liz will give her all to serving the Lord. She will be baptized next Sunday and will invite everyone she knows. She will start praying to receive the Holy Ghost so she can shout and dance around the altar. She will sing with the choir and eventually teach Sunday school and go on retreats with the young people to Gatlinburg. She thinks it is funny, how the church-people all say "young people," as if "teenagers" is a bad word they can't fit their mouths around. The young people will like her because she will not be a prude. When they ask her if she thinks rock n roll is bad, she will lean forward and say "Of course not" with a great air of confidentiality. Because really, she doesn't think it's bad. Sometimes music like that makes her feel even more in touch with God. Sometimes when she is dancing, she feels like she is celebrating life, and that has to be a good thing.

But she can't think about that right now. She will sort all of that out later. Because she knows that dancing is against the church. So is rock n roll. Still, the teenagers will think of her as the cool Sunday school teacher. She will never call them "the young people" to their faces.

She wonders how she can still have her Sunday grill-outs. All her friends like to drink. They sit out on Charma's back deck and drink beer. Liz always fills the baby's plastic pool with ice and bottles of Michelob. The baby is too young for the pool anyway, and Liz has no idea why Charma has bought it. This is something that she is known for—the ice-filled baby pool—and she likes doing something no one else does. After they eat her salads and her steaks and drink her beer, they like to sit around and play poker. They cuss and sometimes get drunk and often get into fights. But then everyone comes back again and they are all the best of friends. She hates the thought of losing them, but a Christian woman cannot have that going on. Maybe she can talk some of them into going to church with her.

She looks at herself a while longer and decides that she will feel differently after she is baptized. Right now she feels exactly the same. At church she had felt a moment of pure ecstasy when she knelt at the altar to pray. There were many hands on her, women who prayed out loud in great breathless pleadings. The women cried and begged the Lord to forgive Liz her sins. The choir started up and they played a real fast song— "God's not dead, oh no no no. He's still alive. Oh God's not dead, He's still alive."—and some of the women started shouting and speaking in tongues and Liz thought she could feel the Holy Ghost running up and down her back, like warm water. She couldn't help but to cry, and it seemed she had never had such a cleansing cry before. When she sat in her room alone and cried over Bruce—knowing that he was off somewhere with his wife—her tears always seeped out slow and hot, but at church her whole body had shuddered and the tears had felt cool on her face. She had tasted their salt on her lips.

"Mother?" Charma shouts, slapping her palm against Liz's door. Liz hates being called Mother. Every other girl she knows says "mommy," but not Charma. Even when she was little, she addressed her in such a way. And to other people she just calls her by her first name as if they are not a drop of kin. "What are you doing in there?"

Liz starts to throw the door open but thinks better of it. A Christian woman has to have a good demeanor. Avalene calls it "letting your light shine." Avalene gave her advice all the way home from church today. She said how Liz had to stop wearing so much makeup and never wear pants and let her hair grow out and stop cussing and quit smoking and most importantly she had to let her light shine. Liz musters up a smile when she opens the door.

Charma greets this with a smug laugh, so quiet that Liz would not even recognize it except for the lift of Charma's shoulders. "Can you watch the baby this evening? Roger Lanham wants to take me to the theater."

Charma always says "theater," too. She will not say "the movies."

"I was planning on going to church tonight, Charma," Liz says.

"Well, can't you take him? It'd be good for him to go." Charma lights a cigarette off the burning embers of her last.

"He's four months old, honey. He wouldn't even get anything out of the Sunday school."

"Well fine, then!" Charma yells and stomps away. At the end of the hall she turns around and says, "See, you haven't changed a bit. Same old selfish Liz."

"All right then," Liz says. This has always been their problem. Liz has never known whether she was the child or the boss. She feels more like Charma is her sister than daughter. Charma seems to go out every night now. She is a good-looking girl and she has this big fine apartment, which the father of her baby pays for every month. He does this because he is a federal lawyer and doesn't want his wife to know that Charma has had a child by him. He even drew up a contract that Charma signed, saying she would remain silent unless he didn't pay child support and the rent. Charma tells all her friends that she is "set for life." Last week she wanted a new living room suite and a big-screen television. When the lawyer refused to buy it, she said she'd call his wife. He reminded her of the contract but Charma simply blew a line of smoke across the telephone receiver and spoke calmly. "That paper might hold up in court, but she'll still *know*." Next day, the Furniture-Town van pulled in and unloaded her order.

Liz watches her own daughter twist her way down the hall and feels as if they don't know each other at all. Perhaps comparing their relationship to sisterhood is all wrong. They are simply two people who have been forced to go through life together.

Liz takes the baby to church that night. Avalene picks them up. It is a hot night but the air conditioner doesn't work and Avalene doesn't want her hair messed up, so she won't roll down the windows and Liz sweats in her new dress, which she bought at the Fashion Bug today. She had to buy something because all of her dresses were for honky-tonking, so they were either too short or too low-cut.

Liz glances back at the baby, who is content—he loves riding in cars— and then cracks the window. She lights a cigarette and blows the smoke toward the stream of air that is whistling in.

"What are you doing?" Avalene gasps. They are stopped at a red light so she is able to glare at Liz for a long moment.

Liz doesn't know what she is talking about.

"Why, you're smoking! I done told you—We'll go to church smelling like smoke, Liz. Just throw that pack out, now honey. That craving will be took from you. You won't want things of the world anymore."

"I doubt smoking will send me to Hell, Avalene," Liz says, watching for the light to change, since Avalene is not.

"But it *will*, honey," Avalene says, as if she is certain not only of this, but of everything. "Your body is a temple."

Liz lets the cigarette drop out of the little space at the top of the window but doesn't throw out her pack.

Everyone at the church is happy to see her. Actually, they look stunned, as if they never expected her to come back, and their big smiles and laughter seems to be out of speechlessness more than anything. All of the woman rub her back in a perfect circle. Liz notices that they all look tired and pale. Maybe it is because they are not wearing makeup. But there is something in their eyes that makes her long for them. She wants to wrap her arms around the women and tell them that she loves them. She doesn't know why; maybe this is part of being a Christian. It seems like something Christ would do.

The baby seems to love church. He bounces on Liz's lap when the choir sings. Everybody plays with him and runs a finger over his soft hair. The ladies in front of her all ask to hold him, and she lets them. He is happy against their big, warm breasts. Liz cannot follow the preacher tonight. He paces all over the church, hollering and stomping. The crowd nearly drowns him out with their amens. This bunch will amen anything; it's as if they fall into a rhythm and know just when to holler it out. The preacher is talking about the Rapture. She catches something about Jesus Parting the Sky and the Twinkling of An Eye. She remembers Zelda, her best friend at work, once telling her that in a Pentecostal church, there are only three sermons. "The rapture, the holy ghost, and the offering," Zelda said. She feels bad for letting Zelda talk this way.

When the sermon is over, she feels as if she has been in a daze. She is only brought awake when the altar call starts. She loves to hear them sing, especially the fast songs when they pound the tambourines and everybody starts speaking in tongues. She can't help moving about in her seat. The music is good enough to dance to.

As soon as she gets home, she calls Bruce. He has told her to never call his house and really she ought to wait to talk to him at work tomorrow. He is her supervisor and she can go into his sound-proof office anytime she wants. They even did it in there once, him standing and her back clattering against the metal blinds on the little window over his desk. That was the best they ever did it, she thinks now, and feels desire stir. She likes the office not only because of him but also because she can't hear the grind of the yarn machines while there. It is like walking out of a storm into a safe place. But she can't wait to talk to him at work. Luckily, he answers the phone.

"Bruce?"

He whispers. She can picture him hunkering into himself as he talks. She can hear a television playing in the background and wonders if he and Lanie have been lying on the couch together, watching the news. Bruce watches Fox News all the time. He cannot get enough of it. He says it is important to stay informed.

"I told you to *never* call me here." He's mad.

"I'm sorry, but I have to talk to you. Can't you act like you're out of smokes or something? Meet me at the Dairy Mart?"

"Ten minutes," he says and hangs up.

Charma is still not back, and Liz had not thought of this before calling Bruce, so she just loads the baby up and heads out. He is asleep anyway and won't know a thing. Bruce will just have to get in the car with her.

He does. He pulls in and simply slides from his car to hers. She thought that maybe that same old feeling wouldn't come to her upon seeing him, but it does. She still feels that sizzle in her stomach. He is still good-looking to her. The only thing is that she realizes for the first time that he knows he is good looking, too. And she realizes that this is exactly why she has always been so attracted to him. Conceit is something that is appealing to her.

It is as if he had been expecting her call, because he is fixed up. He is wearing dress shorts and boat shoes. And he is wearing a shirt that Lanie must have bought for him, a green polo shirt with that little horse emblem over his heart. Her favorite shirt that she bought him is one that he never, ever wears. It says FISHERMAN DO IT IN THE WATER. She wonders what he has done with it and bets Lanie has sold it in one of those huge yard sales she is famous for. She probably won't let him wear such a thing. Lanie is Presbyterian. Liz doesn't know much about that denomination, but Bruce says they worry *a lot* about what other people think.

"Where have you been, all decked out?" she asks.

"We went to the steak house this evening."

Another place they can't go. The only place they ever eat is at the boat dock. Greasy hamburgers wrapped in wax paper. Or in the break room at work. Nabs and a Pepsi, or sometimes a bag of popcorn they put in the microwave. Every time she smells microwaved popcorn, she thinks of him. It is the same with the air on the lake and Eternity for Men cologne. These smells are her connection to him, and she will never be able to rid herself of him in this way. By way of scent, he will always be with her.

"What is it?" he asks. "I don't have much time."

She lights a cigarette. Although she knows this act won't go along good with what she is about to say, her nerves need the nicotine. "I got saved this morning. I'm going to start going to church."

"Church?" A laugh unclenches itself from the back of his throat. "Have you lost your mind? You're not ready for that."

"I have to do something. I've got to have some kind of life. I'm not going to have one with you—you're never going to leave her."

"I can't, Liz. You know that." He looks around to make sure that no one can see them. Her Mustang has tinted windows, so nobody can. "What's the use leaving her if she gets everything? Would you want a man with nothing?"

Liz looks at her cigarette and throws it out the window. "I've never had anything before. Why should now be any different?" She holds onto the steering wheel very tightly, as if she is driving around a sharp curve. She watches her knuckles whiten. "It don't matter now, anyway. I want you to come to my baptism."

Bruce makes a sound like his words are caught in the back of his throat. Then he assembles them properly. "Now I know you've lost your mind."

Liz doesn't feel anything at all. She feels empty. There is not even that yearning of wanting to be filled up by something. She looks straight ahead. "I'm going to try to do right, Bruce. We have to quit this."

Bruce flips down the visor and looks at himself in the mirror. "You're not church-going material, Liz. You're just not made that way."

Before she even realizes what she is doing, Liz starts the car and checks the rearview mirror, which she has adjusted so she can see the baby. He is still sound asleep. At first she thinks she might just start driving, but she doesn't. After a long silence of Bruce just staring at her, she says, "Get out, Bruce. I'm done."

"We'll talk about this more at work," he says, not even looking at her now. Scanning the parking lot. The lights from the store are bright and his face looks very pale in their glare. She thinks of his brown shoulders, speckled by water. Sometimes they go up into a cove and skinny dip. They lie back naked on the boat and the sun catches in the little wet orbs on his slick skin. She shakes this image out of her mind.

"There's nothing else to say," she says, and with her foot on the brake, slides the gear down into reverse. "Go on."

He doesn't argue, but he lets out one of those sighs that used to unnerve her. It used to send her into a frenzy, thinking she had upset him. But now she doesn't care. She is at peace with the world. He gets out and shoves his hands deep into the pockets of his Duck Head shorts. He stands there only for a second before darting his head around, looking about to make sure no one has seen him. She sits there with the car running even after he has driven away.

That week, Liz avoids Bruce at work. She ignores him when he taps her on the shoulder and tells her to come to his office. When he walked by, the musk of his cologne trailed behind. She even ignores him in the break room, where he stands by the microwave, waiting for his corn to pop. But she has to make herself not look at him. He always wears Dockers to work, and they look so good on him. She has always liked to see him in dress socks and penny loafers.

She tries to not think about all that, though. She focuses on her yarn line and lets the noise of the factory force Bruce out of her head.

On break, she talks about church to the rest of the girls. None of them can believe it. They want to know what they will do about Saturday nights, when they all get together and go to The Spot, where they each take turns buying pitchers of Michelob and are the most popular table of women in the whole place. They want to know how they can talk to her like they used to. They all claim to respect her decision, though— even Zelda—and she thinks they are genuinely happy for her.

Avalene bought her a whole garbage bag full of skirts over at the Redbird Mission Store, and Liz wears them to work. She doesn't feel right in pants any more. It is what Avalene called "being condemned." Avalene said, "If wearing eye makeup and pants condemns you, then you ought not do it. That feeling of being condemned is God whispering in your ear. Doubt is just God, warning us."

The closer it gets to Sunday, the more nervous Liz becomes, as if the baptism were an impending job interview that she is not prepared for. Avalene talks about it all the time. She verses Liz in all the ways of the church, as their mother never had taken them growing up and none of Liz's ex-husbands ever wanted to go. Avalene told her that it is the freshest feeling, when you rise up out of that water. "It really feels just like they say—as if your sins have been washed away," she says.

The Pentecostals practice total immersion, and this is the main thing Liz dreads. She can't stand being under water. It smothers her to death. Once she had been on a pontoon at the lake, everybody drunk, and somebody had pushed her in as a joke. Although she is a good swimmer, when she went under, she lost it. She came up hyperventilating so hard that a bunch of men had to jump in and pull her out. She had done it with one of the men that night, right up on the bank while everybody else partied. She remembers him moving on top of her, throbbing and breathing hard. She wonders now if anyone had seen them, and is amazed that she had never even cared before.

Still, she wants this. She wants a change, and in a town like Black Banks, this is the most you can change. There are only two kinds of people here: sinners and Christians. She wants to try a new crowd.

She is happy when the preacher calls to tell her that the church has decided it will be best to use the river. In the winter, they use the baptistry that they had built in the church, but during the hot months they like to use the river. She can picture it, all of the people standing on the bank singing and slapping tambourines. She loves the feel of river water, as it is always moving. Pushing on, not letting anything stand in its way.

On Friday she calls everyone she knows to invite them to her baptism. Most of them say they will be there, but a lot of them have excuses, too. Excuses Liz herself has used many times to escape similar situations. She is no fool. Everyone sounds genuinely shocked at the prospect of her going to church, too. One of her honky-tonk friends laughs out loud when Liz invites her. "Lord, Liz, if you start going to church, the roof is liable to cave in!" she says. Liz can't help herself—she hangs up on her.

And now, on the very morning of her baptism, Charma says she is not going. The baby is crying, but she stands at the stove, stirring eggs and bouncing him on her hip. She talks over his cries. "I'm not going to go there and watch you make a fool out of yourself, Mother." She shifts the baby to her other hip. "Because you know good and damn well that come next month, you'll be right back at the Spot. You'll be down on the lake with Bruce. You are not going to change, and we both know that."

"Can't you give me the benefit of the doubt?"

Charma doesn't look at her. "I've never understood that phrase," she says. With one hand Charma pours the eggs out onto a plate. Behind her morning light falls in the window in a white glare, so that Liz cannot see her face.

"Can't you believe in me this once, Charma Diane?"

From halfway across the kitchen, Charma throws the plate onto the table. When it hits, the eggs bounce off and scatter off the edge and onto the floor. "When the hell did you ever believe in *me*?"

Liz wants to tell Charma that she is right. She knows that she was never a good mother. Marrying one man after another, sleeping with men she brought home from the Spot. People always at the house, drinking liquor and smoking dope right in the living room. Once she had been sitting in a man's lap and taking a shot of bourbon he had poured for her and just as she brought the glass down, she saw Charma standing in the hallway, watching her. She was only four years old, and she had dragged the bedspread from her room. "I had a bad dream," Charma said, but instead of going to her, instead of packing her back to bed and tucking her in, Liz had shouted, "Go back to bed! Quit spying on me." And Charma had simply turned around and shuffled back down the hallway, the bedspread trailing along behind her.

Liz thinks now of how Charma must have felt, lying there in the darkness, afraid, listening to her mother's laughter in the living room. Liz is more ashamed of that moment than any other in her life, and she wants to ask for Charma's forgiveness, but she can't find the right words. She knows if she doesn't say it exactly right, Charma will just laugh at her, or get even madder.

Without another word, she stands and takes her purse, which is hanging from the back of the chair, and puts it on her shoulder. She walks outside and waits on the porch for Avalene. She is dying for a cigarette, but she doesn't smoke one. She concentrates on the blue mountains in the distance until Avalene's car coughs its way up the road.

It is an impossibly perfect day. The sky looks like something out of a movie—completely blue—and a little breeze moves through the willows lining the river. The people are all standing on the bank and seem very far away. The preacher puts one hand into the small of her back and whispers, "Take a deep breath, now."

Before doing so, she scans the crowd one more time. She doesn't know whom she expects to see, but there is not one single person she knows besides Avalene, who is bawling into a ragged Kleenex. Avalene is her sister, but she doesn't really know her at all. She doesn't even like her. None of her girlfriends, not even Zelda. Had she really thought Bruce would be there? He is at home watching the news while Lanie is at the Presbyterian service. Worst of all, Charma is not here. She had hoped she might come up out of the water and see Charma, approval stamped across her face.

"Liz?" The pastor says. "Here we go, now."

He caps his hand over her mouth—his fingers smell like onions and Coast soap—and then "In the name of the father and the son and the Holy Ghost," and he is leaning her back. It is like being dipped during a dance. She is underwater for what seems a very long time, but she is not afraid. She feels like she could lie there in that water from now on. She can hear the river moving beside her ears, like time, like death, like every bad thing she has done her whole life. She can taste the water (mossy, sandy—like the underside of a rock way up in the shadiest part of the mountains) that seeps in between the pastor's big fingers.

She is under so long that she has time to open her eyes. And all she can see is light, slanting down onto the river's surface.

Contributors

RUSTY BARNES grew up in rural northern Appalachia. He lives now in Revere, Massachusetts, where he maintains a blog-azine of rural and Appalachian literature (www.friedchickenandcoffee.com), as well as the well-known literary journal *Night Train* (www.nighttainmagazine. com).

SHELDON LEE COMPTON's work has appeared in numerous journals including most recently *New Southerner, Keyhole Magazine, Emprise Review, Fried Chicken and Coffee, Staccato Fiction, Corium Magazine*, and elsewhere. His short story "Bent Country" was nominated for the 2010 story South Million Writers Award. He survives in Kentucky.

JARRID DEATON lives in eastern Kentucky where he has worked as a journalist for close to a decade. He is currently teaching English at Big Sandy Community and Technical College in Prestonsburg, Kentucky. His work has appeared in *Mud Luscious, Underground Voices, Fried Chicken and Coffee, Pear Noir, JMWW*, and elsewhere. He is a big fan of the music and writing of Nick Cave. He once painted his face with blood during a recreational league softball game.

RICHARD HAGUE is a native of Steubenville, Ohio, in the Appalachian country of the upper Ohio Valley. He is currently a high school teacher in his forty-first year at the same institution, and a small-scale urban farmer, and an itinerant college instructor, most recently at Northeastern University in Boston. His books include 11 volumes of poetry, a multi-genre poetry collection/teaching memoir called *Lives of the Poem*, and *Milltown Natural: Essays and Stories from a Life in Ohio* (nominated for a National Book Award). His *Alive in Hard Country* (Bottom Dog Press, 2003) was named Poetry Book of the Year in 2004 by the Appalachian Writers Association. His work has appeared in dozens of journals, reviews, anthologies, magazines, and on-line sites, including *Appalachian Journal, Now & Then, Appalachian Heritage, Sow's Ear Poetry Review, Smartish Pace, Poetry, Nimrod, Creative Nonfiction*.

CHRIS HOLBROOK grew up in Knott County, Kentucky, and as a native of Appalachia his masterful command of detail reveals a personal familiarity with the people of this region, from the cadence of the language to the food on the tables. Holbrook's Appalachia, however, is neither the sentimentalized Appalachia of Dollywood nor the demonized Appalachia of *Deliverance*. Instead, his stories reveal the thorny, contradictory, and at times funny complexities of Appalachian life. His writing taps into the fierce desperation and unsettling pain of characters that seem primed to explode at any second. In tense, measured dialect, he leads the reader into a world that is frightening and yet familiar. He received the Thomas and Lillie D. Chaffin Award for Appalachian Writing for his first book, *Hell and Ohio: Stories of Southern Appalachia.* His second book of stories, *Upheaval,* was published by the University Press of Kentucky in 2009. A graduate of the Iowa Writer's Workshop, Holbrook is associate professor of English at Morehead State University. SILAS HOUSE is the author of four bestselling novels, including *Clay's Quilt,* and *Eli the Good,* a work of nonfiction, and two plays. House is a two-time finalist for the Southern Book Critics Circle Prize and the recipient of many honors, among them the Appalachian Writer of the Year, the Appalachian Novel of the Year, two Kentucky Novel of the Year Awards, the Award for Special Achievement from the Fellowship of Southern Writers, and others. For his activism he has received the Helen Lewis Award for Community Service. House's work has been published in such publications as *Newsday, Oxford American, The Beloit Fiction Journal, The Louisville Review,* and others. A native of Eastern Kentucky, he serves as the Chair of Appalachian Studies at Berea College and on the fiction faculty at Spalding University's MFA in Creative Writing. He lives in Berea, Kentucky.

DENTON LOVING lives on a farm near the historic Cumberland Gap, where Tennessee, Kentucky, and Virginia come together. His story "Authentically Weathered Lumber" received the 2007 Gurney Norman Prize for Short Fiction through the journal *Kudzu.* Other work has appeared in *Birmingham Arts Journal, Appalachian Journal, Somnambulist Quarterly, Minnetonka Review* and in numerous anthologies.

SCOTT MCCLANAHAN is the author of *Stories* and *Stories II* (published by Six Gallery Press). His other works include *Hillbilly, Stories 5!, The Nightmares* and *Crapalachia* (all forthcoming). He can be reached at www.hollerpresents.com.

JOHN MCMANUS is the author of three widely praised books of fiction: the novel *Bitter Milk* and the short story collections *Born on a Train* and *Stop Breakin Down.* In 2000 he became the youngest-ever recipient of the Whiting Writers Award. His fiction has also appeared in *Ploughshares, American Short Fiction, Tin House,* and *The Oxford American,* among other journals. Born in Knoxville, Tennessee, in 1977, he lives in Virginia and teaches in the MFA creative writing programs at Old Dominion University and Goddard College.

MINDY BETH MILLER lives in Hazard, Kentucky, where she was raised and her family has lived for generations. In 2008 she became the inaugural winner of the Jean Ritchie Fellowship in Writing, the largest monetary prize for Appalachian writing. Her creative work has been featured in *Appalachian Heritage*, *The Louisville Review* and *Still: The Journal*. Miller holds a Master of Fine Arts in Creative Writing and is currently writing her first novel.

JIM NICHOLS was born and raised in Freeport, Maine, and now lives in the little river town of Warren with his wife, Anne. He has published work in numerous anthologies and magazines, including *Esquire, Narrative, Zoetrope All-Story Extra, paris transcontinental, River City, Night Train, American Fiction, The Clackamas Review* and *Portland Monthly*. He is a past winner of the Willamette Fiction Prize and a prizewinner in the River City Writing Awards. His collection *Slow Monkeys and Other Stories* was published by Carnegie Mellon Press, and his novel *Hull Creek* (Downeast Books) will be released in spring, 2011.

VALERIE NIEMAN worked for two decades as a newspaper reporter in northern West Virginia while honing her skills as a poet and fiction writer. She also homesteaded a hill farm and did a bit of fishing. Her third novel, *Blood Clay*, set in Piedmont, North Carolina, will appear in 2011. She is the author of a collection of short stories, *Fidelities* (West Virginia University Press), and a poetry collection, *Wake Wake Wake* (Press 53). She has received an NEA Creative Writing Fellowship in poetry, two Elizabeth Simpson Smith prizes in fiction, and the Greg Grummer Prize in poetry. A graduate of West Virginia University and the MFA program at Queens University of Charlotte, she teaches writing at N.C. A&T State University and is a regular workshop leader at the John C. Campbell Folk School and the North Carolina Writers Network. She is poetry editor for the on-line/print literary journal, *Prime Number*.

CHRIS OFFUTT grew up in Haldeman, Kentucky, a former mining town of 200 people. He writes that "The dirt roads were recently blacktopped and the post office shut down." He attended grade school, high school, and college within a ten-mile radius of his home. He has published five books about people from the hills of Kentucky. The work has been recognized by fellowships from the NEA, the Guggenheim Foundation, and the Lannan Foundation. His works has also received a Whiting Writer award, and an award from the American Academy of Arts and Letters for "fiction that takes risks." He's also written comic books, essays, stage plays, and screenplays. His work appears in many anthologies, is widely translated, and taught in high schools and college. He has many interests but no hobbies. He lives with his family and two dogs. He loves people but prefers to be alone.

MARK POWELL is the author of the novels *Prodigals* and *Blood Kin*. He has received fellowships from the National Endowment for the Arts and the Breadloaf Writers' Conference. Born and raised in the mountains of South Carolina, he now teaches at Stetson University in DeLand, Florida.

RON RASH is the author of four novels, four books of short stories, and three books of poems. He has been awarded NEA fellowships in fiction and poetry. His short story collection, *Chemistry*, and the novel, *Serena*, were both Pen/Faulkner Award Finalists. His most recent book, *Burning Bright*, won the 2010 Frank O'Connor Short Fiction Award. He teaches at Western Carolina University.

ALEX TAYLOR lives in Rosine, Kentucky. He has worked as a day laborer on tobacco farms, as a car detailer at a used automotive lot, as a sorghum peddler, at various fast food chains, as a tender of suburban lawns, and at a cigarette lighter factory. He holds an MFA from The University of Mississippi and now teaches at Western Kentucky University. His work has appeared in *Carolina Quarterly, American Short Fiction, The Greensboro Review,* and elsewhere. His story collection, *The Name of the Nearest River,* was published by Sarabande Books in 2010.

CRYSTAL WILKINSON is the author of *Blackberries, Blackberries,* winner of the 2002 Chaffin Award for Appalachian Literature, and *Water Street,* a finalist for both the UK's Orange Prize for Fiction and the Hurston/Wright Legacy Award. Both books are published by Toby Press. She is a recipient of awards and fellowships from The Kentucky Foundation for Women, The Kentucky Arts Council, The Mary Anderson Center for the Arts and the Archie D. and Bertha H. Walker Scholarship Fund at the Fine Arts Work Center in Provincetown. She is the recent winner of the 2008 Denny Plattner Award in Poetry from *Appalachian Heritage* and the Sallie Bingham Award from the Kentucky Foundation for Women. Wilkinson currently teaches writing and literature in the BFA in Creative Writing Program at Morehead State University. She and her partner, artist and poet Ron Davis, are editors of *Mythium Literary Journal.*

The Editors

PAGE SEAY is an avid outdoorsman who lives in Nashville, Tennessee with his son and daughter. He is currently an MFA candidate at Spalding University where he is completing his first novel.

CHARLE DODD WHITE is the author of the Appalachian novel *Lambs of Men* (2010). His short fiction has appeared in *The Collagist, Fugue, Night Train, North Carolina Literary Review* and others. He teaches English at South College in Asheville, North Carolina. His website is www.charlesdodd white .com.

LaVergne, TN USA
02 November 2010
203116LV00002B/45/P